LILI COMES TO HERSELF

a novel

Zoe Carada

The characters and events portrayed in this book are fictitious. Any similarity to real persons, living or dead, is coincidental and not intended by the author.

ISBN: 9783000 812965

Cover design by: Zoe Carada

CONTENTS

ENDORSEMENTS

"An affecting portrait of love gained and lost... a delight, both whip-smart and searching... Carada opens a window into a world that few in the West know anything about."

Junot Díaz, Pulitzer Prize-winning author of
The Brief Wondrous Life of Oscar Wao

"Nothing goes as expected for the protagonist of this engaging coming-of-age story, from academic success to friendship to romantic love. Readers will find that the many challenges Lili faces in the communist 1980s in Eastern Europe remain all too relatable in our modern western world."

Roz Warren, author of
Our Bodies, Our Shelves: A Collection Of Library Humor

CHAPTER ONE

"Whoever can carry a mountain, shall carry a mountain; and whoever can carry a grain of sand, shall carry a grain of sand," Val Nestor says, his eyes piercing her.

She feels a thud in her chest. That was so precious. But it hurts, too.

So he thinks she can carry a mountain, but she's not pulling her weight. Next, she feels anger. Why has he singled *her* out for his wisdom? Why couldn't he say what teachers usually say, or at least what he's telling the other parents sitting here about their kids: how well they're doing in the tests, what extra homework they should do, or how they might work on their exam nerves if they're taking chemistry for admission?

Why must he get so personal with her alone, and that only to make her feel inadequate?

Yes, sure, it's because he cares about her future, more than he does about the other students'. Maybe. But why is that, again? Who does he think he is, to judge her, instead of simply grading her performance?

What does he think his bloody chemistry is, after all? The hub of the universe, the Earth's belly button? Is she a failure just because she's not getting top grades in his subject? How about the other subjects, where she *is* getting top grades? And how about – well, how about herself? She's far more than her grades, and he knows that, or he wouldn't talk to her in riddles.

Launching this gem of wisdom at her, knowing she can't reply, in front of the head teacher and the crowd of parents.

At least Father's not here to pick up the tune and start a situation analysis, the science professor way.

Mother's cool.

She's suddenly thankful that Nestor will no longer be teaching them this year. It's his last chance to put up his act, in this last meeting. The parents are sitting quietly, squeezed in between the wooden panels and the iron skeleton of the students' desks designed for skinny teenagers, looking up to Nestor as he's turning the pages of the class list and glossing on the performance of each kid. It's his farewell feedback.

Lili is the only student in the crowd of parents, although the meeting was open for students, too. Mother's standing aside, leaning against the wall, watching Nestor with her big blue eyes.

To think how fond she's been of this ridiculously little guy, with his theatrical fits of anger and piercing remarks – the sports-coach-inspirational way, assuming the tougher he is, the more motivated to go-get-it they'll be. But she's not like that. He might delude himself he knows her buttons, but this illusion of his offends her. She has no buttons. And if she did, it's not for him to be sitting in the driver's seat, only to keep grumbling about what an inefficient machine she is.

She's human: she's got her motives, her dreams, and her valleys of despondency in this strange, unsafe world.

She only needs to hang in there for a little longer, keep up her studying streak, and next summer, Nestor will see. She'll show him what a mountain she's been carrying while he was suspecting she might be taking things easy. Just this final school year, and then it will all be over when she's at university.

She's tired of being singled out. Her own feeling of being different is already a nuisance; the teachers' and parents' appreciation sometimes gets too much. She wishes she could join the crowd and be liked by her school mates instead: surrounded by buddies, be inconspicuously good.

But at least she only has to handle their admiration; Val Nestor's appreciation, on the other hand, is inside out. It's implicit in his constant reproaches that she hasn't done as well as she's capable of doing, in his goading her on, calling her a dreamer, a girl without a scale of values.

Lili is eighteen, in her final year at school. University entrance exams loom ahead, merely ten months away, spreading restlessness and anxiety. Lili can barely wait to be through with them and finally start her life and get the space to be herself. Amidst the tight school desks, wearing her Young Communist uniform, she is choking with estrangement.

It's September 1986, far behind the Iron Curtain: the Socialist Republic of Romania.

She has always been a one and only.

Her father is a physics professor at university, and her occasional intuitive responses to challenging problems in the physics class, which set her apart from the others, would make the Professor chuckle with imperfectly hidden delight.

She's his clever Lili girl; Professor Dimi Danes is her Yimmi Papa.

Or was, early in her childhood and primary school years. In the times when it was all right to dote on each other.

Father had been there like a sun, central to everything. Beaming down to her. She beamed back, all powerful.

She would have a tantrum whenever he had to leave home for classes. She would leave him no way but tell her a story, whether good-night or not.

"Come, Yimmi Papa, tell me a story, will you?"

"Oh, no, not right now, I've got things to do, Lili."

"Oh, come on, Yimmi Papa."

"No, no, no, not this time."

"Oh, come, yes, pleeaase, Yimmi Papaaa!"

He rolled his eyes, though smirking, secretly delighted with her pleas.

"Oh, come, Yimmi Papa, you're such a dear Papa."

He laughed. "You're not going to give up, are you?"

"Oh, come, Yimmi Papa, you're such a kind Papa..." and the squash game began, ball after ball.

"And such a clever Papa...

"And such a sweet Papa, and I love you soo much....

"And you're such a handsome Papa, and such a good Papa...

His laughter got louder and louder, seeing himself cornered tighter and tighter with each ball of flattery thrown at him, leaving him less and less room for No. He'd eventually yield, half exasperated, half delighted, and she knew this too well.

His stories were always engulfing, like a magic cloak conjuring up a shell over her little universe. Her own, imagined, universe.

There was an evening star turned into an enigmatic prince.

A master builder who had to entrap his beloved wife within the walls of his masterpiece, to prevent them crumbling down every night.

A father and a son gluing themselves wings to escape captivity, but crashing into the sea from flying too high under the sun.

The creation of the world out of clashes and explosions.

The invention of numbers and the ancient times when people mapped the skies, long before there was any going-to-school, let alone kindergarten.

She asked, in turn, all possible questions: why stars were sometimes twinkling, why some were small and others big, what was beneath the earth if that was what was above, how long it would take to get to one of those twinkling dots, and what light-years meant.

Later, in school, she knew she could get him to solve a maths problem for homework if the solution was not straightforward. His logic felt like a firm hand gripping her elbow before rashly crossing the street of reasoning in the wrong place.

"You do it yourself, it's your homework, and actually, you know very well you can do it," he'd tell her.

Yes, she knew she could do it. As papa's clever Lili girl, she hadn't yet come across a problem she couldn't solve; but she also had her unlimited powers, in that cosmos of their own. For all his protests and scruples, he would end up giving in.

A one-to-one, two-way avenue of bias for each other.

But at some point in time, their cosmos had stopped throbbing, and had turned outside in, going sulkily into hiding. At some point, she had stopped pleading for stories or help with homework, and he had started looking away with a grim face.

It was Father who had tantrums now, and turned out to be a thundering troublemaker who ended up retreating to his study bedecked with books, slamming the door behind him. Home had turned into a theatre of conflict, conflict avoidance, and lulls.

Lili couldn't remember any open confrontation of her own with him. Their fronts were removed from each other and locked in unspoken frustration.

It was the conversations between the two parents that escalated into thundering yells: one moment it was quiet in the house, Lili reading or listening to her John Lennon tape, and the next moment there were howls and crashes, doors banging, heavy objects (most likely books) being dropped on the floor. The Professor was always the origin of these big bangs. At first, she would come out of her room to check what was going on, but would bump into him slamming the door of his study, disfigured by rage.

"Go back to your room and mind your own business," he'd growl at her.

Soon, she knew she was supposed to keep under, until the storm was gone. Locked in her room, she would cringe at the noise, skin growing tight, emptiness in her chest, and would retreat step by step deeper into a self-made bubble of safety: turn up the music, and shake her head back into her reverie.

She had first felt that frozen cringe one March evening in second grade, just before she'd wrapped up her drawing to go to bed, when the walls, the floor, her bed, the wardrobe – everything started shaking, and kept shaking for almost a minute: a devastating earthquake. Their house stayed in one piece, but she had learned the fear preceding disaster.

A few years later, Professor Danes' rage sent shock waves that threatened to shatter walls, doors, and everything alive behind them.

The sun at the centre of her world had become the eye of a hurricane.

In his devastating whirl there was debris of hurtful insults, hyperbolic reproaches, swear words, and inevitably reckless curses against Ceaușescu and his omnipresent secret police. Lili could never make out what the trouble was between her parents, but the one thing that was plain to see was his aversion to state power, which was enough reason for anyone to cover one's ears: one was made unsafe by simply hearing his complaints.

No wonder the phone line made funny clicks. No wonder Mrs Escu, the busybody in the house at the street corner, was taking such a keen interest in the Professor's guests, who were allegedly visiting for private lessons. Anything private was bound to stir interest, and her father clearly was a magnet. Stepping back between your four walls, playing music and reeling films in your imagination were the only sure ways of keeping safe, while resting in a place of your own.

As a silent witness to their fights, Lili chose to side

with Mother as an obvious victim of his temper. And yet, Mother seemed to disapprove of this and defended her husband, which infuriated Lili. Mother kept holding forth about the Professor's hard time at the Physics Institute, where he was apparently treated unfairly; his file seemed not to be clean enough, and his lectures and books not Marxist enough, which was why the secret police harassed him and listened on their phone.

Lili wouldn't hear about that. The Physics Institute was another world. What mattered was the inferno at home, which he alone was responsible for. He had made the world outside her room an alien place where dangers were lurking at every step.

Yimmi Papa's clever Lili girl had become the emblem of a lost paradise. So much for being singled out as anyone's clever girl. So much for being a magnet of attention.

She does take it for granted that she's clever, nonetheless. She also knows that there are yet unexplored depths in her heart.

She's not sure about much more than that about herself, so she's piecing up the evidence she has collected over the years: the impressions she has made on the others, the hearsay, the testimonies of those who have crossed her path.

For now, walking on the stage set of her daily life, she feels like a graceful flower – a lily, maybe? She's tall and slim, taking after the Professor, they say. There is a certain lightness in her step, as if slightly detached in an air bubble of her own. This is vaguely familiar, because Professor Danes seems to walk with his head in the clouds, chin slightly turned upwards, navigating his path by casually peering under the rim of his glasses.

Occasionally, she examines herself in the tall window of her wardrobe. She isn't exactly pretty, she believes, but she does get noticed. Gabriel, her first love, had spotted her walking to the beach alone that summer, and had followed her to say hi. He told her later that from a distance, she'd looked a few years older. More womanly, he meant. He was twenty-three, but she was sixteen back then.

She assumes, therefore, that there's a potentially attractive woman lurking in her, waiting to mature. But it's not her time yet. She's still Lili Danes, the brilliant schoolgirl, dreaming of going back in time and saving John Lennon.

Otherwise? Val Nestor told her once that some girls envied her looks. She opened her eyes wide in disbelief. "What for?" She'd always assumed she looked clumsy and stiff, too earnest and nerdy to be attractive.

"Well, some of them think there's something very feminine about you, which you are not faking with makeup or other frills."

"Feminine?" Lili wondered. That might tie in with what Gabriel had seen in her from a distance. "Is it something on my face?"

Makeup was inconceivable at school anyway, they'd be sent home and the parents would be called in. She only had an eyeliner pencil stump which used to belong to Mother.

Val Nestor laughed. "Not entirely, Lili. There's a gentleness in your features, yes, but you stand out with something both aloof and graceful about your whole person. Like a rare flower. Keep that as long as you can!" he'd added without a smile.

Lili was dumbstruck. She'd never thought the lily in herself might be visible to others, too.

She can't find anything else remarkable about herself when looking in the mirror. She has the same dark brown hair and eyes as most of the others.

Except, maybe, for the fact that her hair is thick and rich. Gabriel told her so many times, running his hand through it, at the back of her head. She holds it mostly tied back in a tight pony tail; it's her earnest, school look. When she goes out with Dana, her best friend, she lets it fall free on her shoulders. That's her 'I'm young and romantic, and life's got so much in store for me' look. It's on such downtown trips that she'll use her eyeliner stump to underscore the outline of her dark eyes.

She has a pale complexion, and her deep-sunken eyes often seem to be gazing from some remote place. With the intense school and study schedule of the final year, she finds she often looks haggard.

She likes her lips most. Nicely drawn. A bit of colour would look good when she grows up, but for now, trying out Mother's only, light coral lipstick, it looks like an accidental smudge. Putting on a mock smile in the mirror, she begins to fathom what people might like about her.

Should she smile more, talk more, so her face comes alive?

One other thing she takes for granted is that being clever is what prevents her from having more buddies. Being clever earns admiration, not popularity. Being clever also means it's hard to feel comfortable fooling around.

She only has Dana for a friend, and there's little to nothing going on in her life outside of school. Apart from their daily triangle of school–private classes–home, they read a book in bed at night, which takes them somewhere else, and enables them to create private spaces that should hold for their lifetimes.

Now and then, there's a birthday party, with last year's music discreetly brought over from the West and copied dozens of times successively as it's passed from hand to hand. There is dancing in a circle, chatting in small groups, or drinking and eating and drinking and drinking. Not herself, of course.

Lili and Dana long for a life lived fully, which tends to be about being in the thick of it, connected. During earlier adolescence, when the school schedule still allowed long leisure hours, they would sit on a bench in the neighbourhood park, on the peaks of boredom, watching others having their fun, being insiders in their connected worlds. Like spectators in a cinema, they would watch, delight, and ache along with what they saw, painfully wishing to stand up and walk into the set.

There was that guy wearing John Lennon glasses and shoulder-length hair, who looked exactly like John's picture that Lili had cut out from the culture journal, when it was running a documentary series about the Beatles, and had treasured in a special folder ever since. Both girls would be looking forward to seeing the neighbourhood's John walk by with his dreamer look. This must be the real John, who must have faked his death to get away from it all. Dana even called out to him once, "John!", and he slightly turned his head; the two girls ducked out of sight, holding their hands over their mouths, eyes wide in amazement.

Their dream team of true buddies would be better than a family: no know-it-alls, no yelling and swearing, no fights, but holding together like one. Together, in those fantasies, with John and their squad, they'd hang out on the main alley, singing, playing ball games, laughing wildly, riding bikes, meeting without any need to set a time, as if the park was their home and their kingdom. A modern version of one for all, all for one.

Sundays and on summer holidays, they'd get up with the hens, grab a guitar and run to the station with a backpack full of sandwiches to go to the mountains, adventurous, jolly, and laid back. That bit was not prescribed in any Young Communist code of conduct.

There were songs about travelling without a ticket, and pacifying the conductor so you could still get to your destination safely. 'Your ticket please, oh here, oh where, hang on a mo, c'mon conductor let me go,' went a popular one.

Lili had no guitar, though, and only a few friendly pals, good kids doing well in school like herself, who had no idea about the timetables of the trains to the mountains.

She turns in unfailingly at the same hour every night. She knows when it's time to call it a day, so she can start a new one tomorrow. Mother and Father might still be smoking in his study, whispering about the latest gossip at the theatre or the Institute. The lights are almost always still on in their house at that time, the gate and the house door not yet locked for the night.

She lies down and watches the diffuse stripes of light from the street lamp, squeezing in between the folds of the curtains and landing on the ceiling of her room. If it's summer, she keeps the window open for a while, before closing her eyes to go to sleep.

She takes it all in: the faint breeze, the distant barks of the neighbourhood's homeless dogs, the hushed chirp of the crickets hidden under leaves – until the four walls of her room are dissolved and her mind is wandering the world.

What world, though? The mechanics of her daily life are not just dull, but downright oppressive. Is there a place that her thoughts can fly to, and find a nest to cuddle in? A place where she's free to be herself?

There's only Lennon and his music. His electrical voice and his words touching her deep.

I'm stepping out, just watching the wheel. Gimme some truth.

Woman, I can hardly express... It's like starting over.

The endless space becomes her home.

She's not in love with any boy, so his love words bounce back. From him to her, and back to him.

But she'll never find a John in her life.

There is no other John.

Unless...

She sometimes allows herself to glide into the fantasy.

* * *

It was dusk and the park across the street, in full blossom, was shivering in the last sunbeams.

"Now's the time," she told herself, watching it from the attic halo window.

She went down the stairs to her room, changed her dress, and took one last look at the contents of the drawers in her desk. There were her letters to John, written of a dreamy night, watching the stars. She grabbed the scrap of paper where she'd taken down the words for *I'm stepping out.*

I gotta make it! she whispered to herself. She closed the drawers, pulled the blinds with jolting movements, and in her rush she hit the vase of flowers. The water started gurgling across her desk, onto the floor. She watched paralysed. Then, she reached out for one of the daffodils, broke its stem short, and tucked it into the breast pocket of her jacket.

At the door, she looked at the wardrobe and a funny thought crossed her mind: what if it's raining *there*? She grabbed her raincoat and rushed out of the house.

She walked straight to the park, her head brimming with crumpets of thoughts. The daffodil in her breast pocket was giving out a hypnotising fragrance. She took it for a good sign.

The park's so eerie now that it won't be hard to lose this reality. What if I go to sleep and I wake up tomorrow morning like a vagrant, on a park bench? Hold on: what's going to happen to me? No, I mustn't think about that now.

What if everything's going to be just a dream? What if I go to sleep and I only dream that I made it, and then the park janitor wakes me up?

What's it gonna be like, being there? Am I gonna be there? I have to be!

I hope no one busts in. And above all, I hope I'm not gonna be afraid, I mustn't, I mustn't!

I just have to make it. I have to. Otherwise, it would mean one human being was born without any purpose, and then everything falls through...

No, that was impossible. Why should she have been born without a purpose? She knew very well what she wanted, what that purpose was, and this alone meant she was going to fulfil it.

After wandering about the park for a while, she finally found a spot where there might not be intruders. It was under an old lilac bush, surrounded by irises and daffodils. If she looked over the flowering jasmine bush, she could see the hazy lake. She could hear frogs and occasional bird squawks in the distance, while she was lying under the lilac, eyes closed.

Okay, hush now. Quiet. A lot of quiet. I'm stepping out.

The flood of thoughts slowed down, until only one was left, hanging like a thread.

I'm stepping out.

The words dripped off one by one, like drops off the rim of a cup, into emptiness. They were the same, again and again, like the strikes of a clock, echoing in a vast, empty room. *I'm stepping out.*

The lilac blossom came down and landed on her eyelids, cheeks, and lips with a caress. The sound and touch vanished in a bottomless abyss. She felt she was plunging into herself, drawn by a force she could not, and would not, resist. The seconds raced past her, or she did past them, catching them up, seeing their faces turned back to her, recognising them and leaving them behind. In that race, she covered vast spaces within herself and countless seconds in the universe. Then, she hung between two worlds.

She felt a light touch on her eyelids. It was the last flower falling from the lilac bush in the park, and the first ray of light.

She opened her eyes and saw the bright sky. Nothing seemed to have changed. There were already early rowers on the lake. The flowers and the blossoming bushes were still there, too. Dew on the grass. She, she was still the same, carrying the same daffodil in her breast pocket.

She had been dreaming, then.

All because of the lilac and the jasmine with their fragrance.

She left her spot carefully, although no one was around. She went out into the street. The same houses and the same little shops. Just –

An old-fashioned car swerved round the corner. A woman came out of the bookshop, dressed like she came from another decade.

The streets were the same, but the people were different. Or they might be the same, just younger.

She'd made it!

She had to hurry to the station. Once there, she got herself a ticket to the big city.

She'd been there so many times, waiting for other trains. Now, finally she would board the right one.

* * *

It was three thirty in the afternoon. At four, she would find John at the corner of this street, walking to the park. At five thirty, he'd be back out of the park, and at ten thirty he'd be walking home. In front of his building, he was going to be shot dead.

While he was in the park, she had to play the card of her life. And of his life, too: at that point, his life became tied to hers.

At four, she could see John from afar, and she took some time watching him as he strolled towards the park entrance. It was the first time she had seen him, and still, it felt as if she'd known him forever. That bouncing step, chin up, gazing around while seeming in a world of his own, a faint smile on his thin lips. His eyes met hers for a second before he passed by. She knew: when she was back home, she would return a million times just to this moment.

She checked back into reality and noticed the stranger lurking behind John. That man must be erased from the picture!

She hurried along a side alley to catch up with John, and waited for him in front of a parterre of roses. And there he came from round a corner, suddenly facing her, briefly recognising her, but walking on. Her face lit up and she rushed to him. He stopped, wondering, while she hugged him. The stranger was there, behind them.

"How wonderful you're here, at last!" she exclaimed and kissed him on the cheek. "I've been waiting here and thought you'd never come."

His confusion melted into hearty laughter. How she loved him for that!

She took his arm and pulled him along.

"By god," he said, "if you're the press, too, I'll shoot myself!"

No, no shooting today, please, a voice screamed in her mind.

"Have you really been waiting for me so long?" he asked with playful irony.

"Oh, not really, just eighteen years," she replied.

A faint shadow went over his eyes for a second, and she felt there was some acknowledgement in there.

"Come with me," she said.

"So soon?"

"Yes, please, as soon as can be."

He chuckled.

"You got me wrong. I meant, this generation is different."

She'd got him all right, but time was running short.

"Please, come along. How can I explain?" She despaired for a moment. The stranger behind might be able to hear. She looked into John's eyes and felt their steel giving her strength. "How can I explain? Forget what I said last night. It wasn't my fault, believe me. But what else could I have said with Steve being there? I wished I could have made you understand, signalled you some way something like *it's all just an act*, but Steve kept watching us and you know he's a son of a bitch!"

Their eyes glistened in complicity, and she pulled him along, out of the park, on to the street. He followed. She called a taxi and off they went.

* * *

"And now?" John asked.

They were standing in a B&B room she had booked before meeting him.

"And now – we wait."

She looked out the window. The chestnut trees were in bloom, and the lawn was sprinkled with wild daffodils and irises.

"Wow. Unbelievable," John said. "All this James Bond action – in a moment I'm going to feel like a kidnap victim."

No. John must never be a victim.

"Make yourself comfortable. We need to wait a few hours."

"Wait for what? Look, do I get permission to feel totally stupid here?" His eyes pierced through her, peeling her like a chestnut of its burr. "I got it that there was some wicked Steve watching us earlier, but now I'm all in the dark."

"Why?" she asked, at a loss for words.

"Why? I'm taking a stroll when a young woman I don't know gives me a big hug, kisses me, tells me she's been waiting for me and pulls me along. I tell her that this young generation has evolved quite a lot, but she won't listen and tells me a story instead about some son-of-a-bitch Steve. We get into a taxi, she pushes me into a B&B, and – crazy! – she hasn't kidnapped me because she's in love with me, no, so god knows what for! And now you're telling me to make myself comfortable for the next few hours?"

"I'm in love with you."

He laughed. She laughed along.

"How very romantic. But I need to be somewhere else at five thirty."

"It's very likely you won't be."

The hours dragged on.

She kept looking out the window feverishly, watching in case the wicked Steve might be lurking around the garden.

He sat on the floor, brooding. Turning hypotheses around, but believing her that there was some vital stake involved. Something was going on. Was she a crazy fan? Was it a bet? But she wouldn't be fretting so much. So anxious to keep him away from the window or the door.

At some point, to kill the tense quiet, they started talking. Memories, passions, miracles.

"Tell me something: who are you?"

"My name's Diane."

"Anything else you'd like to share, Diane? Like, why I'm here?"

"I can't answer that. Not now."

"When?"

"At midnight."

"Is it a spell?"

"You might call it that, too."

"How else might you call it?"

"Don't know."

"Try."

"Maybe time. Or love. No idea."

"A spell, time, and love. Whose love? For what, or for whom?"

"A broader concept."

"And if it's a broader concept, what's making you so anxious?"

"The time. Or maybe all three of them. Or their reverse. Oh, no idea, let's stop talking about it, please!"

"What should we talk about, then?"

"Mmm... miracles."

"— ?"

"Let's take one: music."

Their half whispered words blended and got tangled together in the dusk. She saw his words dancing in the room, become real, while time was being filtered through a sieve, the time that she was taking apart, twisting and untangling, but which was so powerful that it could turn on them at any moment.

It grew dark outside, almost too soon, as if time was running short. It was eight.

"Time's flying like crazy," he said. "Are you waiting for something to happen?"

"No. No, on the contrary."

"On the contrary?"

"Yes. If it happened, then everything was in vain. And I'd go nuts."

"What about me?"

"You..."

She wouldn't think of it.

He stood and came up behind her, at the window.

"It's got so dark so quick," he whispered.

What if wicked Steve was hiding out there?

"Get away from here," she said, pushing him aside in

panic.

They sat down on the settee, but then she stood up again, rushed to the window and drew the curtains. There.

"I have a slight feeling I might be thankful to you for something at midnight when you tell me what this was all about."

"No need for thankfulness, John. Just... live on."

He sighed.

"You know, I was raised by an aunt, Mimi. She's in all my childhood memories. An unusual woman. Her life is still very much about me, almost as if she lives in the past, somehow."

"And she contaminates the others, too."

"What? You know her?"

"She's my neighbour."

"You're kidding!"

"No. That's where I come from. My childhood is also full of the memories of her house, and her stories about you."

"Who are you, Diane, and how come you're so close?"

"I'm one of the kids in that neighbourhood, who Mimi grew fond of, and so she'd spend hours talking to me about her kid called John."

"That's unbelievable. Did she send you over?"

"Not directly, no."

"God, she never talked to me about you. I wish she had."

Diane laughed.

"She couldn't have told you about me."

"Why?"

"That's part of the midnight mystery."

"Okay. Fine. I'll wait. But tomorrow, when all this is over, I'm going back with you. I wonder if she still has those roses."

Tomorrow! What meaning would this word have? She had no idea if she'd be able to find the way back home. But that didn't matter. Not now.

She checked her watch. It was eleven thirty. Time suddenly seemed to come to a halt. She decided to keep her eyes on the watch, to keep watching those stubborn seconds crawling on their way, hoping she'd nudge them faster over the rim. When all this was over, they would laugh at all this anxiety. Or maybe they wouldn't?

And then, suddenly, the wait was over, time was over and broke into millions of pieces. Then, there was just the quiet.

John looked up at her as she stood like a shadow in front of him. Was it her face, or Mimi's? Was he a kid again? Had he gone back to some state he'd lost over the years?

"Diane?" he whispered.

"It's over, John. You're safe."

She let herself fall on her knees, holding her head in her hands. It was another day, and John was alive, defying his fate.

* * *

Lili sits up and sobs, her shoulders shaking.

The fantasy feeds and drains her at the same time. The draining is good, too: it shuts off the mundane reality, and thus brings release.

Weeping all that loving pain out – the love for Life, out there in the world, the pain of being stranded in the wrong time and place. She can almost feel the invisible string tying her to the other, grand world where she belongs, which she was cut off from, being left helpless in this alien dimension.

But hush now, she's alone with her pain. No one can know.

School had become a heavier burden these past two years.

It wasn't only the dull, irrelevant classes. She gradually became more painfully aware that she wasn't fitting in with other people.

There were party fellowships, as she and Dana called them, and the pale, stranded apparitions like herself. The former with the never-exhausted appetite for extroversion, the latter social aliens in danger of withering from so much cramming.

The fellowships were impossible to ignore. She found their relentless partying almost disgusting, with their endless resourcefulness about how to have fun, ranging from drinking bouts to stupid gurgling laughs over gross jokes, and disrupting classes just to play cool. A pitiful counterpart to the squad of besties she and Dana had dreamed about as younger teenagers.

They had an obnoxious habit of showing up at every given party, whether they were invited or not, apparently keeping a log of everyone's birthdays. The party fellows would pop up at the door with a cheap bottle of vodka and a merry "happy birthday" as a pretext to be let in, then hijack the party for themselves.

What made the matter complicated was that she wished, in fact, that she was cool in the eyes of the fellowship, and maybe even belonged as an insider. The besties squad, partly come true.

Was she clumsy because she didn't know how to act, being stranded with the wrong people, in the wrong setting – her school – her life? Or was she stranded because she was such a hopeless weirdo? She was caught between the wish to be seen, liked, and allowed to join in – and the realisation that she didn't like, let alone belong with them. As a result, she sulked, and then cringed at the thought of how much worse her sulking was making things. She disliked the clique, but blamed herself for not mingling.

If only she could be given the right part in the right story, she would be glowing and flowing with it. But as it was, some inadequacy prevented her from acting out the brilliance that the clever Lili girl carried inside.

She's not at home in her world. At home, as well as at school.

So no wonder she's crossing out each week on the paper calendar in the kitchen, as the final exams are drawing nearer, week by week, month by month. Soon she'll be delivered, and find a home.

Teachers had been pompous or hilarious figures exerting their authority to reward or punish. Some gentle, others dreadful. Never on both sides of the teacher desk.

Until Val Nestor came along to shatter their assumptions.

He didn't look like a cut-out from a photo album of the fifties; he didn't have grey hairs; he could get mad and thrash things around, on the brink of calling them all mentally retarded. He brought his temper to the school, and wasn't afraid of letting it come forward.

Which was also why he was the confidante of many of his students, who rightfully estimated that they could trust, more than fear, him.

Some of the cocky ones would mock him for being so short, and so disproportionately choleric. In truth, however, they only had the guts to do it when he turned his back.

He got quickly mad when kids got an answer wrong, as if their failure was an insult to the beautiful galaxy called Chemistry. He would be silent for a few seconds, then unexpectedly, he would swirl around and chuck the piece of chalk against the blackboard, or hit the nearest desk with his palm in wild frustration, his eyes drilling holes in whoever dared to glance back. They would all freeze. Then came the worst – his words.

"This was a science high-school the last time I checked, not an evening school for Second Education Pathway!"

Clever Lili, who finds school so not herself, and the party fellowships so silly, dreams of becoming an astrophysicist, so she might skip the grey alienating world and find a home in the cosmic harmonies. The only vexing thing is that it might be interpreted as the daughter following in her father's footsteps.

She had first set her mind on medicine, and had made the mistake of telling him, in the first term of high school. For admission to medicine, Lili would need to take chemistry, so Val Nestor had all the more reason to become invested in her performance.

She continued to excel in the physics class, but she would no longer bring those trophies home to her father. She stopped giving them any value, as if her talent for physics was a bond with him which she was taking for granted as a genetic gift, and shrugged at it in indifference. The gift, she believed, was a predilection for crazy-scientist abstractions. She wanted to do things. Here, on earth, not in the galaxies of atomic forces. As a medical doctor, your work made a tangible difference.

Her parents had been happy with her choice, if only with a shadow of concern over where the placement may take her at the end: medicine graduates were sure to be sent to a village. There were the envelopes of money, or the wine hamper and the pork chop, which the peasants would humbly hand over as a matter of course, to balance against the rubber boots that would be the daily gear, and the damning life without running water, two hours away from the nearest train station. If qualified to do a technical job, however, you were bound to be placed in a town, often one which was developing around a large industrial plant.

Admission came first, however. Few got in at the first attempt; most of the medicine candidates needed to stay on track and re-sit the exams for as many as seven or eight years. Getting in was a proof of intellectual brilliance and fierce determination.

Val Nestor had, therefore, the perfect pretext of bullying her into getting higher grades. He could blend fondness, empathy, and brutal verbal showers. The fonder he was of one of them, the more ruthless he became, and Lili got to learn that on her own skin. What she delivered was never good enough to match her talent, nor the demands of medicine; he whipped her, estimating she'd feel pushed to stretch herself more.

The outcome was, however, the opposite. She started doubting herself and the point of cramming biology and chemistry in the first place. It took shame and guilt at the thought of disappointing him, but one day, inevitably her resolution was made: medicine was not for her.

She couldn't remember when exactly she'd given up the idea; maybe she'd already suspected it when, aged fourteen, her pet dog had been run over by a car and she'd fainted at the sight. Everyone commiserated and comforted her, but she knew she would never be able to handle suffering. Not somebody else's; her own suffering she would know how to carry around, safely locked in her chest, put away, sealed under wordlessness.

It took years for that insight to turn into a decision. She kept it to herself, however, so that the family continued to assume that she was going to become a medical doctor. Secretly, very secretly, she made up her mind about focusing on physics instead. It was her element, after all. So much of her known universe was about her fascination with the sky, her father's books, his stories about atoms, quasars, and gravitation, or the homework he'd solved for her with his elegant reasoning, like a stylish signature over her schoolgirlish handwriting.

It was not a straightforward process, however. Going for physics was such an obvious choice, with her talent, and her father being there both at home and at the university – but that was also a reason for resistance. The useless theories and endless, pointless research; was her father researching his life away from the stifling daily routine of average mortals? How pitiful!

For her part, she was choosing her favourite subject not just to pass admission more easily, as many of her school mates did, but as a profession for life. That was her bold statement about making intransigent choices, away from the instrumentality of passing admission or securing a safe position in a town after graduation. She took secret pride in that dose of idealism.

But in a secret nook of her mind, she knew that physics offered her, too, that escape from the stifling, but mostly alien, daily life.

Going for pure physics meant choosing a world of ideas, instead of the motherland's building sites and industrial plants. Ideological imperatives were suspended in such worlds, where phenomena occurred by virtue of universal laws, in a chain of cause and effect. That provided the foundations for her to rely on facts and their logical consequences, the perfect example of which being: she was a brilliant student, hence she'd succeed.

In physics she could say, this is me. Physics would be her safe home.

But her father must not know. No way was she going to give him the satisfaction that his clever Lili girl was taking after him!

It was up to her whether she was going to become the same scientist as her father, locked in a tower of engulfing theories, putting out spiteful verdicts about their lives in the real world.

Maybe she would become a physics teacher, as the placements after theoretical studies were always about teaching posts. Physics meets reality. The physical laws of inertia, resistance, friction, entropy – she might be able to convert them to order, harmony and inspiration for a bunch of kids. At least at the beginning. And then somehow, in ways she could not yet imagine, life would make it possible for her to explore the skies.

But her father must not know.

Now, in the final year, she takes private classes in physics and maths, which are the only admission subjects for physics at the higher level. At home she claims that she's also joining the chemistry after-hours coaching in the school, which would have been necessary if she was going to apply for medicine. Maths is not needed for medicine, but at home it goes that she needs maths for the school-leaving exam.

Her father has dropped a few comments about why someone like her needs extra tutoring for the school-leaving exam, where every pupil is to pass anyway, since the Party insists that everyone has equal chances in life, so they all need to get out of school with good grades.

To counter his suspicions, she told him that she was having problems with integer analysis and strings, and nothing further was exchanged. Which goes to prove that there are also advantages to not talking to each other much.

Mother is proof to her that one can be both passionate in the bubble of one's personal life and reasonable in one's interaction with the outside world. She's a technical director in a theatre. She has to make sure the performances run smoothly, with all the actors properly coordinated, stage set in place, technicians at hand. Lili senses that Mother must be good at organising and know how to handle people. A bit of diplomacy here, a bit of familiarity and even belly patting there, a bit of motherly strictness, cracking a joke, or whatever does the trick in the moment. She has to be alert and permanently watch out for any potential ambivalence that might expose her to criticism in the Party Committee meeting, or in the Working People's Committee meeting, or in the Women's Committee meeting. If that should happen, she needs to be equipped with arguments to clear her name, which requires constant forward thinking to anticipate pitfalls and procure herself the proper cover in advance.

It is on the strength of such forward thinking that Mrs Danes joined the Party as soon as she started employment, which happened even before going to university. With that cover, she would not stand out, nor give reasons for questions to be asked, especially regarding her commitment to the Party's mission. By virtue of a precept generally accepted, it is best to stay under the radar, so as to keep oneself and one's family out of harm's way. Minding one's own business, materialised in doing one's job conscientiously, is the best strategy.

Lili intuitively trusts Mother's problem-solving skills and her ability to steer through rough waters. It is safe to be with her.

By contrast, her father is a constant hazard. He is stuck with his principles of how the world should be ruled, Lili finds, and keeps countless tabs on how the political system fails. To her, this intellectual habit amounts to reality loss. He keeps growling about the oppressive state spying on its citizens, but then he doesn't seem to care that his growling is exposing them all.

The Professor only condescended to join the Party when it became obvious that his academic career was being deliberately sabotaged by some elusive, mysterious entity high up in the stratosphere of their little socialist state. But then it was too late to join, and the mistake would stay forever in his file; he had unmistakably stood out.

As a teenager, Dimi Danes had pedalled his way to school fifteen kilometres every day. He was the miller's son, which counted as a stain in his file. With a few land plots, and a steady income generated by the mill, his father had been stamped as "bourgeois," and therefore, part of the oppressing class, when the communist party took over.

Dimi was a boy when, in the late forties, his father was dispossessed and sent to work in a factory as a welder. The village school only went up to grade eight, but Dimi went on to high school in the big city. His physics teacher and the books in the school library put an irreversible spell on him, which made the daily ride on his rusty bike a necessary pain.

The one avenue, of science, opened the universe's grand order to young Dimi, by explaining how phenomena fell into place within the cosmic picture. The other avenue, of the classic thinkers, revealed the significance behind the phenomena, and the harmonies among the scientific laws at work in the outer space as well as in the human mind.

Dimi Danes had no civic goals, only a fascination with his work. To him, forward thinking referred to understanding the effects of physical laws, the conclusions of mathematical equations, or the outcomes of chemical reactions. Broader still, his forward thinking took him to reflections on the ultimate coherence woven into the universal fabric, and pointed him to the discrepancies, the knots and loose ends that needed remedying in the imperfect human world.

It was on the swing of his twofold fascination that he became the outstanding pupil, later the brilliant university student. He did menial jobs in a newspaper office to pay the rent on a downtown studio flat; instead of riding his bike from his village into the city to go to school, he now did so from the city centre out, to the Physics Department, on a special site located beyond the urban boundaries. "The platform," as it was called, hosted not just the academic department, but also a nuclear research facility.

Each term, he would pedal his way between the platform and the city-central university building for the odd course he was keen to visit as an invisible guest student: Ontology and Ethics, Romanticism and the Birth of the Nation, or The Rise and Fall of the Hellenic Culture.

On graduating, he was offered a junior teaching post in the Physics Institute. He was praised for his unifying, cross-disciplinary visions, his compelling papers and his addresses in the lecture halls. Soon there were philosophy students pedalling their way from the city out to the Physics Institute to attend his thought-provoking seminars, or his dissertation speeches. He was merely a junior assistant lecturer, but he was often trusted with the task of standing in for the professors.

"We can only start grasping how the natural forces work by exploring the vacuum – that is the El Dorado holding the mysteries of science and of the three fundamental elements: space, mass, field. Since the beginning of the century we have known that mass is only vibrating energy become material. Nernst, who postulated the quantum vacuum, Planck, Einstein and a few others have shed light on non-zero vacuum state energy fluctuations, which fundamentally refer to the indelible existence of an underlying energy field that persists even in a mass-free space, or what we would otherwise call a vacuum. Even at what would be a zero-point energy, as Planck and Einstein demonstrated, harmonic oscillators still possess an energy value. There is no absolute zero-point. There is only zero mass. The material vacuum, the one we can perceive as an absence of matter, is never a quantum vacuum. Never zero: remember this as what you might take away as a guiding principle for our lives, too. Every day, take even a tiny step; but never stand still."

Soon, Dimi Danes was standing out not just by not applying to join the Party, but also by drawing audiences with speeches that induced the subversive idea that there was a whole universe, and a mysterious, enduring and all-pervading entity, beyond the Party's Bright Future and New Citizen.

If action could be effected not from matter over matter, in the rationalist, Marxist and Newtonian spirit, but from energy over matter – would the working class stop working to build the multilaterally developed society, on account of the quantum field solving all the problems for them? The class struggle, the bourgeois oppressive rule, the cult of labour, and the question of ownership over means of production were but ephemeral phenomena at the periphery of a cosmos emerging from, and crumbling back into, invisible ether. If people understood that spirit was above matter, they would trust God more than the Beloved Leader.

Could there be more threatening ideologies than those backed by science proving the inherent mystery of the Cosmos, and acknowledging the illusion of human power? Against the cosmic impenetrable forces, the life mission and code of conduct provided by the Party appeared ludicrous and downright futile. What was the point of proving socialism superior and building a new citizen, thereby accepting shortage and want of pluralist options, if forces were at work that could blow the Party into dust within a fraction of a second?

And did that mean that the spirit can never be truly subdued, there being no absolute point zero? That oppression, no matter how systematic, could never entirely delete the last trace of resistance, be it in the form of protest, or mere mockery?

"The enduring mission of both physics and philosophy has been to uncover the unifying principle of life and the universe. Philosophy defines itself as the very unified vision, integrating scientific insights across disciplines into an all-encompassing view that might explain who we are, how our human plane reflects and interacts with the universe, and ultimately, what the meaning of life is. Explore the macro, and you'll understand the micro. Look to the stars, and you'll grasp the secrets of our human body. Everything – everything – is interconnected and can be traced back to the ultimate element: space. There we find the subtle, still unmapped energy complex that generates matter and all its subsequent patterns of interaction, studied under the names of physics, chemistry, biology, psychology, and beyond. Elucidate these forces, and we will understand what forces govern our lives, and how we can fit into the universal harmony, as individuals and as a human race."

The universal harmony was a seductive construct, but one that spelled bitterness, too, in the friction with a single-minded state. Uncovering and fitting into that harmony was pushed behind the requisites of daily living, which may have been infinitely less important on the grand scale, but were incomparably more urgent.

Unless – unless one found a way to skip this trivial plane as a nonsensical, ephemeral disruption in the grand order, and settle oneself above it, on a self-made dimension. From that higher standpoint, one could dedicate oneself, most likely through one's profession, directly to the grand harmonies. Truths and exploration were not hindered by closed borders or ideological cleansing.

From that higher standpoint, one easily got the impression one could afford to sneer, even at the much feared secret police, part of the Department of State Security within the Ministry of Interior. The Security, for short. Madam Secu, in Professor Danes's sarcastic terminology. Unlike the regular police, who dealt with trivial matters such as traffic or crime and stood out in their grey-blue outfits, the secret police hunted down anti-state "subversive elements" and kept its soldiers discreetly omnipresent. The civilians, they were called.

"They're so adamant against the retrograde, oppressive bourgeois regime before the war," Dimi Danes would declaim at the dinner table, with or without guests sitting by. Mimicking sudden realisation, he would tap underneath the edge of the table, as if checking for bugs. He would carry on nevertheless, unstoppable in what he was keen to articulate.

"The bitter irony is that Madam Secu is the exact replica of what the corrupt bourgeois state also employed, and called The Safety. At least safety hints at people being kept safe; the Security is keeping the state safe from its people – but who cares, anyway, since the state *is* the people. Whatever keeps them safe from each other must be good."

Lili has learned, over time, the Professor's theatrical routines and noticed with growing anxiety how Mother keeps her eyes down during these speeches, sometimes shaking her head with pent-up annoyance.

It's a Madam Secu civilian squad of three that drives Professor Danes off to a vague address one late January evening in 1987.

"How's your love life?" Val Nestor puts an arm around her shoulders, head bent, as if to listen to her earnestly, although his tone is half playful.

She's been waiting for him to come out of the staff room, wanting to talk, and he's walking her along the school corridor to the science lab, where they can sit undisturbed.

It's late January, not nearly half-way through the ordeal of the school year, and something's terribly dreary in her life right now. She's not sure what she wants to say to him, or what she needs to hear, but she knows she doesn't need to worry about steering a conversation with Nestor: he'll be the catalyst and the pilot, and she needs his adrenaline. Her father was seized by the police last night. She would like to take that bang to someone trusted, but she doesn't know the language. A kick in the bottom and the thud of his head against the gate pole, goaded on like a donkey. The obscene haha laugh of the two grey-clothed, faceless intruders.

Instead, she sighs, half exasperated, half amused. She's going to miss this theatrical, obnoxious, impertinent, bullyish, and yet so lovable teacher when high school is over.

"Love life? What's that?" she asks in mock confusion.

Nestor lets out the gurgling laugh he's been holding back while acting the earnest teacher.

"A girl like you, what a shame," he teases. "But I guess it's fine as it is. It's only six months to go," he says, suddenly game aside, and he raises his dark, bushy eyebrows.

She takes the familiar seat at a pupil's desk, and he grabs the teacher's chair and sits down opposite her. Then, he remembers something; he stands up, walks over to the corner behind the teacher's desk, and switches on the radio.

He looks at her with a complicit smile. Better to keep the conversation for themselves.

My home is a song with graceful tones, holding me gentle, holding my life. The lady of Romanian pop music. What does her flat look like? Lili wonders each time she hears the hit. Surely it's not cold and draughty, with sooty ceiling corners. The gossip goes that she's with a Western big shot in the Diplomatic Corps.

"Come, it's been a while, what's up in your life?"

Lili browses quickly through her routine, but can't find anything worth proclaiming as news.

"Well," she sighs again, "nothing's up. That's the point, I guess."

Nestor keeps quiet, waiting for more. His piercing gaze, this alone was worth coming to talk to him for. It's sharp and alive, unlike her daily life, which feels blunt and blurry.

"I'd imagine a lot of studying's up," he offers, "or I should hope so, at least!"

She rolls her eyes; there it goes again, his old obsession that she's not working hard enough.

"Oh, please, I thought we were past that!"

"Past what? Past the fact that you're still not pulling your weight, because you're in a perpetual daze?" he machine-guns her, retaining half of his playful smile. It's the point where Lili can't tell if he's still only teasing, or if he means harm. How does he know about her school performance at all, now he's no longer their teacher? Does he question other teachers in the staff room?

"You still think I idle my days away? How, could you please tell me, how could I do that? I'd love to have half an hour to just daydream, or worse, just to stare into blankness, but no, I've got the next private lesson to hike to, ninety minutes on the tram there, and ninety minutes back, not counting the class itself! I can't believe you still bear me a grudge for not getting the grades you thought I should! After all these years! When all I want is to feel there's some room for me in this routine, too, not just drill, drill, drill."

She stops short, almost bursting into tears. But that's also part of why she's here. He does that to her, and it does her good. To feel alive, even if it hurts.

My home is the best that I have, and I'm the heart beating within its walls.

"Remember that – " that rubbish, she adds inwardly " – remember what you told me in September, at your farewell parents' meeting, in front of the whole crowd, that I wasn't carrying my mountain?"

He grins.

"I didn't say you weren't carrying your mountain. Maybe you aren't carrying your grain of sand, if that's what you're only capable of," he says, mock shrugging.

She scoffs and slaps her thighs in frustration.

"Why, I thought that was a good one," he goes on. "Deep. Just like the fancy readings you enjoy," he teases further.

Lili frowns, briefly intrigued.

News bulletin. The country's president, Comrade Nicolae Ceaușescu, has undertaken a work visit at the steel plant in Galati. He was welcomed by the crowds of workers with—

"Is Raskolnikov still your favourite hero? Surpassing even Winnetou?" He grins again, revealing his crooked teeth.

She blushes. So he remembers that, too.

"Winnetou was the hero when I was thirteen. Now, it's John. Lennon."

Nestor whistles in appreciation.

"So now we're finally getting closer to real heroes. That's progress. Knowing you, I'd say you like *Imagine*," he struggles to hold back another laugh.

Imagine is all people know about John.

Still, she knows better than to get carried away with vexation. This is Val Nestor, and she expects he'll never change, even when he retires, many decades from now.

—the quarterly targets have been achieved ahead of term, in alignment with the five-year development plan—

"No, you see, you don't read me like you think you do," she takes her turn teasing him. "It's Lennon's mastermind, and clever, killing irony, and for all that, he's a man in love, who's capable of love – " she lets her short rant trail off. He'll tease her for being sentimental next thing she knows.

"Wasn't Raskolnikov the same?" he questions her instead.

"Raskolnikov was – he was the inverted hero. The one nobody suspected, while he was being chased for murder. Look, let's forget about heroes, at least today," she pleads.

"Heroes are great, they inspire us," Nestor probes.

Lili swivels her head to look out the window. The dead, frozen January.

Comrade Ceaușescu congratulated the workers and gave guidance on the way forward—

She wants no hero status. They have been expected to impersonate heroes from pre-school age: a Motherland Scout at four, a Pioneer at seven, a YC – Young Communist at fifteen. Always part of a patriot squad, divided by titles, endowed with ceremonies, salutes, and red hard-cover codes of conduct.

As far back as she can remember, school has made her feel out of place, out of character, and awkward: dressed in school uniforms that were either the wrong size or the wrong state of wear, singing the stiff verses of devotion to an abstraction she was too young to grasp: a motherland, a multilaterally developed society, a new citizen, and a bright future.

It never had anything to do with herself.

Standing out means you would be converted to the squad, which takes your merit and dresses it up to match its colours. You're good at science? Fine, you'll serve the motherland as an engineer, pushing its development and progress to unprecedented peaks.

Lili? She wants to keep her best for herself.

Her school performance has been too good for her to have reason to feel a misfit, but the hero persona never fitted her. Unlike her one-for-all, all-for-one fantasies, being a hero is a single-minded, one-way business: one for the Party, all for the Party. The Party above all.

"Well, yes, that's the problem, sometimes. They inspire us with impulses we can't follow through." Like travelling across borders and time. She keeps staring at the woolly sky. "And sometimes I'm just sick and tired of heroes. Aren't we all constantly supposed to be great heroes in our shabby school uniforms? Aren't you still reproaching me for not rising to the brilliance you expect of me? Maybe I just want to be left alone to do what feels like me."

"But what is it that doesn't feel like you at the moment, Lili, come on?" Nestor stands up abruptly and starts pacing the length of her desk, back and forth, with a hand in his trouser pocket, gesticulating with the other. He always does that when he gets irritated, or simply wrought up in conversation. "I mean, good, you gave up medicine to follow your talent for physics, now you do that, what's bothering you? A bit of hard work? You'd better get used to it." He stops for emphasis and shrugs with the obviousness of his last point.

"I have no problem working hard!" Lili counters. This is once again outrageous: having no social life, only school, homework, and private classes, but still getting this talk, making her look like a spoiled girl putting on airs.

"But then what *is* your problem, Lili?" Nestor shrugs again, with a mix of impatience and consternation.

Yeah, what is her problem, precisely? Her thoughts are racing through her head, giving her no time to find the words. But it's got something to do with what she can't articulate, not today.

"I feel like I'm being chased all the time, do this, do that, you must, you need to, there's a good girl..." That's not it, he'll go again that she's not tough enough to take hard work. "It's not the work, work is fine, but just not having a place, you know, like a garage!" she grabs the idea from the air, "to pull in to at the end of the day. You know what I mean? The only other thing than the chase is sleep, but I wish I could feel alive, I wish I could feel alive with the work, too! But here's the problem, I don't! You said it, I'm working on what I like and that keeps rewarding me, at the end of another tricky problem I've solved – and yet, and yet – it feels so tight, like I'm marching, hands tied, everything aligned for one goal, those exams, the golden future—"

"That's exactly why you're working so hard now, Lili," he suddenly says the magic words, acknowledging her. He has placed his hands on her desk, and is bending slightly, looking at her intently. "To be through at last with this silly school," he carries on passionately, but keeping his voice subdued, below the decibels of the radio, "and leave the pigeonhole behind. No more YC's, best-of-the-year contests with prizes, no more achievements boards. No more alignment – or, well there's always some alignment, whether of our own or prescribed, but it'll be easier to live with it. Just a few more months and it'll be over and you'll feel alive again: you become a grown-up, you take your life in your hands, and you're free!"

She nods, looking down. That's how she sees it, too. The admission, and then she's delivered. Or is she?

It's how to make it through these months, living with the terror of the possible consequences of what happened last night, having to put her inner life on hold and keep pushing the cart. Until she reaches the place where she can be herself.

"Well, as free as can be," he adds, checking back the heat of his previous sentences.

—in the context of the growing threat of the military race, the Warsaw Pact countries vow to safeguard peace and unite their efforts for the alignment to the desiderata of the—

"My father says, this is life, and the patriot squad goes

on. You may no longer be a YC, but you become a Party member, and that's for life. He says you must finish a school, go to university or straight to the motherland's factories, and then do your duty building the bright future: work, get married, have children, attend the political education meetings, dig your plot to become a lower-rank hero within your little patch, and then retire into insignificance. The path has been drawn for you, he says, the choice is only what to study, and who to get married to. Build yourself a home in your vocation, that's the best you can do, he hammers on. But my father's too fond of theatrical verdicts and is thrashing his own home."

Her father's verdicts – look where they got him.

Maybe it's now she can find the words to say what happened last night.

The heroic voices of the choral music after the news bulletin are pushing up the decibels in the background. *We have the motherland's son as most beloved leader, the Party, Ceaușescu, Romania—*

Val Nestor lowers his eyes, nodding, with a faint rueful smile on his face.

Will he tell her to focus even harder on her studies?

"Professor Danes is right, of course," he assents. "But then, Lili," he resumes his usual passion, "if this is our only chance to choose, go for it. To get anywhere, we need to do the work first. You must do what it takes so you can choose your tiny slice of freedom. That freedom to forget about any socialist heroes and the golden future. You can keep your Lennon and Raskolnikov for your own, private, heroes, because no one can ship them off. It'll all be stored safely in that garage of yours, that place you own entirely."

"As it is stored now, only you keep blaming me for daydreaming and being idle. Now you understand it's not that?" Lili retorts, eyes wide open, leaning forward.

Val Nestor looks at her with a mixture of compassion and sadness.

"It's your place to be, Lili, yes, I know that damn well, we all need that place. I'm just worried sometimes that you might spend too long hanging out in there, neglecting this side of the threshold. That's all. You're such a great girl, Lili, don't lose yourself."

She can't believe she hears that. It's precisely the fear of losing herself that keeps her seeking out that place where she can say, this is me.

"Mr Nestor, I—"

"I've told you so many times you can call me Val," he interrupts her.

She pauses.

Today's YC's, tomorrow's communists, the motherland's evergreen trees, today's YC's—

The voices sound brave and determined, jolting in an inspirational cadence of enthusiasm for work and progress.

"I know, yes, thank you. It's just, I can't really get myself to call you that. We don't call teachers by first names, you know—"

"You don't talk to teachers about such things," he replies. "Plus, I'm no longer your teacher."

"True."

But she still can't bring herself to call him Val. So she avoids the choice, by using no form of address at all.

What was it she was going to tell him?

She forgets. There's a lump somewhere in the dark, but she can't seem to find how to grab it.

"Well, you needn't worry. I'm doing all the work I can possibly fit in. There's no space left for Raskolnikov, not even for Lennon, except playing two or three songs before going to bed, during the week. Sundays I try to catch up, but there's so much homework to catch up with, too, so—" She purses her lips and shrugs.

He nods in approval. "Fine," he says. "And I bet you're relieved I'm no longer your teacher this year, or you'd have had even more homework to catch up with." He winks at her and gurgles out his laugh again.

She stands up, vaguely aware that something has gone missing in the conversation. But it'll have to do for now.

A few weeks before, just before Christmas, the Danes had asked several acquaintances over for dinner. As always at such gatherings, Ms Danes would outperform herself cooking and entertaining with her sunny smile, while Professor Danes would excel at telling anecdotes about famous figures, from Galileo to Stalin.

That night, Mother drew Lili apart with a secretive wink.

"I need to ask you something, Lili." Mother held her shoulders and looked her in the eye intently. They were standing in her father's study, where all matters from god's existence to the month's domestic budget were conferred on.

Had she done something wrong?

Mother took a step sideways and extracted one from the pile of books that stood huddled tight on the shelf, like little soldiers. *Molecular Electrodynamics*, by Tase Bodu-Beran. Lili raised her eyebrows. The same Bodu-Beran who was sitting in their living room right now, listening to Professor Danes' stories?

"I want you to take it," Mother pressed the book into Lili's hands, "and ask Mr Bodu-Beran for an autograph."

"What? No!" Lili cried out with a wince.

Mother nodded, closing her eyes, acknowledging her protest, but not giving in.

"Please. Lili, please. Just do it."

"Why? No! Why don't you do it?"

"Because it's got more impact from you. I work in a theatre – do I look like someone who might read such stuff?"

"And do I?" Lili hissed. "What is this, some good-night reading for an eighteen-year-old high-school student?"

"No. But it may be at some point. You're growing up. You might read it someday. You're growing amid all these books," Ms Danes pointed at the walls decked with crammed bookshelves, "so it makes sense that you pick up one of these today, another one tomorrow. And tonight," she paused, raising her eyebrows for effect, "you're picking up this one, and noticing the name and wondering if the author is the very same guest sitting in our living room. You don't know yet what's inside, but you're going to read it some day and find out, and when you do, you'll have his autograph on the front page."

"So what do I care about his autograph? I won't do this!" How could Mother expect her to put up such a false act? As if she cared what father's boss had written in his stale career! "I won't do it! Why should I act like I'm a fan? He's just a big-belly pompous big shot, what do I care? Leave me alone!"

Mother nodded again to quiet her down.

"You'd do your father a great service, Lili."

"No! I don't care!"

"Lili, please listen to me. Your father needs any little help he can get. You know how upset he is every time he's skipped for promotion, which has been long, very long overdue."

"To hell with his promotion. You want to use me for him to get a bloody promotion I don't care about? What's the big deal about it anyway?"

"It is a big deal, Lili, trust me."

"Well, he should see that he does the right thing himself then, don't push me to the front of stage!" Lili writhed out of her mother's hold. "Did the two of you plan this together?"

"No!" Mother sighed and looked sideways, at a loss for words. "He has no idea. He'll be so much more pleased when you go in there and do this. Just do it for his sake," Mother touched her hands pleadingly.

She wouldn't do it, certainly not for his sake.

"I realise you wonder what this has got to do with you, and you're right. But – I wouldn't ask you if it wasn't so important."

She didn't care what was at stake. She didn't want to be made to grovel. To be made to say words she didn't even dream about, to be made to act in such an unlikely way.

She remembered primary school kids dressed in their gala Pioneer uniforms who were selected to scurry out of the chanting crowd to offer a pompous flower bouquet to the Beloved Leader or his wife. The Beloved Leader or his wife would bend and acknowledge the lovely dwarf with a smile, then hug and kiss the little one as a reward.

The dwarf would have no idea who these grown-ups were. The flowers would have been individually selected and placed in the little hands at just the right moment, with clear instructions. The innocent child making an offering to the grand heroes of the country – what a touching picture! Sometimes with a short verse, expressing gratitude and love, wishing the grand Mother and Father good health, so they might carry on leading the people and achieving universal peace and happiness.

"You know everybody calls him Professor Danes," Mother carried on after a pause. She seemed to be searching for words carefully. "In truth, he's not a Professor, Lili. He teaches, all right. But his rank is still the one when he joined the faculty over twenty years ago, it's called an assistant lecturer."

The guests in the living room were laughing. Professor Danes was good at telling about curiosities that few people knew.

"He met the requirements to become a full lecturer in the first few years. He got his PhD at twenty-six, you know when Bodu-Beran got his? Forty-one. He was appointed head of department right afterwards, and Associate Professor, too.

Your father has kept publishing articles in the university's journals, he wrote two books and co-authored a couple others. His seminars are visited by students coming out of central Bucharest just to hear him, and he even often stands in for full professors and gives lectures. There's the university in Aix-en-Provence that has been trying to hire him on a temporary contract, and a few Western journals that have tried, the clean, official way, to get him to publish for them. That's something, Lili! That's a lot! He should be at least an Associate Professor, like Bodu-Beran, but he'd be happy to hop on to the lecturer rank at least."

Lili looked down. Her father seemed brilliant all right, and maybe a great victim, too. But she had nothing to do with all that.

"And still," Mother went on, "he's being consistently pushed back. He's not the most comfortable voice, you can probably gather that."

Oh, yes, his voice was anything but comfortable.

"Nobody's still an assistant lecturer at fifty, Lili! It's like he's being punished. But make sure nobody finds out, will you? Your father, too, mustn't know that you know. He'd be torn with shame. Each time someone calls him Professor, as people do, you know, like peasants bowing to the scholars, cap in hand, Professor Sir, Doctor Sir, Counsellor Sir— he feels a lurch in his guts. I'm telling you all this so you understand it's not like he's chasing promotion for his ambition."

"But for what, then, if not ambition?" Lili countered.

Mother paused, with the same intent look.

"His current rank and what he's allowed to do professionally – it's not who he is, Lili."

Professor Danes's voice could be heard from the living room, at the height of excitement. It sounded like the Einstein visiting Harvard story.

"And all this time, others are placed above him, in roles that are not who they really are, either. It's just that their files are clean. Year in, year out. Deliberately. He needs some positive little note to his file, anything that can create even a tiny breach—"

"Oh, and that should be me, right, creating that tiny breach?"

"Yes, Lili, that's right, why not. You just take this book, go in, ask for an autograph, and leave again. That's all. No big deal. Bodu-Beran will be pleased, doesn't matter whether he believes you're going to read his book or not. If he leaves this house pleased, your father might have one little plus on his tab."

No. No, she wouldn't do that. It was disgusting. All this purposeful pretending. Being sent into that room as an innocent lamb to come out smeared by the paunchy guy's satisfaction. To help get a promotion for her father.

"But that's not who I am either!" She stepped back.

"Lili, you've got to do it. Please. Do it. You go in there, say a few words, he scribbles his name, you come back, and there's nothing more. You can forget it the next second."

Mother had a way of cornering her and making her do things, without raising her voice or threatening any punishments. Her pleas were flooding her, giving her no more room to step back and shut herself off in opposition.

She clutched the book, which Mother had been pressing her to take, and headed for the living room. Her skin felt tight. She only saw the narrow channel ahead of her, her peripheral vision shut out. The glowing lava and the greenish puke held back.

She opened the door to the living, holding the book in her hand. Father looked down with a grim frown. As he should.

Just a few more steps; the minimum number of words mumbled enough to be heard, but not to count as her own; and it would be over.

After Professor Danes' arrest, Mother is also summoned to the police headquarters to be interrogated, and she comes back home each time with a puffy face and eyes red from crying. A few weeks later, they dispatch him to one of the country's building sites, where he can atone for his transgression and contribute to the bright future of the socialist motherland.

"They say he's been making illicit money with his private lessons," Mother explains to Lili.

The word illicit is always used in connection with sources of income, implying that the person has flouted two fundamental laws: to sell means to own, and neither is conceivable at the individual level. The Professor may own his intellect, but selling its product is supposed to go only over the institutional counter of the university.

"In reality," Mother goes on in a faint voice, looking down, "you know so well, almost every kid in years eight, ten, and twelve takes private lessons for the exams." Which shows that the system tolerates such private enterprise by pretending it isn't aware. Until it has reason to become aware, that is.

Lili doesn't need to wonder about the reason they became aware of the Professor's private lessons, and spares Mother the question. Everyone sees his students coming and going at set hours, one by one, or in twos.

Sometimes, Lili realises now, they don't exactly look like high-school students preparing for university admission.

Sometimes, the Professor's voice cannot be heard from his study during his lessons, as usual. Lili always assumes the student must be doing some work on their own, which would explain the stillness. Her father refers to his students by name, or as "the one from Oltenita," or "the mechanic's daughter"; but some of the faces showing up at their door he simply calls "the student".

With father gone, it has been quiet at home. No more having to disguise her reluctance at family dinners, no more starting at each noise – although she senses that her secret relief is not exactly right.

Out of habit, she keeps listening for what is going on in the house; the only sound she can hear now is Mother crying on her own. She cringes at the wailing that seeps through the walls, but she's afraid to go and try to comfort her. What could she say? "Now there's no one to fight with"? It would only hurt her more.

She vaguely suspects that her father has been more than the impulsive fuss-maker raising his voice so often. Mother's continued support of her husband, both within the family and beyond, points to that.

On the other hand, it is Mother who has occasionally grumbled in the past, dropping the word "divorce" in the wake of their fights, letting out her own anger on the pots and cutlery, Lili standing by with a blank stare.

How is she supposed to make sense of these grown-up things? Why did they fight? What did they really want – were they enemies, or friends after all?

It doesn't really matter. It's none of her business.

In her deep self, she's not surprised that her father has been removed from their lives. It has been long coming. She only finds it somewhat disconcerting that her secret expectation is now being met, and she's not better prepared on how to feel about it.

On the day after Christmas, grey civilians had come to give them their last warning (grovelling for Bodu-Beran's signature wasn't any good, obviously.) No knocks, just butting in while they were having dinner around father's desk in his study. An unassuming Dacia car parked right in front of the gate, as if to bar any exit. "Lili, please go to your room. Now," Mother had said, her eyes set on the men.

That New Year's Eve, there was as usual the endless

succession of dishes that Mother brought out from the kitchen; the rolled cabbage leaves at eleven and the meat shortly after, so the wine would go down well at midnight. An endless anticipation of TV highlights, which were getting scarcer and sorrier every year – the odd music video clips from the West, New Year's messages from celebrities, *Laurel and Hardy*, or even *Tom and Jerry* – and the disappointment when they were over too soon. The growing numbness from sitting in the chair from nine p.m. to four or five the next morning, only to find that the first of January was quite a grey and ordinary morning, not worth the exhausting celebration.

As if all this was not enough, her father had insisted on their traditional father–daughter walk in the park before lunch on the first of January. With a clouded brain after a sleepless New Year's night, a walk in the park with the Professor was the last thing Lili wanted. She was eighteen now, and he was no longer the story-telling Yimmi Papa.

A reckless, pitiable big mouth.

Protesting was useless. Father pursed his lips and looked away in annoyance, but Mother took her aside, looked her in the eye and said, "Lili, please, it's New Year's, we don't want any bad mood today, the first of January, do we? It's only a walk in the park, and he's your father."

They headed for the park, desolate on a downcast frosty morning, walking side by side, both muffled up in their winter coats, simmering a frustration they wouldn't voice, but couldn't leave behind either. Lili was determined to give him just that, the walk, nothing more. She uttered no word. Her father bitterly waited to gather the evidence of her resentment, and make out how far it went. He walked in his own, grim silence.

"We walked for an hour like complete strangers," he reported to Mother, back home. "We didn't find a single word to say the whole time."

The one thing she blames him for, on her own account, not Mother's, is spoiling the original paradise of her inner home, the perfect harmonies of their symmetrical love. That symmetrical love turned into symmetrical avoidance.

She sees now, looking back, that she may have been clumsy hiding her resentment, and he clumsy handling it. Sulking fuelled the resentment, which caused more sulking in turn.

The same looping mechanism that constantly holds her frozen into clumsiness at home, as well as outside of it.

She tells Mother at some point that she has changed her mind from medicine to physics. Mother is happy to hear that, but Lili suspects that it is partly because she's taking Lili's choice for a touching tribute to her father, which it isn't of course.

Unlike the Professor, she will not expose herself unnecessarily. No need to sneer at Madam Secu, nor fascinate crowds with brilliant visions and dangerous understatements. She'll avoid standing out and giving reasons to be watched, as she has learnt all these years. No speechifying on political oppression, on favouritism, or Buddha for that matter.

She'll just keep herself to herself, and mind her own physics.

CHAPTER TWO

"So, how did it go with Val?" Dana enquires with big eyes.

Every other Saturday afternoon they go out for a pizza on the main avenue, or a profiterole ice cream at the one and only fancy café downtown. It's preferable to the cinema: there are either Romanian or Soviet films in the revolutionary realism vein, or a Bud Spencer movie from 1972.

Today it's ice cream.

Lili rolls her eyes, amused. "You know him. Ever the same. Worried I might be dallying too much, not giving my best. First thing he asks, how's my love life!"

Both girls burst out laughing.

"What did you say?"

"What could I possibly say? I mean, come on, can it be even more obvious?"

"He's just teasing. Of course he knows it's all about private classes this year. For many, it started last year already. And he knows that better than anyone, giving the dozen private classes a week himself!" Dana winks at her. She's taking these classes, too, squeezed in with four other school mates. She has a crush on him, but she's cool about discussing Val Nestor with Lili in a detached way. "But silly jokes aside – and I mean, his silly jokes aside – how did it go?"

Lili wags her head from side to side, gazing through the large windows. She likes this café for being so sunlit, high ceilings and window panes the full height of the walls. It feels spacious and airy, if only it wasn't for its blankness.

"Well, it was good, I suppose. As usual. You always get something out of a conversation with Nestor, though almost always it's not exactly what you'd hoped for."

"But you just wanted to talk, didn't you?" Dana checks. "No particular problem, right?"

That's too complicated to go into. And the words to describe it must stay locked in. Plus, it would hijack the conversation and the whole mood of the outing. No point wasting this leisure time on gloomy subjects such as her family.

"No, apart from the obvious – like, not having a life at all? But yes, I wasn't expecting a specific answer, maybe just a bit of 'cheer up, girl'." Which he had given her, in his way, teasing and all. "You know, I'm always so hopeful before talking to him, as if expecting he'll give me some clarity, some solution, he'll wow me with a deep insight that'll open a fully new perspective. Sometimes I guess I just need to feel he understands, and supports me. But in the end, he sort of leaves me high and dry, you know?"

Dana keeps nodding, and replies knowingly, "Tell me about it, Lili, tell me about it, I should know best!"

Before high school, Lili had taken Dana for just another nerd, but one with a biting tongue. She was thin and had frail bones, a pale face with edgy features, carrying thin glasses on an outstanding nose. Her clothes often seemed to Lili to make an overstatement through bold patterns and emphatic cuts, as if a full-grown woman in her was stage-directing her appearance, in order to command awe. Lili still remembers Dana's trouser skirt – old-fashioned and excessively baggy, while the white dots on the turquoise dress were too large, and too much. She looked like a nerdy kid who had dressed up in a diva's outfit.

She may have looked like a cut-out from a fashion magazine of the early 1970s, but when she was mocked, Dana possessed a wide vocabulary to retaliate with. "That goes to prove again how endlessly inept and vile humans are," she would proclaim, then swivel round, turning her back and lifting her chin.

It was through Val Nestor that they had become close, the summer after junior year in high school. Dana's stage appearance had cooled off somewhat, and, on a summer camp in the mountains led by Nestor, Lili had discovered the avid reader and dreamer hiding in Dana's skinny body.

"And it was the same this time," Lili continues, "I mean, I did get that feeling of talking to someone who understands, the feeling of a deep conversation, not just someone preaching this and that to you. But as always, he drops bombs on me that I need to shake my head and ask myself what was that, please? And this derails the whole conversation, of course. What he says is always dense, I need time to digest it, and when I'm done digesting, days or weeks later, I need to talk again. Mostly, to disagree with what he told me," she adds ironically.

Dana nods, with a tender smile. Her tenderness goes to Lili, but also to Val Nestor's unpredictable temperament.

"You know, after all these years knowing him," Lili goes on, "I have the feeling that he doesn't actually get me. He probably understands life and is truer, as a human being, than the others, whose emotions have got fossilised with the routine, but what he tells me is often so off the mark that he catches me unprepared and my mind freezes. Like that preposterous gem of wisdom about the mountain and the grain of sand in that epic parents' meeting. Or when he told me in tenth grade that I haven't got a bloody scale of values. Where does he get all that from? What scale of values did he mean, I was only sixteen, for hell's sake? He should point out one of our school mates who has a scale of values! And what does it even mean, the scale of values? He means maybe, yeah, those who only know cramming and do it without wailing, their scale of values is: I must get into university, dead full stop." Lili sips at the soda to give herself something to do with her agitation. "Maybe I have my own values about that: I must get into university to get rid of stupid things like Nestor's bullying – should I tell him that so that he knows my values?"

They both laugh and duck their heads as if to keep the laugh under.

"He sees you, Lili, and maybe he thinks that in your place he'd make tougher choices. Maybe he thinks you deserve much more."

"So do I, maybe, thank you very much, but what am I supposed to do? What exactly is there for me to choose that I'm not choosing already?"

Dana shrugs and looks away thoughtfully.

"Maybe he wishes you'd shine the way he thinks you should."

"Yeah? Shine, like – like your Hemingway guy?"

"Yeah, sort of like my Hemingway, I'll get you all, I'm the coolest sort of thing. He can't – won't accept you're no Hemingway type, but more like what? Your Dostoevsky guy?"

They chuckle in complicity, Lili rolling her eyes.

"Yeah, Dostoevsky was on the agenda, too, imagine! Along with Winnetou, gosh what an embarrassment. As if I was there to talk about my literary preferences, starting from sixth grade all the way."

Dana's gaze slides downwards. "Well, I'm sure he was trying to make a point, you know?"

Lili shrugs, "Like what?"

"No idea, you should ask him – and be ready for another rant," Dana adds her usual ironical punchline. "I didn't know about Winnetou. When was that?"

"Sixth grade, I guess. Yeah. He was my first role model. Don't show wild emotions, that kind of thing. Be tough and dignified."

Dana smiles and gazes at Lili as if she's picturing her dressed as Winnetou right there, in front of her. She seems to like the picture.

"There were four of us," Lili resumes, "sitting together in two adjoining desks at school. We met in the park and acted out various imaginary feats, whereby one of us was Winnetou – unfortunately, not me, the other girl was quicker to pick the role – and I was Old Shatterhand. The other two were Old Surehand and Nscho-tschi. We played a combination of Hide and Seek and Cops and Robbers, we had the whole terrain to ourselves as the prairie, and we were earnestly searching for tracks of animals and kept only finding dog poop. But it felt good to be Old Shatterhand, you know." Lili's voice gains a nostalgic undertone.

"Yeah, I think I can see that in you. Winnetou's counterpart, maybe even his better version. Winnetou was a victim, but you are not," Dana adds, raising an eyebrow emphatically. "And Raskolnikov seems like a suitable expansion, walking through disaster carrying his own meaning."

Lili glances at Dana, surprised. That sounds so beautiful, but somehow like an ill omen, too. Disaster?

"But what did Val tell you this time that was so off the mark?"

Lili heaves a deep sigh to cool off the heat of rebelling against Nestor's verbal bombs.

"Not one thing in particular. But he was teasing me again about my imagination, dreams, you know, Lennon's *Imagine*, my imaginary heroes, along those lines. I don't know what he wants me to do, what he wants me to be, but it's definitely not me."

The brilliant scientist walking with her head in the clouds is definitely not her, and this must be how he sees her. She's only gasping for air, struggling with the single-mindedness that is expected of her, whether it's studying or striving for the motherland's prosperity. That air of detachment might be the extra space she takes every moment to work out her next move and way to act. Except she calls that her self, not detachment.

"But I guess, what the hell, at least he's got his own head, and he talks in real words, no slogans. He certainly challenges you until you see red – or hear little birds." They both shake with laughter and lean back on their chairs. “And he’s crazier than any of us,” Lili adds, chuckling.

“Oh, yes, Val’s the first to challenge you to go wild. Remember when he dived into the mountain lake?”

It was at the summer camp when Dana and Lili had made friends, in the gentle wilderness of the West Transylvanian mountains. On one of the hikes, they came across a pond. Val Nestor took off his clothes and screamed, “Whoever’s last diving in does the dishes tonight,” running the few yards before pulling his knees up and jumping into the water. Lili was not the only one standing by doubtfully, afraid of the contact with cold, unknown waters. But in the end she made up her mind and took off her clothes and went into the pond, step by step, not diving, watched by the others with awe and disbelief.

“That was ages ago,” Lili smiles nostalgically. “High school’s best. One summer camp, ten days, that’s it. So much for high school being the best years.”

“Yeah, great memory,” Dana echoes her nostalgia. “Not much else we had fun doing, I guess, all these years. But then, this is it, isn’t it? Nobody’s having much fun, look around, we’re all about getting that stupid admission right.”

“Oh, I can see some having fun all right, at least more than the two of us are having,” Lili replies grudgingly.

“No, I don’t think so, I know who you mean, the merry party fellowship – but even they’ve had to slow down this year, haven’t you noticed? They’re not planning how to get Pepsi and brandy like they used to.”

They laugh again.

“All the things you overhear, I can’t stop wondering...” Lili admits.

“Well, they’re doing it right behind us in class, I can’t help overhearing them, I wonder how you can’t. It’s not like you’re enthralled with the political economics lesson,” Dana teases her.

“So has Nestor’s demon of getting their asses down to

work finally caught up with them, too?"

"Sure, two of them are going for medicine, even though the bets are split whether they're going to make it the first time. I can see Adrian having to try several years. He'll never make it from the first attempt, I could hand it to him black on white. The others are going to the Polytechnic, nothing very demanding, except for Theo and Maria, who're applying to aeronautics, which, again, is going to be tough."

Lili draws imaginary doodles on the shiny surface of the table. Their ice creams are coming, looking gorgeous, as always.

Both of them raise their eyebrows in appreciation and fall to eating right away.

"You know, I was thinking just now," Lili says, swallowing a smooth mouthful of vanilla ice cream. "It's funny how we talk of ourselves. Before this year, there were the party fellowships, the nerds, the nice people, the weirdos, the stars – you know what I mean. Now, suddenly, we're the medicine bunch, the engineering bunch, the architecture bunch..."

"Yeah, sure. But that's also because we hang out more with the same people, what with the private tutoring, if we go to the same teacher, like we go to Val, you know," Dana says.

"Sure, but most of us take private lessons with teachers elsewhere, often university guys, who know admission inside out, so it's not so much that we hang out together. In fact, you said the parties have slowed down, it looks like there's not much hanging out these days."

"Yeah, you're right," Dana reflects. "We come together in school, but each of us is busy getting through their individual study plan. So, with not much else in the picture, we are what we're going to study!" she proclaims jokingly.

"Precisely! That's strange. And terrible, in a way. I'm that crazy scientist girl going for fancy physics, instead of a down-to-earth engineering programme."

"Oh, no, there's secret admiration for you over this choice," Dana counters.

"You're kidding!"

"No! I mean it. Look, sixty percent of us go into some sort of engineering course at the Polytechnic. The others are statistically irrelevant anyway, but among the science people, you're the one that stands apart, in a follow-your-passion kind of way."

Lili scoffs. "Then so do you, with your industrial chemistry; it's not the Polytechnic!"

Dana grimaces. "It's not pure chemistry, as in your case, pure physics, which is all right; what placements are there for pure chemistry?"

"And what placement do you think I'll get with pure physics? But I'm not thinking about that now, it's admission that matters."

"Well, your pure physics might be good, you want to go on to astrophysics and you're passionate about outer space. You wouldn't belong in an engineering programme," Dana explains emphatically. "For me, if it couldn't be medicine, then I suppose industrial chemistry is just fine. It's something dull, for sure, but I guess it might just do, to get a safe placement in a town, and a decent living after. That should be worth this dog's life now, and foreseeably throughout the four study years," she adds with mock indifference.

Lili looks into her ice cream cup, hiding her disapproval.

Dana had dreamt of medicine, too, but had given it up, not feeling up to it. Lili still thinks it's wrong of her to go for something she doesn't truly like, with a sense of resignation and implacable doom about the rest of her life. But she has nothing solid to oppose that, other than her own aversion to it. It's certainly not the attitude she wants to have going forward into her own adulthood.

Maybe she's privileged, Lili suspects. She loves physics,

focuses on physics for admission, and is going to do just physics as a profession. No hybrids, no compromises. Maybe that's why Dana says she stands apart. Pure physics. Pure passion.

"But are you sure medicine's out of the question, Dana? Why don't you think again?"

"Are you nuts? Come on, Lili, you can't be serious. I can't sleep at night without my mum's pills as it is, you think I'd need any extra pressure? The three private classes I have on top of school each week is more than enough, with the homework in between, let's be clear. What if I knew I had to scramble my way between a nine seventy and a ten, so I might even start dreaming of being admitted? No, thanks, I'm already overcapacity. My industrial chemistry will have me if I get an eight, too," she concludes on a tone of self-irony. "I'm not like you, Lili, don't forget that. You skim through your notes during the break for the next class, and if there's a test, you get a nine just based on that skimming. If I'm to get a nine, I have to cram a whole afternoon for it."

Their chatter goes on: shreds of school gossip, moans about their routine, updates on how far they've come through the syllabus, all sprinkled with reflections from the book they're reading, and pervaded by an underlying yearning they're unable to name.

Surrounding them is a grey and dormant city, pulling itself together each day for the next round of building the bright future. As a mirror reaction, the people inside wake up only to step back and evade it. Like Lili, they may be yearning to be able to say, this is me. As it is, they leave their cubic flats and go about their daily lives steered by the one instinct of shutting off the intruding outside world. At the end of the day, they compulsively switch their TVs from the daily reports of stunning results in the socialist competition over to the Bulgarian channel. At least the Bulgarian socialist reports are in a language they don't understand.

There is hardly anything, therefore, in the way of distraction, that might put Lili's and Dana's work at risk by bringing them off-track. The track is all there is.

Seeing themselves on a good train is what matters, or seeing their bags loaded on the cart, as popular wisdom says. The rest of their lives is drawn out in advance once they're on course, but it makes a difference whether they travel first, or third class. Or not at all for that matter: stuck with back-breaking labour in the fields, watching the trains go by.

She goes about her daily routines mindlessly, changing buses and trams across the gloom of the city with no concerns about the future or the past, suspended in a race that she never questions for a moment.

The school timetable is the only way she can tell days and years from each other, but that's what the blind race is for: to enable her to be empty on the exam day, focus pure, zero friction and maximum mental agility.

All the classes, the tutoring, the hours spent waiting for tram 32 to ride it through the entire twenty-three stops from one end to the other of the line, the homework, the tight sleep schedule, all of this is just a necessity before the time comes for her to be delivered, to be made, to start living, to start being. As a student in physics, on track towards her life.

Yes, the exams are tough. But she'll be quickly through with them. Just two exams. Go there, no feeling, no nerves, as if under anaesthetic, answer the questions, through.

It's thirty degrees Celsius outside at nine in the morning, and there she is, sitting at her desk, thighs sweaty and burning, but with one hour still to go until it's time for a break. She's drawn the dark orange curtains as a sunlight screen, but the room feels like an oven in the new, fiery light.

She knows exactly what she needs to cover each day. She listed every chapter of maths and physics of the four high-school years, and divided them by the number of remaining days. This way, she has come up with a sound schedule that ensures she navigates the syllabus systematically, without the risk of missing anything. Mornings are for physics and afternoons for maths in weeks one and three, with the order reversed in weeks two and four: that's a smart way of making sure she gives both subjects equal attention.

She's aware her body and her brain need refreshment, too, so she has scheduled a fifteen minute break every three hours; at lunch, thirty. At six p.m. she puts away the papers, changes clothes, and goes out for a constitutional in the park. Sometimes with Dana, but often on her own.

The goal is near.

She doesn't need Val Nestor to tell her what she has to do. What goes in will come out the other end: her conscientious work, her brains, her determination on the inside equals the going through, getting in on the outside.

Half an hour lunch. Mother is tiptoeing in the house so as not to disturb her. The meal is ready on the kitchen table.

"How's it going?" Mother asks, her large blue eyes beaming at her.

"Fine," she replies. "Finished thermodynamics today, as planned. Just need to get my head free a bit before I start optics. But that'll be tomorrow."

"So now the afternoon...?"

"If it's afternoon, it's maths," Lili confirms.

"Yes, maths. Wish I could be of any help," Mother smiles and pats her on the shoulder.

"You're not eating?"

"I have to go now. We've got dress rehearsal," Mother says before she leaves the kitchen.

The months since her father has been gone have forged a new solidarity between them. They have been forced to accomplish the tasks he used to take care of, such as carrying diesel jugs from the cistern at the back of the garden all the way into the house, then pouring their contents slowly lest the dregs are stirred up, and finally, lighting the fire and watching it in case the burner gets clogged.

Digging the flower beds and trimming the bushes, the apple tree, and the roses. Fetching heavy supplies from the market. A twenty-kilo potato sack was about everything they had to eat until Easter, because Mother had been too drained by her heartache to be able to queue for food. Lili had volunteered to queue up when needed, but now she's always on some tram across the town to her private classes when she's not at school.

At least it's just the two of them, Lili comforts herself, watching out for each other whenever possible. In the middle of a disaster that everyone is commiserating with them for, they have grown closer in a solidarity that they often speak of: "All I have is you; all we have is each other."

Mother had seen Father in February for the last time, just before he was taken to the labour camp. She had told him at that point that his daughter was actually going for physics. He had nodded, Mother told her afterwards between sobs, and had pursed his lips. He wrote them a letter in March, saying he was doing fine under the circumstances, but they lost trace of him after that. Visiting was out of the question, as the site was of strategic importance, so no visitors were allowed. Underground stories went that you simply had to keep hoping for another letter, as there was nothing you could do from the outside.

She hopes remotely that Mother will gradually see that life is moving on without her husband, and that Lili can fill up the space he's left by helping with the household chores; this way, given a little time, she might realise that the husband's absence is not such a pain after all, and the two of them might start enjoying their togetherness.

She'll soon become a university student and most likely get a grant too, and she'll also give private lessons and so be able to contribute to the household even further. They're going to be fine, she's sure!

For now it's just this narrow tunnel she has to keep running through and come out at the other end. No feelings, no yammer, no discomfort caused by the long hours spent on the chair or by the late June heat. Dispassionately breaking down the syllabus items and matching them to the unit of time for revision over the remaining few weeks; dissecting the chapters, assembling the notes and summaries, reviewing calculations; check; move on.

Just keep going, stay focused, hang in tight.

The day before, deliberately kept free. No studying on the eve of the exam: expert advice for a light and focused brain when you most need it, which is during the test itself. Lili follows the guidance thoroughly, along with further tips. She has regular meals, takes her constitutional in the evening, when the heat has subsided, and makes a point of thinking about nothing, especially about nothing to do with maths or physics. If she feels anything at all, it's what a high-performance athlete must feel before the grand day: her whole purpose is to deliver and get the results. The rest, whatever else there might be, is immaterial.

At times, she gets a pang of panic that she may have omitted something to revise, or forgotten how it works, but she knows this is normal, too, so she dismisses these pangs promptly. She must stay away from a muddled head: it's safer to walk on clouds, without looking down, holding on to the hope – no, the certainty – that she has done her bit. Her log list is covered with green checks.

Mother has managed to procure chicken and has made a nourishing stew with potato mash; there's butter, too, for sandwiches on the exam day. Not that eating is allowed during the exam, but she's going to take a long tram ride to the end of the line, where the city ends; there, get on a bus that goes down a bumpy road for another twenty minutes to the platform.

Lili is not hungry, her guts feel numb, but she knows she has to eat, especially as Mother has taken so much trouble. She appreciates the delicious taste of the stew with the detached attitude of an observer. Mother keeps fretting around to fulfil Lili's wishes that she's trying hard to fathom, and Lili takes note of her efforts with a remote tenderness.

Tomorrow, and the day after, and then it's over. She can have her feelings back, and she can have the freedom she's been craving for so long. No more having to put up with silly, pointless school, and no more drilling to be admitted to adulthood. Freedom is near, yet not near enough to sense it just now. Not yet. These two days are a time warp, but even they will soon be over. A relative eternity in time-space. Just dive in, and she'll come out safely at the other end.

She goes to bed at the same time she regularly did throughout her school years. Disciplined, but also finding nothing worth staying up any later for. She's smart and sensible. Everything will work out fine. Tomorrow, and the day after. And in general.

She goes to her bedroom, puts on her pyjamas and prepares her clothes for tomorrow morning on the chair. She sets the alarm clock for five thirty, counting once again, satisfied that she's getting about seven hours sleep. Optimal, or at least sufficient, considering the early schedule tomorrow. She gets into the bedsheets, closes her eyes, and lets herself sink into the void.

Waking up, brushing teeth, downing the cup of coffee and the bread and butter sprinkled with salt, getting dressed, watching the time, briefly checking she's got everything in her bag – laying her hand, for a quick reality check, on pen, ID, bus tickets, tissues to wipe sweaty hands, an ancient corked up Pepsi bottle for water, check. That's it. Go.

She leaves the house right on schedule. The trams arrive reasonably quickly and she sinks into her numbness. Walks on a cloud, sits on a cloud. Breathes, and watches her steps. Moves her mind's radar to the next leg of her journey.

Sees the crowd waiting outside the building from far off. A slight pang of anxiety, then gone as she dives in and accepts it. The crowd, yes. They must obviously be waiting to be let in, one by one, parents left behind waving and shouting "good luck" – as if it was good luck, not hard work that mattered.

The parents' restlessness is the worst. The shivery look of the candidates, her own opponents, with their dark rings around the eyes from a sleepless night, their pale skin from having been sitting indoors for many weeks and months, out of touch with life and summer – that's easier to deal with; there's almost a solidarity when you can recognise on their faces that they too, like you, are in the same game. This means that the fear is theirs as well. Some of them she'll meet again, maybe even make friends with, as first-year students.

She's a bystander watching the film reeling on. Inside, she's unbending, with a remote but distinct feeling of superiority. She knows something they don't: she's already in. Her side of the equation is flawless. She only needs to show up for the grand test, and show up she will.

But the parents – they're the noise in this before-the-big-bang picture. Almost spoiling the composure before she's spreading her limbs in flight. Reminding her of what's at stake, of the unpredictability of luck, of fear.

She holds the candidate ID and her personal ID in her hands. The latter, a grey, dog-eared little book; she never quite understood why you needed a little book for an ID; would the small pages be covered, in time, with the story of who you are, for proper identification? Right now there are only blanks apart from the awkward, silly photo of a fourteen-year-old child girl.

The candidate ID is light-years better. Just a small card with her name and her photo, taken a week ago for registration. Her long, wavy hair spread on her shoulders, she's peering above the camera with a smile, and the feeling that's been around lately is now back: "I'm ready!" A smile of tenderness, one might think, towards the present that will step out of her way, letting in the future that is waiting for her to catch up.

The first bottleneck is now behind her, she's inside the building, sensing the smell of ancient, dank paper and wall plaster, which is a distant home, from the childhood years when Father sometimes took her with him to show her around. Her father is no longer here, but that home is, and will soon transcend memories and become real.

A few bottlenecks to go still. On the landing just before the exam rooms, and on the doorstep to the room itself. Her name reads loud and clear on a list of twenty-five rows typed in faded grey: Lilian Danes.

She's too early, as usual. The railway station is swarming with people: a faceless crowd with huge shopping bags repurposed as travel luggage, shabby trunks like dog-eared cardboard, and a blend of odours ranging from smoker's clothes to early morning sweat and spirits. She looks down at her own travel bag, as if checking how it compares to the rest of the world, but the bag will do. Considering where she's going for the next few days, it'd better do.

As a favour to her mother, Cora Balș, the literary manager at the theatre, offered to take Lili to the mountains for a week. She's staying at the exclusive hotel for Party bosses, while her husband is abroad with an official delegation. Mrs Danes was pleased with the favour, although she was not sure how to account for it. She wondered what favour she might have to return to settle the account.

It's not the first favour Cora has done for Lili. She's got a good hand for making clothes, and she creates her own designs. She might as well sell them in the artists' designer shop downtown, for what Lili can tell. It's cool to make your own clothes. It means you've got an artist's eye, and are smart enough to use your hands and brains together. Professional tailors do more pompous, conventional outfits;

the trick of the creative people is to find the easiest patterns, even improvise without a pattern, and compensate for a lack of formal instruction with fancy ideas and shapes.

Cora makes baggy skirts and lavish blouses with a laid-back dexterity, and then wears them, or gifts them, with a matching ease. She simply hands a plastic grocery bag to Mrs Danes, saying "This is for Lili, hope it looks good on her!" Mrs Danes looks inside, and cannot believe it. Lili, at home, can't either.

"Just like that?"

"Just like that, honey," Mother smiles. "She's a very kind woman, and seems to be fond of you. Having no kids of her own..."

Lili nods, but dismisses the explanation. It might be that Cora can have no kids, or that she's blessed to be part of a well-off family, or that she simply takes things easy, laying no price tags on things she does as a hobby. Lili feels like a young laid-back queen wearing Cora's clothes.

Cora, in her mid-thirties, is the daughter of a sculptor held in favour by the Party for his works depicting peasants and workers standing up for their rights in an exemplary class battle. She's married to a Party Central Committee member, which gives them access to the Party's closed-circuit network of hotels in the best parts of the country.

"Morning, Lili, hope you haven't been waiting long," Cora suddenly shows up from behind her.

"Good morning, Mrs Balș, no, not at all!" Lili puts on her smile.

"It's Cora, Lili, I'm not an ancient aunt," Cora says, winking at her. "So let's get on, the train seems to be at platform ten."

Cora turns around and leads the way through the crowd. Lili can't help but examine her outfit from behind. She wears black, as usual, although it's early morning and elegance isn't normally expected. Cora's outfit strikes her as eccentric and unassuming at the same time. It seems to say,

I'm cool, but I don't need to shout it out. The black trousers of a slightly shimmering fabric are tight on her shins, but flare up unexpectedly on her thighs, only to be pulled tight again at her waist. Over the black sleeveless top she wears a light velvety jacket with kimono sleeves and no buttons in front, of a faded dark violet-grey. Cora walks ahead at a steady pace, heading to the platform as if her personal limo were waiting for the two of them to board.

Lili must acknowledge that she could have been more creative choosing her own clothes for the journey. Instead, she's picked jeans and a light green tee, thinking of it as a journey on a dirty train (trains are by default dirty), heading to the mountains – therefore, a casual outfit was the right choice. Cora's style, however, makes such preconceived ideas look silly.

Off it goes now: a cool chaperone, vacation, mountains, comfortable hotel, being served decent meals, new scenery. The entire study schedule and the daily race are over and shelved.

They get off the train two hours later, and are picked up by the hotel's chauffeur. The resort lies on a plateau at over one thousand metres altitude, surrounded by spectacular peaks. Not a place that anyone can happen to drop by on the way somewhere else; one needs to drive up a winding, steep mountain track off the main road. Not like the crowded resorts huddled along the north–south highway.

Some of the few four-star hotels in the country are here, such as the Alpine Bliss, or others bearing names of local peaks or rivers. They can hardly be booked through the National Tourist Office; the "no vacancies" sign hangs on the wall behind the receptionist like a permanent decoration.

The driver swerves into a shady dead-end lane, and stops in front of an unassuming building, only two stories high, which seems to be saying to the casual hiker, "There's nothing for you here, just walk on!" There is no sign. It doesn't need a name, because it's not open to the public. In the records, it might be called something as dull as

"Accommodation unit no. 5". It stands off the resort's main grid, in the shadow of evergreens. Nothing to see from the main street. Only foreign tourists, or the well-connected ministry directors can enjoy the fancy visibility at the Alpine Bliss.

Lili is not sure at first if she has any business joining the group of spoiled brats meeting up every day in the lobby. They all went to the same school, it seems, and have been here apparently every year since childhood. They know the bar where you can get whisky, the disco that plays this summer's chart hits, the bowling alley, and the behaviour codes.

There is so much fun being had in that group, but she doesn't quite share in it. The old tug-of-war is revived in herself – wanting to join in, but not wanting to after all. Disliking the people, but feeling clumsy for not playing along. She puts it down mostly to the fact that her nerves must be on edge, after the past weeks and months, and now the added pressure of this vacant time, suspended in the clouds of the mountain resort with no news from home, no signal yet to go ahead towards her future.

There's a guy in the group who puzzles her with his interest in her wellbeing. Why would any of them notice her in the first place? Her self-made clothes are nice, by her world's standards, but nowhere near the laid-back, feel-good-in-my-skin style of the others. She doesn't have jokes to tell, or at least doesn't tell any, and her dad isn't like the other dads.

True, the guy isn't the coolest of the gang either, and that might account for it. One from the periphery is more likely to notice her.

Is she being vaguely tickled by his interest? Redeemed, if only a bit, from insignificance?

Nonsense! He isn't even handsome, or funny; in fact,

she's pretty sure the others are sometimes secretly making fun of him.

He is tall and slim all right, but seems to be wearing a grimace across his face all the time, a sort of rictus, especially when laughing. He's dark haired with a swarthy skin that makes him look as if he has dark rings around his eyes. He chatters most of the time, without getting to a point, and everyone soon loses interest. Yes, well, he does tell jokes, and the guys do seem to like him, the way you like someone because they're trying so hard that you feel you need to oblige.

He is busy mentioning his dad: he's the chief surgeon at the Ministry of Interior's Hospital.

He is also busy mentioning his mom: also a medical doctor, if only just a general practitioner.

Both parents doctors? With the added perks of the dad being a surgeon, and a closed-circuit hospital?

On top of that, somehow predictably, he is also studying medicine, third year. There you are. Some people are just that privileged.

She cannot quite remember when she last checked how interested boys are in her. These past two years have been disproportionately, she now finds, about studying, coping with her father, dealing with her own coping.

Gabriel was shorter, wore glasses, and had a fair complexion.

And now this guy, ticking almost all the boxes, crossing her path and keeping her company. She's just not sure those boxes are hers to tick.

Vlad is his name. Vlad the Devil, or Vlad Dracul, better known as Dracula, that might be a bell to ring. But also blah, flat, bland, vapid, or simply dull. She's got rhyming connotations to choose from. The worst are the nicknames, stretching from cuddly to slightly ridiculing, which he is called: Vladut, Vlady, Vladyboy.

So here it is, a puppet theatre. She's a pale Lili standing

aloof, looking on, upgraded by the interest a guy shows in her, who is himself only an insignificant Vladyboy, upgraded by his family and his study choice.

She might be able to sell the plot to Cora; as a literary manager, she could see its value and put it on stage for unsuspecting young audiences. In reality, Cora seems to be engulfed in the mini-universe of the resort herself, and she has clearly got wind of the budding romance.

She won't mother Lili; she'd much rather sister her, if possible. Cora's hot for news, and can hardly stop herself questioning her each morning, over breakfast. What did you guys do? What did Vlad say? Did he offer to take you out on a date? Who did you say his father was? He must be so sweet, go get him, Lili!

"What music do you like?" he asks while playing his favourite tape of the summer's disco hits.

What music does she like?

Some sort, any sort, or several sorts at least. (John doesn't count as favourite music. He's her one and only.)

What the music is for, that is the question. If partying, yes, that tape he's playing is good. If it's for studying – or for daydreaming – or for a dreary Sunday afternoon anticipating another week of pointless school—

Should she say all this, as when solving an equation and listing the if-then, or just pick the first kind of music that crosses her mind and leave out the rest? Or just pick the music that's already being played, to make things simplest?

Never mind. Before she can come up with an answer, another guy is telling about a trick they played on a teacher before the end of term. They're sitting in the hotel's common room, each sipping at a pink or turquoise cocktail.

"I had this new Minolta that dad had brought me from his trip to Belgium—"

All this Western country name dropping, impressive and unnerving at the same time.

"— and our teach found us out while we were fiddling

with it in the break, and wanted to show off his importance and started preaching on me as to why am I bringing such stuff to school and so on, so I said hey, teach, why don't we all take a photo at the school main entrance? And he smiles, you know, it was so obvious he didn't want to show it but he liked the idea, and so he played tough but let himself be persuaded in the end, you know, and we all head to the main entrance, what with the end of the school year and just before the final exams it all makes sense to shoot a group photo, so we all huddle on the stairs together and shoot it, all solemn and important, the teach quite stiff, and—" he starts laughing "—you'll never believe it, when I had the film developed that night and I looked at the picture, I said hey, what's this? Outside the building, just imagine, above the stairs there's the flagpole, and instead of the motherland flag someone had hung a uniform shirt, which was waving in the breeze like a rag!"

There's a collective roar of laughter, they all bend over their cocktail glasses and then backwards.

"So guess what," the guy carries on when he's recovered from laughing so hard, "I draw a circle in red ink around that rag and pin the photo up on the billboard for top socialist school competition results in the main hall. And then comes a bit of a show, of course, what can you expect, 'Who hung that rag up there?' They threaten me, 'You're going to get expelled and kiss final exams good-bye, how dare you,' and all that boo stuff about unworthy YC behaviour." He downs his cocktail.

"So what happened in the end?" one of the girls asks.

The guy shakes his head as if saying 'The obvious, of course!'

"Well – my dad had to make a few phone calls. He did give me a long preach, sure, but it was all right in the end."

They give another round of laughter; life's so much fun.

They go hiking or picnicking during the day, and the evenings they spend either bowling, or at the disco, or both.

Vlad gets her drinks, asks when she's hungry, tells her jokes to make her laugh. She chuckles, not convinced, but willing to be nice in response to his kindness. He gives her a full, though unsolicited, picture of his background. Beside the dad – and mom – there's the grandpa, their flat in Bucharest's exclusive district of high party officials, and their cottage in the mountains, not far from here.

He lets her in on why they're part of an elite although they don't have the credentials one might imagine. For one thing, he's not actually staying at this hotel, obviously, as nobody in their family is a Party Central Committee member. He only comes over each morning after breakfast to join his pals here. Most of them live in his neighbourhood back home. And then, their flat on the posh boulevard – that's because of his grandpa, a retired army general, only two specimens left in the country, who got it way back in the fifties, when the games were made.

There you are. They're normal people after all, just very lucky and successful.

His fact sheet reflects top eligibility, she sometimes catches herself thinking. As if his family past, present, and possessions were not enough, he's doing medicine, and he's five years older than her, which already places him high in an eligibility ranking.

And then, his persistence in trying to cheer her up is touching. Bringing her closer to being inside a group, although that's not his deliberate intention, is a spin-off effect of his interest in her that she's putting down on the positive tab. She may have been too clumsy to join in with the party fellowships in high school, but now it's becoming clear that, given the right context, she can access the cool circles, whether they're worth accessing or not.

"I come here actually in winter only, summer's for the seaside, winter's about skiing – do you ski?" he turns briefly to her, sees she's shaking her head, and goes on without waiting for her to elaborate. "I take the medium slopes just to relax and enjoy the view, but when I want a challenge I take the Kanzel – do you know it? – no, yeah, well, or Ruia. I almost broke a leg there once, my dad was with me and gave me first aid, you know, first aid from the experts, I was lucky wasn't I?" He chuckles, looking at her with eyes wide in excitement.

"So you know this place well," she puts in.

"Oh, yes like the back of my palm, as they say," he picks up her thread before she can even wink, "I'm here at least ten times a season, what with our little cottage just forty kilometres away; we have a little house down in Busteni, you know, where the Caraiman peak is best visible, the mountain feels as if it's crashing over the place, it's just a village, well, they turned it into a mountain resort, it's a bit crowded and you can't ski, the mountain's too close and too rocky. My dad went to Innsbruck for a surgeons' conference and he says Busteni is just like Innsbruck, only much smaller; sure, there are other differences, too," he acknowledges with an attempt at irony.

She's never crossed the border, but she has heard of Innsbruck, whereas she's pretty sure nobody out there has heard of Busteni—

"Yeah, well, so we often take a break there from Saturday to Sunday evening, and we drive this stretch over here for the slopes. Lucky we don't need to book a hotel in this expensive place," he winks at her. "My dad taught me to ski, he's very good at it, I'd say almost still even better than me," he adds modestly. "I'm pretty good at it, I have good motor coordination, Dad finds it amazing because when I was born I was pulled out with the forceps, you know? Yes, of course you do, you're also a bit into these medical things, well, and you know what they say, right? They say, this might affect the baby, well, it obviously didn't affect me, as you can see, no one beats me at bowling either, ha ha, just can't wait to get the drinks for the bet I won last night!"

She remembers he left the others no hope of winning on the bowling alley. Skinny and bony, walking briskly, with his skeleton wriggling like a marionette, Vlad proved his motor coordination last night.

"Well, yes, and the other thing that my dad finds amazing about my skills, when I was three I got meningitis and you know what they say, right? The doctors, they say, with meningitis you either kick the bucket or you stay an imbecile for the rest of your life, and look at me, alive and kicking, best grades at uni, I'm going to have to take a specialisation from the fourth year, and I'm going for surgery just like my dad—" and he goes on and on, she keeps quiet, wouldn't have much chance to chip in anyway, but at least time goes by, and every day she's closer to getting that phone call from Mother telling her the wait is over and she can finally start her life.

Vlad's medical record, fact sheet and property review are a bit of distraction she's thankful for.

Lili is back in her room, tired after a day of smiling and searching for what to say next. Cora is still having drinks with a small but merry group out on the hotel's terrace.

Amid the blankness of the recent weeks and months, she suddenly feels a presence. Is it Gabriel's memory, back before her eyes? He seems to be smiling his half tender, half sarcastic smile.

He hated being questioned.

"Where are you from?"

He had just said hello on the beach, "My name's Gabriel, how are you?" She had no idea what people were supposed to say after that. She was just a sixteen-year-old ignorant goose.

"From Sighet."

"Where?"

"Sighet."

"Where's that? Never mind," she added, afraid of some embarrassing explanation. Later, she looked the place up. It was a little town on the edge of the map. "And what grade are you?" she went on, to show a friendly interest.

He paused a little.

"Eleventh."

She laughed again. Eleventh grade would be just like herself, but it had sounded funny.

"You needed some time to think before answering, eh?" She could feel he was giving fake answers, but it didn't stop her. "And what do your parents do?"

Gosh, she'd asked that, too, within five minutes of their acquaintance. Checking his credentials, trying to make small talk, no idea why. She could have just let him take care of it, but she didn't want to seem shy.

"My mother's a weaver, my father's a foreman."

That sounded cut out of the communist working class propaganda, so she burst out laughing, but immediately checked herself, for fear he might have meant it and her laughter would offend. It was only half a year later that she earned the privilege of knowing what his parents did, when he told her without her asking, because she never asked any questions of that kind again.

"What are you doing tonight?"

"I see you're forgetting to ask me the one essential thing," she said.

"What?"

"If I'm alone."

He frowned for a second.

"Why, you've got a boyfriend or something?"

She laughed. What an idea! Boyfriend, together at the seaside, at sixteen?

"No, I've got an aunt."

"And she won't let you?"

"I don't know that, I haven't asked. But we're together and I have no idea how I can go out by myself."

"Lock her up in the bathroom. You'll work something

out," he reassured her with a wink, stood up and went away, leaving her to work something out.

She turned her head towards the sea. Something was telling her she wasn't going. Lili, going out on a date? With a guy who just came up to her to say hi and ask her out? Just like that? And lying to sneak out by herself to run to a disco? How wild – and complicated! But then she realised that that was what she had been missing: to feel like a young girl. Flirting, lying to sneak out to a date, going out to dance in a disco, wasn't it just that?

The little lie about the town on the edge of the map was cleared up soon, when he asked her phone number that first night. It was her turn to tease.

"Why should I give you my number? I'm in Bucharest, you in Sighet. What's the point?"

"Come on, maybe I can come to visit you."

"Sure, a six-hour stay in the main railway station changing trains—"

"And what if I'm not really from Sighet?"

"Hmm, and what if you're a fake?"

"Not a fake, no, but well, okay, I'm from Bucharest too."

She felt as if she had regained a little bit of face. But when he showed her his student ID, she got dizzy. His name next to a strange picture – a Gabriel wearing glasses and looking a good few years older than the guy standing there.

"You wear glasses?"

He'd finished third year at the Technical School and was twenty-three years old. She'd never met anyone in that age category.

And it made a great difference. She hadn't cared a bit about his age or home town before, but now that she knew, she couldn't go on ignoring them. She felt not small, but worried. What should she say, how should she act, so she didn't come across as the little high school girl she was?

But for a few days, they still had the beach and the

summer hits – "I wanna know what love is, I know you can show me" – cocooning them. He put on no cool-guy act, played no games; he was there. It all felt easy.

She looks out the window, onto the terrace. Cora is laughing and gesturing vividly while telling a story.

And Vlad? Who's Vlad?

On the fourth day, just before breakfast, she gets the phone call. She's summoned to reception and picks up the phone, and then she hears Mother's voice, warm, smiling into the receiver at her end, it seems, but with a sort of restraint.

She says, "Honey, everything's good, my clever girl, you got nine fifteen in maths – well, and erm – something's happened in physics, well, we'll need to see, I'm already talking to people, you know—"

"What do you mean, something's happened in physics?" she interrupts, her breath gone white.

"Well, yeah – you know," Mother keeps smiling in her receiver, but inhales with some difficulty, "you got a good mark there too, it's just – well, it's not as good as it's supposed to be, there's a mistake, I'm told, and they're rectifying it soon, so—"

"They're rectifying it? What mistake?" she wrestles with the nonsense of it.

Mother sighs, then hurries to speak again. "Yes, well – the thing is, right now you're not yet in, you know? But as I said, they're working on it, I'm working on it, talking to people, and people are calling me to tell me what's going on, you know, colleagues of your father, they do know what's going on, and things won't stay like that—"

Mother's words trail off and she listens to the silence, listens for some sense.

"So what exactly is my final grade now?" she enquires, trying to go about it systematically.

“Seven ninety-eight,” Mother replies, as if relieved to be talking facts.

“And what’s the last grade above the line?” Lili asks.

The line, how strange to be interested in it, the line on the results list, separating success from failure. Above the line / below the line has never occurred in her universe until now. There never used to be a line there.

“Eight oh one,” Mother says after a moment’s hesitation.

There’s an air pocket in her breast and she feels the momentary jolt.

“So I got nine fifteen in maths, but my final grade is seven ninety-eight, that means in physics I got—” She halts in disbelief. She could never, but absolutely never, get such a mark, and in physics of all... The simple arithmetic tells her it must be five something, which she never got in high school even for chemistry, or political economics; this is mad, this isn’t happening. Five is the absolute minimum pass grade in school.

And hold on.

Seven ninety-eight, eight oh one.

“How far below the line am I, then? I mean, until this – mistake – is rectified?”

“Well—” Mother breathes in with some flutter again, “actually – you’re the first below that line – but as I said,” she hurries to fill the space that’s suddenly gaping, “it’s not going to stay like that, don’t worry, I’m doing everything here, and your father’s colleagues are helpful, and on our side, and supportive. I’ve already drawn up some papers and I’m going to the Institute, so let’s just wait and be patient a bit longer, it’s all going to be fine, you’ll see,” Mother ends on a tone that suggests she’s not just smiling in the receiver now, she’s downright beaming, visualising the victory.

Lili hangs up, restless with the pile of questions that are wobbling in a state of entropy. Strangely, and irritatingly, the entropy is not in her head, or else she would be able to formulate the questions and proceed to find answers, as she did about the thousands of problems she has solved along the years. No, the entropy is going on elsewhere, behind a screen, or below a massive lid, and she can't quite locate it.

That five something, that just can't be, she knows too well, she can still see with her mind's eye the problems written in careful handwriting on the green board in the exam room, and she knows the paths to the solutions; the reasoning and the evidence were there, in her test paper, beyond any doubt. Okay, she did forget to make references to the relevant theorems, as tests traditionally require, but she applied and integrated them in that crisp and elegant manner she knew was what mattered in science. Right, so maybe that has cost her a few marks as per the rigid marking scheme typical of admission exams – bureaucratic marking schemes, or sensible marking schemes used bureaucratically by assessors with a civil servant mentality, too afraid they won't be able to justify why one candidate was admitted and the other not. Many candidates just have to fail.

But the references to theorems can't possibly account for half of the overall mark, so how did this five come about? Had the others, above the line, done both problem solving and quoting theorems? Since none of them got the maximum grade, ten, which hasn't been awarded for at least a decade, it must be that they had attempted both, just not to one hundred percent accuracy. So her perfect reasoning was worth less than two failed endeavours.

But what mistake did Mother mean? And what exactly was she doing about it? Have admission results been displayed? The rolls of paper glued on the inside of the windows, so they can be read by the crowd outside, listing the candidates and their grades, both above and below the line – if those rolls have been glued already, then what is there to do? Her fate is glued and sealed.

But that just can't be, this is the wrong fate, the wrong script, it just makes no sense.

And what exactly are her father's colleagues doing,

being supportive and all? What papers does Mother mean? That's just a conglomerate of absurd phenomena which would never occur, would it? The five in physics, the being-first-below-the-line, grades being "a mistake," results being displayed and still, Mother talking about changing them (or what else was she fretting about?) – all of this is nothing but impossible events, in an impossible causality chain, in any given physical system of the universe. Which theoretically allows for the possibility that once a fundamental law has been flouted, a whole chain of divergences follow, so the question is what was that original divergence, where is the flawed premise?

But then, Mother was so confident on the phone. She reassured Lili several times that it was all going to be sorted out. Errors would be corrected. Rectified was the word she had used. Is Mother working on turning the time wheel backwards and generating a different chain of events? Lili knows time travel is a holy grail, but things always start small, don't they, who knows; turning the process of this admission exam backwards might be the start, and the rest would follow.

The laws would follow, or our recognition of them would adapt to accommodate this new finding, namely, that processes can be reversed, indeed, that nothing is set in stone, that people, and tests, and fates are subject to error, they're bound to incorporate some deviation, at least now and then. Statistically significant deviation.

Can it be, then, that she's part of such a deviation? This would account for all things going wrong in the impossible causality chain she's reviewing in an endless loop. But what is the way out of this, then, how can deviation be redressed, corrected, rectified? She's always been an outsider, true, now she thinks of it, it all makes sense in a way, what with the party fellowships, her clumsiness, her aloofness, it may all mean that she is deviant indeed, her brilliance included. But that isn't making things any more transparent or comprehensible.

She's used to wrestling with a problem in her head

while having lunch or doing her constitutional. She goes downstairs to have breakfast, conscientiously, observing the timetables, but she hardly hears or sees anything. She sits down at the table, opposite Cora, who would be reporting what she sees people doing at neighbouring tables, as she always does.

A cup and saucer, cutlery, and a napkin take shape before Lili out of nowhere, then some brownish liquid is being poured, a plate with a few plastic wrappings lands before her, they read butter, jam, honey, processed cheese respectively, all portioned, weighed and packaged with mathematical precision.

Someone sits down by her side and is trying to make himself heard, oh, yes, that Vladyboy, what is it? She raises her eyes to meet his.

"Something wrong?" he asks. "The results?" He raises his eyebrows with a sudden tearful look in his eyes, his head lopsided as if ready to comfort and cuddle. She has had to let him in on the fact that she's waiting for admission results, even if she doesn't do much talking otherwise.

She shakes it off and replies, "No, of course not, nothing wrong" hurriedly; she's not to let out anything before she has made sense of it by herself.

He discards the cuddly pose just as instantly as he'd put it on, as if relieved that he can go back to his light-hearted chatter.

There's a different sort of numbness she's feeling. Background noises and bustle, such as Vlad's voice, the people walking by, the sun changing angle in the sky, it all feels different from yesterday. As if there's something else going on now, between her body and the outside world, a perpetual, remote purr of a system working endlessly, like a mill rotating on and on. Half-questions are being tossed up like rags, chunks of answers are being tried out and disposed of almost instantly.

She calls Mother back an hour later.

"Hi my love, there you are, I'm in a bit of a rush, going

right now to the Institute, I've got an appointment to talk to the dean, you know," Mother chirps in a tone of delight.

So...? she wonders.

"What exactly is this appointment all about?"

"Well, this situation, honey. It's unacceptable, of course!"

"What exactly is it, I still don't understand, Mom, what has happened, can you please just explain it to me from A-B-C?"

"Lili, honey, I will, but no time now. I can only say, they've made a mistake marking your physics paper; I've made an appeal of course, and I've been getting phone calls from your father's colleagues who are telling me what exactly has happened, I'll tell you everything, better when you're back home rather than on the phone!"

"Okay, but if it's a fact that they made a mistake, where's the problem? I mean, where's our problem? The error will be corrected, if they know about it," Lili presumes.

"Well, honey, that's why I say, let's talk about it off the phone. It was a mistake, true, but that's what I'm being told, just, you know, through the grapevine. Apparently the results have been displayed, they're out, and it takes a lot of bureaucracy to make changes afterwards, but don't worry. They don't expect us to know, but today this appointment, they're going to see we do know, so they'll have to find a way, otherwise the cat's out of the bag and so on." Mother is almost panting into the phone with excitement. "So let me just dash off for now, and I'll give you a call maybe tonight. You're coming back home the day after tomorrow, it's only a short while left and we can best talk then."

Lili nods, lost in thought. Something's not right there, too many things that should be happening for the first time – results being changed, appeals being granted, appointments with officials bringing a resolution. Mistakes being acknowledged and remedied, outside a maths problem or a physics lab? Father would snort.

But then, her father, with his know-it-all professor attitude, sneered at everything.

Vlad and his clique would be able to testify to other ways things can work. To things getting solved no matter if mistakes were involved. It must be a matter of leverage.

Sometimes the system does get cornered and must acknowledge wrong decisions, and go back on them. But certainly not with her father's attitude; that never solved anything. Mother can make it happen. When it becomes clear to them that the truth is out there about the marking mistakes, they'll have to amend it. What would they have to lose if Lili gets admitted?

And besides, the Party's ethics-and-equity ethos, socialist integrity, the New Citizen, Mother can embody that, the New Citizen engaged in the fight for justice, with hard evidence in her bag, demanding no favour but merely righteousness. She does have a case there, and a chance.

Lili must just find a way of making the next forty-eight hours go by, but she's used to that, after hovering through the last two years of school, crossing out week after week in the kitchen calendar. This now is a trifle: she has Vlad chattering the hours away, a bit of nice scenery, and a forced relaxation programme.

CHAPTER THREE

"What's wrong, kid?" Cora sits down by her side, on the terrace. "Did Vlad do something wrong?"

Vlad?

Of course not.

But then, oh, yes, she remembers. She and Vlad are the latest gossip as the new couple. She shakes her head slightly, dismissing the trifles.

"No, nothing about Vlad," she replies in a faint voice.

"The results?" Cora probes gently.

Lili shakes her head again, not knowing exactly how to sum it up. Is it the results? Is it the nonsense?

"Oh, no, kid, what's the matter, tell me!"

What can she tell? That she failed, but is the first below the line? Some compensation. That she failed, but Mother says there's been a mistake? Don't they all think it's a mistake when they fail? But then, numbers don't lie, there clearly must be a mistake. But won't it make her sound pathetic, as if inventing excuses? And then, Cora – which side would she be on? She's with them, that's how they are in this hotel. They shouldn't know what Mother does and knows; she mustn't give away their underground sources.

"Lili, listen to me!" Cora shakes her arm. "Kid, tell me what's wrong. Is it the results? Did you talk to your mom?"

"Yes, I did, twice," Lili replies in a thin voice.

"What did she say?"

That's an easier question to answer.

"She said that I'm the first below the line, but there's been a mistake, I don't know what, but she's busy putting in appeals, she says—"

She stops short. Cora sighs and squeezes her arm.

"I know your mother, Lili. She's a fighter and a no-nonsense woman. If she says there's been a mistake, she knows what she's saying. Trust her. And she's going to do everything that's right. But tell me exactly what she said about this mistake. Can it be helped, perhaps? I mean, in parallel, if we throw out several fishing rods—" Cora leaves her statement suspended.

This is a good mental exercise for Lili; gathering her thoughts to relay the information in a way that makes some sense to a third person might help her make sense of it herself.

Cora listens and occasionally butts in with a question, but then prompts Lili to go on. Lili pours everything out as she recalls it, almost word for word. She can't take the trouble to filter anything out, it would be too much to decide what might be strategically wise to keep a secret, and what not. Cora nods and she can tell she's scheming, taking it all in.

"Honey, look, go for a walk, for a hike, take the ski lift up to the peak, go to the pool, do something with yourself. And tonight – have you got any plans?"

Lili halts with a blank stare.

"Plans? Oh, yes, Vlad said something about—"

"OK, forget Vlad tonight, please, give him some excuse – just don't tell him anything, OK? Act as usual, but give him some excuse, and you're coming with me tonight after dinner and we're having drinks here, there might be someone joining us who – well, who knows, might be able to help."

Lili opens her eyes wide.

"Yes," Cora nods, "don't get your hopes too high, and don't say a word to anyone, not about the results, not about planning to talk to this person, just let your mom do her work over there in Bucharest, and we take our shot here, just to see where it might take us. All right? But do something with yourself to pass the time. And chin up, kid, OK?"

Lili nods, but can't tell what exactly she might do for her chin to go up. She'll fill the time with something until tonight, that's the one thing she can do.

Cora is keen to inspect her evening outfit before leaving the room for dinner.

"No," she says curtly, "this is too bland. Too 'I'm mama's little brave girl and I do whatever I'm told'. We need a bit of salt and pepper. Got anything fancier?"

Lili stands still, her mind frozen. She's got her best skirt on, which she made herself, baggy and reaching way below her knees, the latest fad, and a grey, equally baggy tee.

"OK, I see," Cora nods. "Let's get you something from my stuff." She opens her side of the wardrobe. Her things are lying neatly folded on the shelves; with brisk movements she taps on several items one after the other. She grabs one.

"What do you think?" Cora holds it up.

Lili's eyes open up wider for a moment. It's a sleeveless black silk piece that looks incredible. She puts it on quickly and turns to Cora for inspection. The silk seems to be flowing around her body and glistening in deep waters.

"Perfect," Cora smiles.

"Erm, don't you find the cut a bit—"

"Deep?" Cora chuckles. "No. Yes, maybe, but nothing too much. Just a bit bold, and that's what you need to make an impression. We both need to make an impression tonight," she adds, winking.

Cora always makes an impression, Lili finds.

Tonight, she's wearing a short, tight black skirt with a large sunflower stitched on the side. Her legs are covered in something Lili can't exactly describe: too opaque to be stockings, but too thin to be trousers; they're tight on the legs like a second skin, and they're cut above the ankles. She's seen nothing like them before. Over a black, close-fitting spaghetti strap top that provides only summary coverage, Cora dons a dark purple kimono-cut sweater knitted loosely, like a see-through mesh. The eye can't help but hover over the dividing lines between the top and the skin underneath.

She swallows her dinner in chunks like pebbles. Who's the mysterious person, she wonders? Cora doesn't seem to be on the lookout for anyone; she churns out theatre gossip merrily. Words keep flying past her ears, muffled: the Party Secretary, the lead actress, the stage director, the hopes for a new possible performance tour in the West, the video night shows as the latest hit—

"Is he here?" Lili interrupts.

Cora stops short, with a slight gasp.

"Erm, no, Lili, shhh, he's visiting – if at all. He was here last night, and seemed to be staying in the resort for a few more days. Let's just wait and see, all right?"

Lili nods, looking down. If he's not staying here, what kind of power can he wield, should he be willing to help at all?

Cora's been talking to Mother on the phone this afternoon, that much she knows. But she sounds secretive about what Mother told her.

They finish dinner and head to the bar. Cora gracefully chirps her friendly small talk to the bar lady and gets an orange cocktail for Lili and a glass of red wine for herself. She turns around and mimics an excited 'Let's go, now's the big time!'

Lili follows her onto the terrace. Are they stepping on a stage, strolling on a catwalk, showing themselves off, making an impression? What impression is it?

At the far end, a small group is sitting and talking quietly. There's a brief outburst of laughter, which is checked back into discretion, and the heads draw close again over the table.

In the momentary opening caused by the merry party leaning back in laughter, Lili can see at the far end of the table, almost as if keeping himself away from inquisitive eyes, an elderly man she hasn't seen around before.

"Just remember, Lili, you tell the story as you know it, in your own words. What matters is that you talk in your own voice, a young person like you, your innocence. He'll want to hear you, you, Lili Danes, not some prepackaged account I or someone else might give him."

Herself. Offer her voice, her candour, her innocence. So as to strike an emotional chord, put down some positive little note to her tab, anything that can create even a tiny breach and help her push her case through. Thankfully, she hasn't got to ask for anything, nor flatter with some book signing, just tell her story. Her voice might do the work.

They keep walking slowly towards his table, as if casually searching for some place to sit. A hand sticks up, waving to Cora, which Cora acknowledges with a broad smile.

"Come on," she says to Lili over her shoulder. "Oh, and —" She stops short and turns to Lili. "This is Gregory Talu, Minister of National Infrastructure we're talking to, just so you know."

Minister! – but national infrastructure? How's that connected? And who are the others? Party Central Committee members? They look a bit merry for that. She's spotted them before, they're staying in the hotel, but she's never been introduced.

"Come on, Cora, we've been waiting for you – and good that you've brought your protégée along, too – welcome dear!"

Lili nods with eyes to the ground. She can hear the cheerful voices, but can see no faces.

"Yes, tonight I bring you Lili Danes, a friend's daughter," Cora replies with her sunny smile etched in her voice.

"How charming, sit down here, next to me, dear, good to have you – just – Cora! Why did you drag the poor young lady along? To sit with us old chaps, instead of having fun with the kids her age?"

"Well, she preferred a quiet get-together for tonight, you know, Lili's not so much into partying – although she is of course, having so much fun with the young people here, no doubt, but tonight's an exception."

Lili raises her eyes briefly and sees Cora watching her with a beaming smile, as if saying, 'Go honey, go'.

"Oh, we're delighted to have her, of course! Luci was just telling us how it went in Prague last month—"

"Oh, Vasi's congress, so you did go along with him after all," Cora exclaims.

"Of course, I did, yes, in the end, how could I let him go alone, I mean, how *could* I..." There's laughter. "And it was good I went. He'd get back from the meetings at about four and say, 'Let's go out, Luci, see what we can get for our pretty foreign currency'."

There's an instant but restrained burst of laughter. The sphinx at the head of the table is smiling faintly, with narrow feline eyes.

Lili sits somewhat stiff, not sure how much she can hunch her back without letting the V cut reveal too much. She clutches at the soft mohair shawl Cora cast over her shoulders to keep her warm in the chilly mountain night air. She must listen for her cue and do her part. This is not exactly her, but it will be over quickly.

Names of some absent people are being mentioned again and again. Vasi, for instance, Luci's husband. It was his congress in Prague. Sounds like a parliamentary committee. Then Fred, who's Sebi's brother, here with his wife Marina. Fred apparently was here the other day, but the driver had to take him back to Bucharest for an emergency meeting with Office 2 (that's code name for Comrade Ceaușescu's wife).

Office 2 seems to be often trickier than Office 1.

Luci is busy whispering to Cora about the darker districts in Prague where it's a bit wild, almost like in the West. This would be unimaginable in Bucharest! Sebi and Marina are entertaining their guest of honour telling him about the expansion plans of the metro network.

With conversations going on and the spotlight temporarily away from her, Lili starts glancing around, at first nervously darting back to the glass in front of her, but gradually taking more and more time to examine the people sitting around. The only picture she had of high officials was one of stern faces clapping hands at Party Congress assemblies. But now it strikes her that there's nothing special or otherwise distinctive about these high-society specimens. They might be decent people, after all. Even nice.

Her nervousness is slowly fading.

With the spoiled papa's brats that Vlad hangs out with, she's but a fly on the wall. They have their insider jokes and their clique act. Although, come to think of it, not even they have anything special about their persons; one has thin, colourless hair, the other a crooked nose, there's one who's so skinny she looks like a spider in tight jeans. They might put on a fancier sweater, or white sneakers with three stripes (the 'original' Adidas, they say) smuggled out of the export factory, but they're just teenagers, after all.

Luci is a middle-aged woman with her hair done up in something that looks like a beehive, clearly a perm. Gold, ring-shaped earrings, the design that's become standard. A dark green cotton sweater with a neat boat cut. She could be a school teacher for all Lili can tell. Her mascara is smudged a bit at the corners of her eyes, which only makes her more likeable.

It's her absent husband that's the real McCoy.

Marina and Sebi sit opposite each other, between them the minister. Lili remembers Cora telling her that they both work in the city hall, the urban development office. Their city hall jobs are solid, but it's Sebi's brother, Fred, who made them possible. There is no hint at Fred's own position, but if he's been summoned by Office 2, one can have the wildest hypotheses.

So, if she's not wrong, none of them, including Cora and herself, except the Minister, are the real heroes, but just their stand-ins: the relatives, the spouses, the protégées. The sponsors are in the shadow.

Her eyes suddenly meet Gregory's. He's listening to Sebi's perorations, while watching Lili. He's got a vague smile on his face and Lili can't tell for sure if it's about what he hears, or what he sees. What is it that he sees? She checks her posture again, suddenly reminded of her purpose in being there, and of the low cut of her blouse. A shame, such a gorgeous blouse, but probably not for the Lili now – maybe years later, the woman she might yet become.

"How's your husband, I haven't seen him in a while?" he suddenly speaks, gazing at Cora. The chatter round the table stops.

"Well, yes, he's been away with the trade delegation in Cuba, and then back only for a week before they went to Syria," Cora replies.

Her voice sounds velvety, to Lili the absolute embodiment of confidence and feeling good in her skin. She can tell why people love Cora. That sunny smile on her face, the dark deer eyes, the straight girlish haircut, seventies style, her petite stature and the cool but always comfy outfits – everything just right. Her look seems to be making a statement, one that cannot be ignored, although it's not one that needs to be shouted out loud. Cora is who she is, unmistakable at that.

Lili was thankful to have Cora as her chaperone. She hoped to get some of her feel-good by reflection, by being in her proximity.

"And how about you, Lili?" the minister turns his eyes on her again. He speaks deliberately, in a low pitch. "What's your story?"

She feels a flutter in her guts. This must be the cue.

"Lili's taking a short break from admission nerves, you know, exam results—" Cora intervenes.

"Oh, exam results. Where did you go, young lady?" His eyes don't leave her, despite Cora's chipping in.

"Physics," Lili answers promptly, with a gulp.

"Oh!" there's a faint rustle around the table, eyebrows raised and nodding in appreciation.

The minister has raised one eyebrow, too. His gaze is somewhat tighter.

"Not a girl for an easy ride through life," he says.

"No, not at all," Cora assents. "Especially as – well – the entrance doesn't seem to be so straightforward," she adds in an allusive tone. She gazes at the minister with mute significance. He frowns and glances at Cora for a fleeting second.

"Why, what's the matter?" he asks with a grunt.

Cora nods to Lili. "It's best she tells you herself."

Everyone is watching her, waiting to hear. The minister's gaze is going through her. What about that bloody V cut?

Here she is, delivering her part, the cue she's been preparing for all evening, while dressing up, rehearsing mentally, pre-packaging herself for something positive to go down on her tab and hopefully push her cause up for consideration and resolution.

The story, as she tells it, is through before she knows it. Was it too short to have any impact? Did it make any sense, for all the gaps in Lili's own making sense of it? Are its implications for her life, for her family, even beginning to dawn on these people, and most importantly on this elderly guy who has no connection to her context?

"Greg, but this sounds awful!" Luci puts in, meaning to elicit his approval.

Greg is still processing what he's heard, narrowing his eyes while they're still resting on Lili's flushed face, and doesn't acknowledge Luci's intervention.

"Erm, yes, well, there's a bit of background to this, if I may just—" Cora comes in, but halts, glancing around, as if she's trying to explain more but is careful not to be overheard.

"Come here, darling, let's swap seats so you can tell Greg more." Luci gets up. "I'm sure he'll want to help," she adds in the way of a compliment to the minister.

There is a sense of approval around the table, nods and encouraging grunts, as Cora advances her position next to the man of the evening. As soon as she has taken her seat, she swivels on her chair to face him, bends slightly and starts whispering. He tilts his head, listening. A one-on-one channel has been created between the two. Occasionally, Greg glances at Cora and puts in some brief question or remark. Cora goes on explaining in a subdued voice and with restrained gestures, so that Lili cannot tell what she might be saying. Did Mother fill Cora in so thoroughly?

Luci straightens her back and leans slightly forward, facing all of them, as a teacher about to address the class. She seems happy to take over and leave the two whisperers to their privacy.

"These admission stories, oh, what a pain for parents, we all know them – and of course, for the kids, too, bless their little souls," Luci declares with a motherly smile.

"You, too, must have had your share of admission fevers some time ago, over Danny's exams, right?" Sebi prompts her.

"Oh, yes, don't even get me started," Luci nods. There's an expectant silence, except for Cora and Greg's subdued murmuring. "Well, yes, Danny went for law—"

"Great Scott, no less than law, was it," Sebi exclaims in the background.

"That's right, Sebi, that's right, no less than law. You know," she adds, turning to Lili and Marina, "you know what that means, don't you, the battle over each hundredth of a mark, the whole list going from nine ninety-eight to – say, nine forty-four – a hundred students squeezed in that tiny range. And, guess what, our Danny lying way out with his eight ninety-three."

"Ouch," Sebi puts in. "Not good," he adds humorously.

Sebi wears thick glasses that make him look funny. He seems to be on the joking trip most of the time. It's his way of being socially adept.

"Not good at all!" Luci nods with eyebrows raised.

"So he did the long army stage?" Sebi wonders. "Or – oh, you found an arrangement—"

Luci keeps nodding, every nod going deeper, with added significance.

"An arrangement, of course, what else? If a kid goes away for sixteen months, how can you expect him to pass admission to law when he comes back, all his knowledge erased, all his study habits blown away, he'll be a different person!"

Yes, Sebi nods, looking down at the tablecloth. Marina nods faintly, too.

Lili is waiting for the rest of the story.

"So you got him to stay home—" Sebi volunteers.

"We sort of got him to stay home, though it wasn't easy. Vasi was mad – 'What if I'm ever asked why my son got exempted from his patriotic duty,' he said, 'how can I justify it?' He was right, in his own way, but then, it was Danny's future on the line. We found a compromise that worked for everyone – Vasi found a compromise," Luci corrects herself. "He put Danny down for the transmissions division, life's more merciful there for the kids, you know, and most of them are the short-term kids who've got their study place in their pockets, which means, it's a better environment, they can make friendships, they're good, smart kids in the same league, you know what I mean – anyway, Vasi got him in there, in a unit just twenty miles out of Bucharest, and he could come home nearly each weekend to get some rest.

"In time, he resumed some of his private lessons, and with a weekend at home, and a bit of sick leave every other week, we managed to keep him above the line. The next summer, we got him leave of absence and he came home and took the exams again. He was lucky and got in."

"What? That's an amazing performance," Sebi slaps his thighs. "Brilliant kid."

"Yes, that's right, Sebi, thank you, Danny can be very ambitious, takes after his father," Luci adds emphatically.

"So, but, wait," Sebi presses on, "what, he passed the exams and then you could get him out of the army ahead of term?"

Luci nods with significance. She mimics something like 'Yes, but don't ask for the details'.

"Wow," Sebi exclaims again, impressed. "Amazing. Chapeau to both of you, Luci, how you got him out of the shit – sorry," he ducks his head in guilt, looking around the table, "but what you both did was truly amazing. And of course Danny himself in the first place!"

Lili blinks and frowns, busy processing what she has heard. Is Sebi so emotional, or is he fawning on Luci?

She ventures, "I didn't know the long army stage could be terminated sooner—"

"It can't," Sebi replies, with the same mute significance on his face as Luci. "That's the point. What Luci and Vasi did for the kid was – can't find my words, Luci, I bow to you, really!"

Luci acknowledges his compliment gracefully.

"Yes, my dear," she turns to Lili, who's still confused. "Obviously, that's not normally possible. But Vasi moved heaven and earth; I mean, on paper, Danny was still enrolled, you know? But he was on leave of absence extended and extended and extended, while he went to school, and by the end of his first semester, his army stage was completed, too. End of story!"

Sebi scoffs and shakes his head in awe.

Lili keeps quiet. Happy ending, indeed. But it's a story about failing and working harder next year. Hers is a story about having done the work the first time round, but some people having mixed things up.

"Does anyone else feel like another drink? Should we get a bottle of wine? But let's wait until they're finished, so Greg can tell us what he prefers."

Sebi moves over to the free chair next to Luci, intent on talking to her about something. There's a murmur accompanied by nods and grunts replacing words. Lili doesn't bother to listen in, especially as they seem, just like Cora and Greg, to be using their own discrete channel.

"Don't worry, it will all be fine, in the end," Lili hears Marina's voice for the first time that evening. It's faint and flat, as if cautious not to come out into the world.

Lili smiles and nods – good manners.

"I tried five times. And then, the sixth year, I finally got in. Architecture. You simply need to know it may take time," Marina concludes, darting a quick glance around the table as if to check if anyone can overhear.

Lili feels the tension in her nape from nodding. Should she just wisely agree? Pay Marina a compliment about having studied architecture?

The murmured conversation between Cora and Greg is over. Cora swivels back to face the table, looking around. Luci and Sebi stop their chat, too, as if awaiting instructions.

"All good?" Luci enquires with a broad smile, gazing at Greg fondly.

Greg nods several times thoughtfully.

"Cora here has been of great help," he says. "It seems to be a tricky kettle of fish." He takes a sip of his wine. "But the girl here has done her part, and now the others must do theirs."

They all nod, impressed by his words. Lili stares at him, waiting.

The waiter is coming up to the table. Luci briefly

hesitates whether to interrupt the great moment, or put off the wine bottle for a few minutes. Greg notices. He keeps silent, allowing her to go ahead.

"Sorry, everyone, Greg, shall we order a bottle of wine, what do you think? What would you like?"

"Just get us red wine glasses, will you," Greg says, barely looking at the waiter. His voice sounds rusty. "I've brought you a bottle of my own," he adds to them with a faint complicit smile.

Lili hangs suspended, watching the glasses landing on the table and the bottle of export red wine being admired, hearing the excitement and the gratitude going around the table.

They're now ready to toast. Greg is holding up his glass with an intent gaze at Lili.

"Let's get justice done, then," he says.

A murmur of approval rises briefly on his words.

Lili feels a thrill about the solemnity of the moment. She bows her head, and only just manages to utter "Thank you," struggling to hold back her tears.

When she has regained enough composure to raise her eyes, the conversation has moved on to expressions of delight about the wine.

A minister is getting involved for her! Mother will be relieved.

Greg Talu is going to fall like thunder on the muddled heads of the faculty staff. Lili has no idea of hierarchies and remits. There's the government, the Party Central Committee, the Parliament, and in between them, Madam Secu. Who reports to whom, who carries more leverage, or can that leverage be reversed? But minister is an impressive title, unlike the other bodies, which are collective nouns of members or officers, deployed in internal ranks more complex than DNA chains. She assumes, therefore, that Gregory Talu can wield more than enough power to save the day for an insignificant girl like Lili Danes.

Vlad's light-hearted disposition hasn't changed since she told him what's going on. She had to, because he kept asking, being fond of her, if she'd had any news about her admission results.

It was a bit awkward at first, having to actually put in words the idea that she failed admission (how absurd!), and then hurrying to explain, but again, without letting it sound as if it was pretence or wishful thinking. Plausibility was so elusive.

Expounding the situation to Vlad has been her first go at achieving this plausibility. Not quite satisfactory, she found, hearing herself during the conversation, but Vlad believed her nonetheless.

"So, I'm not sure that's so convincing, Vlad..."

"There's no convincing, Lili, I absolutely believe in you. You're an amazing girl, the most amazing I ever met."

How comforting! Vlad doesn't need any persuasion, because he isn't questioning anything. Not many people will pledge so much on her, under the circumstances.

It's just – he keeps mentioning the topic.

"When the results thing is sorted..."

"How exactly did your father's colleagues...?"

"Something just like this happened once at med school, and they..."

She understands he does it out of his keen interest in her, but she wishes he wouldn't poke so much around it. If truth be told, she'd rather be home, talking to Mother and planning what to do. Tomorrow she and Cora are going back.

The other thing that feels off is Vlad's funny side-remarks tagged casually to whatever he's talking about. Things like, "My mom's hydrangeas, you'll see, Lili, they're really amazing and she's crazy about them," or "The park restaurant – have you been in their garden? No? Never mind, we must do it together, you'll love it," or "We've got dozens of video tapes, they're Dad's actually, well, but we'll be watching together, we've got movies, and music, I'm sure you'll love them."

All that future tense. Once again, she and Cora are leaving tomorrow. Vlad doesn't seem to realise that. Or is he doing it on purpose? What makes him so sure they'll see each other again once they're back in Bucharest?

She watches his face next time he mentions it. He's earnest. There's no question lurking behind his eyes, no particular intent. He doesn't seem to have even the shadow of a doubt. So – are they going to be girlfriend and boyfriend?

She's immersed deep in her problem-solving reasoning, in her eerily emotionless tunnel of waiting for things to happen. Vlad, the happy-go-lucky clique, the mountains, the hotel and its quality meals for its oh-so-special guests, Cora's friendly attempts to distract her with her chat – all of this has been but a stage set; it all melts into the background, inconsequential to her.

It's been of course good to enjoy a bit of distraction, and she's thankful for it.

A bit of kissing, with Vlad, too. Some curiosity involved: how does kissing feel again, after all this time since Gabriel? And what kind of kisser is Vlad? Is he a chatterer when he kisses, too, or is it maybe in his kisses that she can sense his depth? Say, like kissing the frog into a prince – oh la la.

She didn't quite sense any difference, though, when it came to pass. Or maybe she wasn't exploring properly.

Maybe because it's all been part of this out-of-the-routine, here-I-am-dropped-in-a-film-set interlude, her life being elsewhere, suspended before it can at last move on.

When he hugged her, she noticed how his lips were closing up, already poised for the kiss. His lips were glistening moist, as if the hormones had already started the secretions ahead of the actual lip contact. His eyes were closed, ready for the magic moment. Should she close hers, too? She did, taking up the cue of the scene she was cast in. And then? Some brushing and rolling of lips on lips, tongues negotiating the narrow space, round after round in what was meant as a heightening of passion.

It was all right for a first time; they could always give it another try, as they would.

Until then, they held hands and displayed their mutual inclination. Lili's inclination was poised against the backdrop of the film set, where she was playing her role patiently; she was half there, basking in Vlad's fondness, half removed in a world he had no access to. Not yet, at least.

It's Vlad's future tenses that stir her out of her detachment and make her realise that a choice is required before closing this holiday.

"—and you'll see when you meet my dad, he's such a great guy, I'm sure he'll absolutely fall for you—"

Really?

"And what about your mom, will she fall for me, too?" she teases.

Vlad nods first, before articulating any word, then goes on, "Yes, Mom too – okay, she'll ask more questions first, you know, moms," and he winks at her, but she keeps quiet.

Mother never questions her. It must be because she trusts her and relies on her as an adult.

Okay, she did ask questions, when she was in love with Gabriel, and she was a bit worried that he was older than Lili when she was only sixteen, so every time she went out to meet him, there was the usual where, how long, what...

Mother most probably feared that he might seduce Lili and treat her badly afterwards, which is what everyone thinks or expects in these boy-girl stories. But that story died out anyway, long ago.

She's sure Mother won't be worried about Vlad. Vlad's got something that works immediately on people, a sort of reassurance that he can't be up to anything wrong. Not even remotely doubtful.

Vlad is safe.

It hadn't been anywhere close to this, last time. With Gabriel. She wasn't called to make a choice: it simply flowed on, like a stream. They, too, had met on holiday, at the seaside, and took their romance back home, making it real.

That autumn? Unbelievable.

She would leave home long after it had got dark, at eight p.m. – which was hardly imaginable for "good kids" her age, barely seventeen. She spent some three quarters of an hour changing buses to get to his school, where she would wait for him to come out from classes. She'd see him showing up on the dark street, just before nine, and they'd go and sit on a bench in the central gardens to have the last pizza that they could get in a takeaway shop. Greasy, but they never minded that, or if they did, they'd make fun of it.

He asked her once: "Are you happy, Lili?"

There was that glint in his eyes, in the dark, that she could sometimes see when tenderness would run over and envelop her like warm lava.

She answered without hesitating.

"I don't know what happiness is supposed to be like, but it sure feels like it."

"Do you need definitions?" he asked, smiling fondly.

"Nope, I'm good."

"Hear, hear, Lili Danes foregoes definitions and theorems," he said, his hand cupping the back of her head.

He felt real and complete. She put it down to him being what they called a grownup man: his self-confidence meant that he didn't complicate things, and that basically he knew what he was doing.

"Come on," he'd pull her by the hand, "let's go!" and he'd start running down the boulevard.

"What? No!" She'd hold back for a second – what a crazy thing to do, run down the street for nothing! But the fun of it!

"Come on!" He'd drag her without looking back, and the next moment they were both running, laughing and squealing, the sound of their steps echoing on the pavement, in the neon light. They had the boulevard to themselves, close to ten at night.

But he was also alert and watched for bikes or cars, or passers-by unexpectedly popping up from round the corner, when he'd halt her or steer her off to dodge the collision. Her hand in his felt safely nested.

Things were running their course with ease, and she had no time or reason to stop and think about how much she was changing, thriving, budding.

Sometimes they'd look back with a laugh.

"My goodness, that day we met at the seaside!"

"Yeah, you were as cool as a cucumber, like some Hollywood star!"

"Yeah, poor me, and look how I ended up!"

"You ended up? Only the first episode."

"Good point!"

Everything got tighter, closer. Tangible.

So Vlad's talking about a back-home sequel? How curious.

What is it that makes him want that, she wonders. She's not talkative, not particularly funny, she's not even in the mood for being funny, but even if she was, she knows too well, from the endless school years, how socially clumsy she is.

Then, her parents are nothing special (or not in that way; actually they *are* special, especially her father, in another way), so what's in it for him?

She's not even a beauty. Right, well, there is something special about her, she recalls past evidence from Gabriel or Val Nestor, but that something must be looking pretty insignificant against the obvious fact of her not fitting in his world.

Is he going to fit in her world, vacant as it is? Fit in with – what, John's music? The park bench where she used to sit with Dana waiting for the neighbourhood's John to show up with his glasses turned to the sky? What else has she got? Not much, now that school's over, and with it, faces and routines will fade away.

That precisely might be good. In the void that has set in, Vlad wouldn't need to fit in. He would only occupy vacant space. Which he's most welcome to do, in fact, if he cares. Why not.

"We're going to the disco tonight, so better take it easy today, spare yourself, it's gonna get veeery late and wild, I can tell you," Vlad announces, raising his eyebrows in warning. "Laura's treat, it's her birthday today, you know."

No, she doesn't know. It's her last night before going home, is all she knows.

At the disco there are lights of various shrill colours, pulsating with the music, as if the lights are needed so people can get the rhythm. Quite a lot of noise, which almost overwhelms the inner mill's tossing and chucking, questions and answers temporarily crushed, even if an occasional popular song does call them up again. Especially Europe's *Final Countdown*, the drama of it, the passion, the pathos, the final countdown towards something once in a lifetime, towards the breakthrough into endlessness; instead, it's the countdown itself that is endless, never quite reaching its breakthrough.

And that Madonna lady daring you to show what you can on the dance floor. Laura does it in full spotlight surrounded by cheers and whistles, getting so wrought up that it's starting to look like striptease, which she quits before it becomes too obvious and might call for an intervention from the security staff. Lili watches and wiggles in a way that might look like dancing. It's a wild night, she tells herself, it's the hottest mountain resort, partying with the popular people.

Laura's the Minister of Foreign Affairs' daughter, and the guy next to her is the son of the editor-in-chief at the one-and-only national daily, which is the Party's proud trumpet. The others she can't pin down, as their parents' identity is never revealed too specifically. Why should it be? It's shared knowledge of each other's shibboleth that secures their belonging here.

And Vlad, yes, that much is clear, who he is, who his parents are, why he's here, whether truly belonging or not. She's reviewing the progress she has made from being left out by the party fellowships to at least standing by in a circle with these so-called cool people, plus the progress from always being on her own to having someone so sweet to look after her like Vlad.

So fine, why not, she shrugs mentally. Let's carry on chattering and kissing back home. It will be nice to feel "together" with someone. Nice to witness his tenderness towards her.

How charming, indeed: fulfilled romance, a sweet guy that sticks with her, a social life among people with the best credentials. Soon, maybe a new Lili, promoted from outsider to participant, or at least bystander, removed from the draughts of her home and its prying ears, with a clean slate, and placed on the list of the good.

Sounds like a promising film.

So let there be Vlad.

"Right, so here's what happened. They marked your paper wrong, which explains why they penalised you for not writing the theorems as text, although the criteria didn't require it—"

"But, hold on, hold on, please," Lili interrupts, her eyes fixed on the ceiling, as if working hard to visualise the problem in the air. They're sitting at the kitchen table having breakfast. "They marked my paper wrong – how do you mean that? How could that happen? I mean the marking scheme is there, right, at hand, and there are two people marking each paper, right?"

"Yes, sure, but that's where it gets interesting," Mother replies, leaning forward over the table, both excited and secretive. Why does this suddenly feel like an action film? Hopefully the Roger Moore of this script will turn up just in time.

"There are two people marking, that's right. Now in your case, the guy who actually gave you that nonsense score, he's a poor idiot, everyone in the faculty is aware of that. He marked your paper wrong – don't ask me how, I can't really imagine how, but anyway, he gives you a five twenty; but now comes the outrageous part," Mother purses her lips and leans back on the chair.

Lili waits with a squeezing heart.

"So," Mother clears her voice and looks down as if uncomfortable, "apparently it's a common practice that they actually – well, you know, everyone's tired after the whole year, wants to go on holiday sooner, so they actually split the papers among themselves; meaning, instead of double marking, each one marks their own batch, then they copy the scores from each other on to their own roll, plus or minus a few decimals to make it look as if they were just a bit different, and so they're finished in half the time."

Mother pauses for effect, for Lili to take it all in.

"So then, the other guy, not the idiot, simply copied the wrong score, you mean, and never had a look at my paper?" Lili says after a while.

"Yes, that's right," Mother nods, peering into Lili's face. "And that's what's maddening, he could have made a whole difference, as he's not an idiot at all – guess who he is."

Lili shakes her head. She doesn't know, and she doesn't

know why it should matter.

"It's the grand Mr... Drăgan," Mother lowers her voice to a whisper when pronouncing the name.

Mr Drăgan is the faculty star, and the physics star in their little country, insofar as stars are tolerated besides the Party president and his wife. He is Honoris Causa with Moskow University, has published a whole shelf-full of books, and attends all international congresses, leading any delegation of scientists, whether physicists or not. Whenever NASA or MIT report something notable, Mr Drăgan is sure to be interviewed by the Romanian Press Agency, and he's bound to have something to report on his own behalf, or on behalf of some research team nobody knew existed, on the very same research topic that has made the press in the West.

"But Drăgan's clever," Lili takes her eyes down from the ceiling, no longer brooding. "Is he aware of what's happened?"

Mother nods quietly, as if just about to speak but considering her words.

"You lodged that appeal, didn't you," Lili insists. "So? What did he do?"

"Well, there was nothing he could do at that point. The results were out, and the appeal was official. He couldn't have just come out and admitted it was his fault, he would be compromised forever, and he simply didn't have anything to say in an appeal process."

Mother stands up to get something but the next moment realises she doesn't need anything. Coffee is out, breakfast is through. Everything's now on the table, half eaten but no longer wanted; she must keep sitting and there's nothing else to it now but to spell out the truth.

"Lili, you need to understand that what I've been telling you is the unofficial version. There's no talk about copying scores from the other marker. This story doesn't exist."

"Then how do you know about it?"

Mother sighs.

"Your father's colleagues have been calling me, all of them compassionate and outraged, and willing to help somehow, how else but by giving us information so we carry on and don't give up."

"And the official story is...?"

"It's that your paper got five twenty in physics, and that's it. Under this final grade there are two names, Mr Drăgan's and the other one's. We've lodged an appeal, and then a complaint, and we'll see."

"But there's still something I don't understand," Lili frets on her chair. "How do father's colleagues know that Mr Drăgan just copied the other half of the scores from his partner?"

"An appeal by Lili Danes was bound to have a lot of echoes in the Institute; it's your father's name, everyone knew you were sitting their exams ever since you registered. So when the appeal was submitted, there was a lot going on behind the scenes. And apparently the poor guy who had marked your paper wrong started wailing in the staff room that he had done everything by the book, why was there so much fuss about it, and people got suspicious and started questioning him, and in the end it was all out – but out in the staff room, you get me, between those walls – that he'd passed on his list to Mr Drăgan and he'd done the same in his turn. Outside of those walls, there's no such thing as copying grades over."

Mother stands up again, this time knowing she needs a glass of water to soothe her dry throat and the heart beating at the base of her neck. Lili watches her, waiting to hear more, to hear it all.

"And then, following our appeal, they had to set up a new commission to mark your paper again, this commission made up of three people. They marked all the appeals, not just yours, and they had no idea which paper they were marking and what the initial marks had been. That was two days ago. And that night I'm called and told that when they unsealed the papers and looked at yours, instead of five you'd got an average of eight sixty-nine from the three markers. Eight sixty-nine!" Mother stresses the last words and raises her voice. She turns quickly, facing away from Lili, and fills her glass with water again. Then she comes back to the table and sits down.

Lili can see the breakthrough: this is it, her correct score, although the eight sixty-nine, that mark's still not her league, but for now it's more than enough. To get the official grade amended there must be a difference of at least one full point against the initial score, and here we're talking about three.

A big smile is spreading on her face.

"So then, it's all settled!"

Mother smiles and looks away for a moment.

"It's settled! Isn't it?" Lili asks, impatient at her Mother's keeping quiet.

"Yes, well, it should be, definitely," Mother replies. "The only thing is," she adds, drawing a deep breath, "the new commission won't admit they gave such marks, except for one of the markers, who said he would stick to his position when questioned."

Lili has big wide eyes and eyebrows knitted together under a crease on her forehead. What was that?

"Yes, well, that's not the end of it. They did give you these marks, but again, I only know it because somebody called me, otherwise your appeal has been rejected – officially."

Lili's got a lump in her throat. The room is spinning and pulling away from where the two of them are sitting with these irrational facts on the table.

"But as I say, it's not over yet, sweetheart!" Mother lays her hand on Lili's. "I'm not giving up, you know me, you know I'm a fighter, and now that it's clear your grade is wrong, I'm going all the way, I promise you that!"

But why did the commission ignore its own marks? Lili's toes are touching a wall that won't budge, and won't let her see through. Where's the cause-and-effect logic? What law is this?

"It's clear why they won't make the second mark official," Mother looks deep into her eyes. "It's the end of Mr Drăgan's career if it comes out that he gave marks on papers he never looked at, it's against basic professional integrity. It's a scandal."

"So what, if he's such a big boss he can weather that all right, who cares after all about his integrity?" Lili's voice is about to break. "And even if anyone cared, is Mr Drăgan's reputation so important?"

That an official commission takes so much account of Drăgan's reputation, to the extent of bending official procedures to accommodate his position, seems absurd.

"Drăgan's a high Party official, Lili. He'd be prosecuted for this. Of course he wouldn't be the only one, so my guess is, it's not just his skin that's at stake. There would be an investigation, against Drăgan and his co-marker, and it would of course transpire that this is a common practice, so what I'm saying, there's a reluctance to disclose these things because it would have too far-reaching consequences. And Drăgan himself, the face of socialist Romanian science, must not be compromised. Not to mention he's involved with the wife of someone very high up."

Lili keeps her eyes on the floor, brooding. She can't look up just now. The ceiling was for attempts to make sense, for drawing and re-shaping combinations; the floor is now for hanging on, for dodging this alien thing closing in on her.

"And what about the marker who maintains his position?"

"Yes, that's another thing that muddies the waters quite a bit. Of course he's not officially contesting the resolution to reject your appeal, but he says if he should be asked, within an enquiry or an investigation, he'll tell the truth – god bless him, what a fine man!" Mother adds.

But Lili's not willing to let the discussion digress in emotional evaluations of this or the other person; she wants to understand, to get to the bottom of it, where things make some sense, so she can recognise what law has taken force here, and so she can see where this is all going, see a horizon, through and beyond this wall that obstructs everything.

She's about to tell Mother about Greg Talu's promise to help, and she wonders fleetingly where his intervention would land in this muddy setup. But she's sure Cora has updated Mother on this possible trump card, so she decides not to mess with the course of the conversation.

"So, you're saying you're not giving up. What is there still to do, if the appeal's been rejected?"

"Well, I'm taking it to the next level. You know it's not wise to try to skip levels, or they'd kick me out saying you should have contacted the other level first, comrade Danes, so I'm not giving them that chance, to kick me out, I'm going by the book, level by level, and if necessary I'll go as high as the Central Party Council itself," Mother declares with conviction.

"And what's the next level?" Lili looks up again.

"The Rector. Maybe they'd like to hear what they do in the Institute of Physics, and I thought, maybe I'm lucky enough that the person I'm talking to feels there are greater risks sweeping such evidence under the carpet than escalating things up. You know, in the event of the tables being turned, there could very well be the reproach why didn't you take action, comrade, to clear the Party of the stigmata of such corruption? And depending on how confident of his own cards that person is, he may decide he could have something to gain out of this, helping communist ethics to prevail, justice be done and all that."

"That's where you were going when we last talked on the phone?"

"Yes, I filed the complaint, but not with some secretary who could make it lost in the archive. I got an appointment, you know, phone calls and connections of connections, so I went straight to the Party delegate in the Rectorate."

"The Party delegate? But appeals are the university's business, aren't they, I mean, it's the university that decides," Lili frowns again at yet another logical flaw.

Mother smiles almost condescendingly. "Honey, the Party decides everything. It's the Party who decided that Drăgan can't be touched, isn't it? Besides, this is no longer an appeal, because your appeal has been rejected, over. No, this is a complaint about misconduct and how things are handled in the Institute. So it's the Party who needs to settle that, it's only the Party who can undo what the Party has done!"

"But how can they do it? Why would they? You say it yourself, it's the Party who decided already against my case!"

"Well, yes, but the Party's not a block, the Party's also the people, the departments, the institutions it's lodged in, and the connections between these institutional bureaus to the central structure; maybe a connection leads to another cell in the big Party organism, maybe if the issue is escalated we come across someone who wants to prove themselves, or who's waiting for the right moment to kill another cell off; you never know. And if the issue gets enough exposure maybe it'll be impossible to cover it up any longer."

Lili's back on the floor, waiting for the conclusion.

"So how did the appointment go at the Rectorate?"

"Well, he listened, a very amiable guy, he listened with quite a lot of interest, and read through my petition as I was talking. He wanted to know, of course, where I had all that information from, but he was also aware of your father, and I made it sound a bit emotional you know, we're all human after all, your father's gone," Mother's voice falters for a moment but she gets back bravely and carries on. "And here's the daughter, hard-working, excellent grades, she wants to become a worthy scientist for the glory of our motherland, isn't this the last thing that should happen to her, isn't it enough that the circumstances in our family are so unfortunate—"

"Did you actually say all that to him?" Lili opens her

eyes wide, blushing on a rising wave of embarrassment.

"Yes, why not?" Mother protests, getting louder with excitement. "It's the truth after all, Lili, it's your work, it's your brains, and what they've done to us and to your father, that's more than enough!"

She keeps quiet, sulking. So embarrassing! She wants no commiseration; this isn't about her father or the family's circumstances, it's simply a procedural mistake that has to be rectified.

"So in the end he promised he'll investigate and we'll be notified in due course," Mother concludes, standing up again and tidying up the breakfast remains, absent-minded. Then she remembers: "Oh, and do tell me, you said you've got an admirer." She swivels back to face Lili.

Oh, that! Lili feels as if she's being pulled forcefully away from the wall she's been trying to break through, up in the air, landing on a hazy island that looks too hazy and rosy to have any bearing on her reality.

"Yes, well, Vladyboy – I mean, Vlad, yeah…"

It's not helpful if she starts calling him Vladyboy herself.

"So what's he like, come, tell me!" Mother plays excited and joyful. The gap is still there, though, between the previous topic and this.

"He's erm," Lili starts then halts in suspension. "Nice, very nice, very considerate, and he likes me a lot, it seems," she smiles, strangely embarrassed.

Vlad's story has no place in this morning's conversation. There are far more earnest matters between herself and Mother than him. She leaves the kitchen on the excuse of having to call Dana.

Dana has passed her admission to industrial chemistry. They meet in the park, on their old, familiar path. There are only young mothers and grandparents sitting quietly in the shade under the trees, kids busy on their own in the sandbox.

She tells Dana the story of her admission results. She goes back and forth between one viewpoint and another, constantly trying to balance them against each other, admitting the absurd, but still expressing hope. A long suite of "While it's true that...," "but still...," and "on the other hand." She's officially failed, but apparently that's just a mistake, although anyone might say, "Yeah, sure a mistake"; but Dana knows her and she has good reasons to believe her. Although the red line has been crossed, that is, the results are out in the open, there are back doors that Mother argues can still be used to reinstate the facts, and she'll soon be rehabilitated. So yes, she's not a student yet, but she's going to be. Soon. It's just a bug in the system that will be remedied.

Dana listens to her and nods, pondering. She asks very few questions, which Lili is grateful about, although vaguely suspecting that it might simply be a friendly tactic to disguise her scepticism about how this story is going to end.

She's tempted briefly to mention Greg Talu, as further proof that things should get sorted out. He asked Cora, before he left that memorable night when Lili had opened her heart, to give her his direct phone number in the Ministry, and Lili was awed by this gesture of kindness. She's got a minister's direct number! Her case is on his mind.

Should she call to say hello, thank you, and hope he might let drop a tiny update? She finds herself near the telephone again and again these days, sometimes picking up the receiver, or even dialling the first digits, but she always hangs up instantly, startled by the thought that it might have already initiated the connection.

Dana has been to the seaside with her father and his wife. She's got a golden tan on her fair skin and she radiates laid-back relief. Typically, she has some trifle or other to complain about in wailing tones, which Lili enjoys imitating until they're both laughing, but today Dana is composed, placid, radiant, grown up. It almost feels as if it's Lili now who needs cheering up, but she's definitely not complaining; she's only presenting the facts and the hypotheses that will need to be proved in the near future. Oh, yes, and besides, she's also got Vlad to report. That's her great news, her new boyfriend, the high-society guy who's so sweet nonetheless.

"Great," Dana says, smiling. Patches of sunshine sift through the tree branches shiver on her blonde hair.

Lili resumes her story-telling when it becomes clear Dana's not going to add anything else. She makes fun of Vlad's perpetual chatter, his dad stories, his granddad stories, cottage stories and medicine stories. All this while Dana is smiling, at times giving out a short chuckle, taking the stories in, nodding along, willing to give her all her tenderness as old best friends; but Lili is finding it vaguely upsetting, and feels a slight squeeze in her heart, so she carries on chattering, hoping to get rid of it. She knows Dana too well to suspect there's pity involved, but there is an insidious suspicion growing inside her that to an outsider, she might be worth pitying.

Lili has always considered herself privileged compared to Dana. Dana's parents have been divorced for ages, which has put, over the years, a permanent resigned, tight-lipped smile on her mother's face. Dana herself has taken after her more and more as she's advanced through teenagehood, growing more sarcastic and pessimistic, making choices based on no-nonsense arguments, to the tune of what is reasonable for a woman these days, and what can you expect from life?

Whereas Lili dreads becoming like her father, or dealing with her parents' quandaries, both as individuals and as a couple. Her life won't be anything like what they're struggling with. She's pulled by a conviction that the future lies ahead teeming with opportunities, like a pack of cards spread wide in front of her, and that doing her best is the surefire guarantee that things are going to work out for the best, too.

That's why she chose physics in the end: she had

to commit to something that was part of her world. She couldn't choose a lifetime of living outside of herself, catching up with the inside part of herself only after working hours.

People constantly do that, living outside of themselves, so they usually choose occupations that allow that space of absence. Dana has made such a choice, too. She has mentioned time and again how she'll be working in a factory as a chemical engineer, making a decent living, keeping safe in tough times. Weathering life, hanging tight.

Lili is horrified at such a prospect. She feels an unfailing urge to throw herself into life, which, she believes, shouldn't need to be weathered, but embraced, if one is living it from inside one's being.

She's never told Dana about her mind movies, whether saving (or loving) John, or any other adventures of her wild future life, even though she knows Dana wouldn't judge her. She would most likely feel like a fool nonetheless if she were to start talking about her cinematic dreams. And strangely, it now crosses her mind, she has no resources to spin a mental film about being promoted above the bottom line results as she might once have done. Instead, all that's inside her is a motionless, dooming blank.

The school years are definitely over, and Dana and herself are sitting in different boats: her own boat drifting in muddy waters, while Dana's neatly heading away, Dana's way.

She believes Mother when she says that things will get sorted out by the time term starts in mid-September. She finds the evidence overwhelming, and the underground solidarity among the faculty encouraging. Everybody knows she's got to pass. Somebody will just need to acknowledge it, and with the pressure of Mother's arguments and passion, alongside the Party talk of communist integrity and justice, it'll work out in the end.

The problem is her neighbours, relatives, former schoolmates and teachers are all eager to find out whether she's in or out. Answering this black-or-white question, inevitably she has to start with the unthinkable: "I've failed", or "I'm out", hurrying to add that big, complicated story. Still, "I've failed" is the answer they'll remember; the rest is noise.

The day after returning from the mountains, she and Vlad have their first date. Following her long breakfast conversation with Mother and early afternoon stroll with Dana, Lili is unsure what else she can handle on the same day. She sways between anticipating the date as a welcome compensation and dreading it as yet another test of self-regulation.

Vlad meets her at the underground station where the central downtown is left behind, and the northern, posh city area sprawls ahead. It's a residential district for the Party's high society, with embassies and foreign trade missions discreetly blending in. The streets are shaded by old chestnut and lime trees, sunk in an aristocratic quiet, away from the vulgar bustle, lined up with villas of various sizes and architectural designs.

"I love these streets," Lili whispers, as if afraid to break the quiet. "Each house has its own personality, incredible!"

She can't help thinking of her own neighbourhood, reminiscent of an early century population of small traders and professionals, resembling a Balkan *mahala*, where kids play ball across the street and the elderly sit in clusters, knitting or playing backgammon. Or elsewhere in the city, the vast areas overbuilt with towering, uniform apartment blocks, tiny window next to tiny window, cage upon cage, compared to which her own house and *mahala* is a privilege.

This here is a different universe, withdrawn behind stylish forged iron fences and neatly paved front gardens. It could be the set of any movie, whether London, Paris, or – who knows? – all the other places on the map.

"Look, this is where the head of the Swedish trade

mission lives. He knows me, sort of, I mean, I've happened to be around a couple of times when he got in or out of his limo, such a friendly guy, he nodded at me with a smile, and next time we waved at each other," Vlad says, his eyes large in excitement.

"Really? Is that safe, I mean, you know, having connections with foreign citizens and all?" Lili wonders aloud.

"Yeah, sure, we just greet each other from opposite sides of the street. No words. There are witnesses, if anyone is watching. But you know who the guy is, right?"

The head of the Swedish trade mission? How would that be someone she should know?

"Gotcha, he's coupled with Michaela Mai."

The diva dressed in the most unimaginable outfits, leaving the other singers way behind her looking like try-hard Cinderellas. The lady singing about her home being the best of herself, her heart beating within its walls. Right. Lili can very well relate; she would feel the same living here. No privilege, just normalcy, and an individual design for each house – unless that alone were to be stamped as privilege.

Her mind's eye watches Vlad and herself from above, walking hand in hand under the shade of old trees on romantic streets, and she feels remote joy. Could this be the first scene of a new mind film? Vlad is wearing a nice tee that flutters on his skinny torso and hangs loose over his jeans, a teenage kid stretched to the size of a grown-up man. She's wearing a pink-and-black outfit she's made herself on cut-out patterns borrowed from Cora Balș, with baggy sleeves and baggy folds, as bagginess, the latest fashion fad, feels like confidence and choice. Which makes them a cool pair of young people who have suitably found each other. Any moment now he's going to swivel her into his arms, against his chest, and kiss her tenderly.

"It's grandpa's birthday tomorrow, we're throwing a big family dinner, he'll be ninety-two but still hale and hearty, the old man."

"Congratulations," Lili utters, not sure what to add. Thankfully, there's no silence to fill with any further words, as Vlad carries on unbothered.

"Thanks, yeah. We bought him a hand-made chess board, ordered straight from Germany. Well, ordered – I mean, erm, Daddy's got some connections from his surgeon conventions, you know..."

Lili's mind wanders. She wishes there was more intent in their togetherness: maybe, if Vlad's voice were to take on intimate undertones, or his eyes glistened with significance, or even just with playful flirtation. Vlad, instead, is very... down to earth.

Which might be for the best, actually. Reliable and loyal. Within reach, at all times. Yes. She can live with that. Mind films are merely hazes wreathing out of valleys of idle daydreaming. Now she's got reality, which is always better than dreams, for being real.

They cross the broad street into the park. They'll come out again, after a tour, and cross over, again, to Vlad's house. He's been planning the route carefully, all the way from the pick-up point at the metro station. Ownership is total: the chic neighbourhood, the largest, greenest city park, his entire domain to show her around.

They stroll up to a parterre of roses, and there, right in the middle, just as she's going to bend over to sniff at a yellow rose, Vlad finally swivels her against his chest. There's a moment's mis-coordination between their arms, chins and noses, she chuckles, but his jaw stifles her chuckle when he presses his lips against hers. She feels his tongue rolling over and between, and she sighs, here it is at last, the kiss, if only she wasn't aware of her shoulder being squeezed under his armpit. She plays along, letting her tongue join his on the aimless tour of their merged mouths.

Then, they come apart again, and Lili can bend to smell the lovely rose.

"Should we get back?" Vlad asks, slightly on edge.

Lili shrugs. "Fine, if you want to."

She realises that he's pressing to get home to introduce her. If walking with a new guy on a first date, some kissing involved, feels a bit awkward, going to meet his parents right afterwards makes it even weirder. Is she becoming official, before even settling in? Where's the insecure flirting, the compulsive clinging to their one-on-one intimacy, away from the intruding world?

So much more awkward is the flutter that grips her when the introductions inevitably come to the question of what she does. Vlad, with his overflowing chatter, rescues her smoothly by telling them she's just been admitted to a physics course, at which both Bacis raise an appreciative eyebrow.

Vlad had repeatedly assured her it was best not to start telling his parents stories. In a way, she could see his point. Why make it complicated? The question of what she studied was straight; the answer had to be the same.

What upset her was that "not telling the story" distorted the facts. By her logic, they should refrain from spinning yarns all right, but say what the current status was. Vlad, however, was anxious about that.

"Trust me, Lili, it's better, I know my parents. They're so sweet and kind, but now, for the beginning, let's not make it complicated. I'm sure you're going to get admitted in the end, and then what's the point in rocking the boat?"

Was he saying that his parents might be against them dating if she'd failed the admission?

The Bacis are friendly, especially Mr Baci, or, in the appropriate form of address, Mr Doctor Baci. His wife is also a medical doctor, so she would need to be called Mrs Doctor Baci, or even just Mrs Doctor. Mr Doctor has a round face and a round body, with big round watery eyes that seem always on the verge of joyful tears. His thick eyebrows and his rather sensual lips, set in a permanent smile, make him instantly likeable. Mrs Doctor is more restrained and if anything, more inquisitive, but she plays along with her husband's gaiety.

Following their first date and her successful

introduction to the family, Lili and Vlad meet on a daily basis; it's summer holiday, so why not. There's no mind film anticipating or recalling these dates, as their reality is right at her fingertips anyway.

What strikes her more is how weird it is not to have to sit on her chair until her sweaty thighs stick to the upholstery and read for maths or physics. Days are assigned a different task now: waiting. And counting.

She counted months and weeks until school was over. Now she counts days until her grades might be rectified.

Lili and Mother get a phone call one of these days. Lili is waiting restlessly for Greg Talu's phone call to give any news, as he promised when he said goodbye, looking her straight in the eye.

But it's Mr Bodu-Beran, the department head. She hears Mother speaking very cautiously over the phone, diplomatically disagreeing and alluding to the turmoil going on in the Institute on Lili's account. He insists on talking to Lili herself at the end. This is very strange. No adult has wanted to talk to her so far, in a serious matter. Except for teachers, of course, but that was just school.

She takes the receiver from Mother. It's hot from her tight, nervous grip, and she puts it to her ear. There is that moment of initial silence before the conversation starts, but the silence is alive and she hesitates on the brink before diving in. What does he want to hear from her? What does he have to say to her, which he hasn't told Mother?

"Hello?" she says in a wavering voice.

"Hello, Lili, how are you?"

"I'm fine, yes, thank you, Mr Bodu-Beran," she answers mechanically. There's silence again, and she wonders if she should ask "And you?" just for politeness' sake, but she finds it would be presumptuous of her, as if they were on equal terms, which obviously they're not. There's the faint rustle of breath, she's not sure if it's hers or his, both of them waiting before the dice are thrown.

"Lili my dear, I wanted to tell you how sorry I am about what has happened. I realise you are such a hard-working girl, and so clever too, taking after your papa, and then this – it's so unfair, life is so unfair," he adds quickly as if correcting himself. "We all know what this means, failing admission, it means a whole year being put off, all the life plans put on hold, and the knowledge that you've worked so hard but to no avail, we know it's so hard – I just wanted to say cheer up, girl, your whole life is in front of you. I mean, a year yes, it's bad enough, but it's just a year, you know what I mean?"

"Yes, Mr Bodu-Beran," she answers mechanically again. What is he telling her? There's something like a spiky lump somewhere in her chest, in her guts, stirring cautiously inside of her, almost as if in hiding, but it's there.

"You need to keep your optimism and get back to your hard work at some point, and next year it's a new chance, a new game, life isn't over, you know, definitely it's not over at eighteen," he chuckles, almost relieved, it seems, to have something funny to say, on the face of it at least.

She nods absent-mindedly, omitting to say anything, feeling that spiky lump stirring inside of her again.

"So, about my paper, you mean—" she ventures, because she sees Mother watching her intently, as if expecting some outcome to this conversation.

"Yes, about your paper," Mr Bodu-Beran hurries to reply, "well, you know what exams are like, Lili, don't you? I mean, there's a marking scheme, you can't help it, even if you do come up with a solution, if it's not as per the marking scheme – and it so happens this year the marking scheme did require solutions to be formalised instead of text annotations, and so what can one do, it's the marking scheme, you can't help it—" but his voice is growing fainter and fainter in Lili's ear.

She's about to shout, "But that's exactly what I did! I just wrote down the solutions and afterwards worried that

I hadn't written the text annotations!" But something grips her by the throat, something like a stream rolling past her, a flood of false excuses that were prepared and delivered by the other side, and none of her objections could make any difference. She wonders briefly if he has seen her paper at all and is deliberately lying to her. No, that can't be. He really must be as much of an imbecile as Father used to tell them over dinner, sometimes. He must be talking through a claim he has prepared beforehand, or one he has been given, and which has nothing to do with her paper.

It dawns on her why Father refused to mark in the admission exams, year after year. They thought he was being difficult.

She suspects the only people who ever actually took a look at her paper were Mr Drăgan's counterpart and the three markers of the appeals committee. This doesn't stop theories from going about, however, about what she has done wrong, according to the mysterious marking scheme.

The deadline for the admission debacle to vanish from the world is fast approaching, namely, the start of the academic term, mid-September.

Although, Mother says one day, well, actually why does it have to be sorted out by mid-September? After all, the term starts with a familiarisation week, nothing that really matters, then they do the practical farming work for four weeks, picking grapes by the Danube, so she could also join her colleagues later if need be, in October. With the added bonus of having skipped the farming experience.

That might also be possible, true, which does give them some more time, but it sounds less than optimal. This suspended emptiness to be extended? What should she say to Vlad's parents? How can she go on keeping up the pretence?

Mother is humming in the house, doing housework or

going to work in a good mood, which Lili recognises from the past. It's Mother at her best, giving off a sort of certainty that the world is all right. And if it should temporarily be otherwise, it will soon be restored with the proper deployment of tactics and persuasion. Or is she faking it, to spare Lili anxiety?

Vlad's parents are ever so kind. They spend pleasant evenings together, in their living room, watching videos on their VCR, chattering away and laughing. Having the choice over what to watch, in your own home, is a privilege. VCRs are rare in their little country. They're one of those things you can't buy in a regular shop, but you never ask where people have got theirs from.

She likes the music videos: so much colour, such smooth, glimmering film, so much fun those singers are having, life's great, life is live. The singers themselves, looking out of this world with their loving eyes, like George Michael begging for forgiveness please stay. There is, then, such romance, and there are such heroes as in her mind films after all, it's just that it's all locked away out of reach, and for most people around her, out of grasp.

Sometimes they watch a movie. *Amadeus*, or *Police Academy*. There are so many exciting things going on in the world. Life lies ahead waiting to be discovered, and from that cosy but understated living room, the path into it feels a tiny bit more plausible.

When she's back home, it feels as if ghosts are lingering: the neglected house with its draughty windows, its cracks in the door frames, shelves up to the ceiling, stuffed with books, hopelessly dusty – all the past is crammed between the grimy walls, all her captivity in school, in her clumsiness, insecurity, and daydreams.

The old TV, placed in a corner just because nobody had a better idea where to put it, shows grey broadcasts with stripes and dots because of poor reception. The fridge has rust stains and when she opens it, there's a cold breath of air blowing out of its vacant body. The water heater needs an hour until you can have a bath, and looks like a thick industrial pipe with the paint shrivelled from the heat over the years.

Mother has started preparing the winter supplies, and the house smells in turn of pickles, of plum jam, and of the stewed vegetable spread. The smells are good, but they're a clear sign of the inevitable advent of winter. Lili dreads winter, which takes about half a year in their house, when the walls, the floor, the bathroom are cold and draughty. The other half of the year she spends dreading the return of the winter.

The Bacis' flat, by contrast, is a warm haven. There is nothing opulent, which might make her feel alien. It feels just right. Spacious rooms, walls smooth with a pastel-coloured wall-paper, solid parquet flooring, no spots, no flaws, no cracks, but no intimidating shine either. Windows are large. The fridge is full. No limits on hot water.

The front garden is neatly paved for the most part, only small isles of hydrangeas here and there. Old trees cast their shade on their windows. A rustle of leaves, no traffic to hear. A place where you can be; where you can be home. Life can be that simple.

Dr Baci is always there with a light-hearted joke or story. He talks to her just as he does to his own son. Teaching, advising, patting on the shoulder. Don't worry. Life is good. He's always wearing a broad smile from above his visible, but not obtrusive paunch; the paunch almost makes him more respectable, and more likeable. The honoured doctor, with a PhD in cardio surgery, the Chief of Surgery in the Ministry of Interior's hospital – and still, no infatuation, just a jovial and warm-hearted man with a paunch.

They have, like any family, their little rituals, which Lili is beginning to discover. For instance, their rhymes or anecdotes. Every now and then, one of them might say as a punch-line:

"— but don't worry," which can – and will – be followed by the others:

"Tell a story."

"While Loretta drives a lorry."

"And the shopkeeper is sorry."

Usually it's Mr Doctor Baci that gives the cue, and then Vlad and his mother promptly add, in turn, the following rhymes, almost as in an a cappella arrangement. Lili watches, amused. A funny and happy family, and she's becoming part of it.

Although, on second thoughts, she's beginning to wonder what she's there for. They set out on the premise that they were a romantic couple. It turns out she's relishing the domestic harmony. Lili cannot tell exactly to what extent she's with Vlad, or with the Bacis. The distinction is rather blurry.

"There's a party coming up, get ready, any time soon I'll know exactly what's on," Vlad announces. They're sitting in a downtown café.

Oh, no! "What party is that?"

He nods while downing the last of his orange soda. He's visibly happy she asked.

"Remember the guy with the Minolta camera?" He grins, eyes wide with excitement.

She blinks.

"Emil, the guy who stuck a rag in the flag pole at his school? Never mind. He's a good friend, and the son of Bucharest's MP," he adds in a subdued voice, with an earnest look in his eyes.

"And how do the two of you know each other?"

"Emil lives a block away from us. Remember when we were walking the other day through the neighbourhood, we passed by a security booth where the poor security guards were having their packed lunch, and it was stinking of garlic ten steps away? That booth was in front of his house!"

"They've got security at their gate?"

"Yes, they do," Vlad nods emphatically, "that's the MP

thing. Whenever I go to his place, you know, have a drink, have a chat, play a bit of pool, I need to remember to bring my bloody ID with me." Eyes rolling.

She's getting gradually used to Dr Baci's Lada, as Vlad keeps picking her up and taking her home in it, or on short trips to woods and lakes out of the city's boundaries. Ladas are no big thing in themselves, but this one is a noble, crystalline white, with a posh number plate with only three, instead of four, digits. That's an unmistakable mark of distinction, granted only to someone high up in the army or internal affairs, or somewhere else where functions are not even recorded in any public file.

It's obvious that Dr Baci got the special licence plate as Head of Surgery in that hospital, which is vaguely reassuring, knowing that this distinction came from his competence, and not some secret, potentially threatening involvement with Madam Secu. (Although the question always is whether one is allowed to be a head, even on account of professional competence, without being on the secret payrolls, too.)

But it's the bumper sticker that's the real hit, showing a pair of lips sending a kiss; *baci* means kisses in Italian, as Vlad explained when they were still in the mountain resort. Who else has seen anything like that? Her father had needed a special approval for a vintage typing machine, and he'd had to register it with the police, in case it might cross his mind one day to type subversive flyers. How about a sticker displayed freely for anyone to see, on the back of a car? And the kiss, such a Western, kitschy thing, how did they get away with it?

The other thing she's getting used to is having dinner at the Bacis' when she and Vlad get back from a date. She's thinking of Mother not having to cook for her, which is certainly some relief. She can't exactly remember when the two of them last had proper meat. It's not so much a matter of money, but of Mother's ebbing motivation to activate connections at local butchers to get pork or chicken after the hours when the restless queues have dispersed.

She's not exactly hungry either, most of the time. But strangely enough, she gets wolfish hunger at the Bacis'. She has to pull a brake on getting herself one more helping. The Bacis have had a calf slaughtered (connections, connections!), and they've got countless meat bags in their freezer. The sweet, tender veal is doing magic to whatever Mrs Baci cooks, from steaks and schnitzels to risotto and stews.

It's not just the savoury taste. It's a relief to see that no one keeps track of how much she gets. No hole is being scooped into the household supplies. If the risotto is gone, no problem, tomorrow there's another menu; there's always more than enough to go round, today, and then tomorrow, too.

"But are you sure that's what you really want, Lili?" Dana asks unexpectedly while sitting in their familiar pizza place. "I mean, it's not so much Vlad you're talking about, but your family get-togethers."

"Does it matter?" Lili replies, frowning over her pizza slice. "There's not much to tell about Vlad and – what, the little nothings we talk about, or the flowers he sometimes brings me?"

Dana smiles. "He brings you flowers? How sweet!"

Lili smiles. Yes, Vlad is sweet. He brings her flowers and takes her to fancy places, which stand out from the greyness: one has a beautiful terrace by the lake in the great park; the other is in a historical hotel recalling the glamour of the 1930s, before the post-war greyness crushed in.

"I'm sorry," Dana adds, "I didn't mean to upset you, it's just, you know, when things were going on with Gabriel, there was so much you were sharing about him. You were all about your last date, and how you sat on the bench in the dark, and—"

"Yes, but what's the point in comparing? I was sixteen back then, and Gabriel was – yes, he was my first love." Lili sees it clearly for the first time. "But that was ages ago."

She believes she's going to fall in love with Vlad one

of these days, seeing as all premises are met and their relationship couldn't be rosier. But there's no way she can reproduce the content of their time together. They seem to be walking in front of a screen displaying Vlad's tender gestures and the places they go, the two of them this side of the screen, chattering about the day's little incidents, mothers, fathers, cousins, grandpas, errands, grades, winter supplies, and the spell of the moment locked away in the film, out of reach.

It's one of the days around the beginning of term when Lili can no longer withhold it. Dr Baci asks her when she's going to the Institute to check her course timetable, what she thinks of the courses she's going to have this term, if she's met any of her new colleagues, or where they're going to do their farming work.

She fetches a deep breath and says, "I'm sorry, Dr Baci, but I have to tell you something," and her eyes shift nervously around his face, trying to fathom any reaction, then to the ground, and then sideways to the hydrangeas in the front garden. Dr Baci watches her, still smiling, but having got the message that something's coming. Vlad is away for the moment, and so is Mrs Doctor. This is good, Lili feels. It's just between herself and the father. He's a kind man.

"You see, it's like this," and she provides a succinct picture of the situation. The bottom line of the results, with the evidence of her brilliant academic track record, and the unconfirmed, but strong, evidence of her entitlement to a study place, despite the official lists. She doesn't mention Gregory Talu.

Dr Baci listens to her, sustaining eye contact, as if he, too, is looking to capture any sign on her face. Is he trying to see if she's lying? Or if she's delusional?

When she finishes, just a few sentences later, she isn't able to raise her eyes to face him yet. Her cheeks are burning, and she curses them. That's definitely not a grown-up look; it gives her insecurity away, and the most important thing in this situation is to convince with confidence.

Dr Baci changes the remote smile of his listening mode to a broad one again when it's clear she's finished speaking. There's something vaguely different about his smile, however. Something more intentional. It's not so much to do with joviality, rather with weighing his response.

"I'm very glad you told me, Lili. I appreciate it a lot," he says.

His voice has the same mindful quality as his smile, as if the small-talk, the chatty story-telling and the rhyme-chiming is put aside, and there's a human being now, a different kind of father, talking.

"And I'm sure it was Vlad's idea to give us the short version of this matter. He's a great boy, but still a bit naïve, sometimes. And he's obviously quite in love with you," he adds, briefly relapsing in his socialising joviality, before going on, "I'm sure you're a very studious and bright girl, we've seen that already, and I hope things will get settled accordingly. So don't worry, we like you just as much for it; actually, as I said, I really appreciate you telling the truth."

The thoughtful intermezzo is ended by Vlad striding in, carrying a bowl of grapes and plums. Dr Baci resumes his jovial smile and paraphrases a health slogan in his baritone voice:

"Fruit every day keeps the doctor away. Very good, my son, very good, ha ha," and he pats Vlad on the shoulder.

A few things have happened that she hasn't logged properly yet.

The amiable Party guy from the Rectorate has set a communication machine in motion, and Mother received a brief letter a few days ago stating regret about not being able to help, because the assessment of Lili Danes' paper has been completed, including the appeal.

Did Mother claim otherwise, she wonders? Would she have been in that office, lodging a complaint, if the assessment hadn't been completed, including the appeal procedure?

Things are not making sense, but it's not the first time, so Lili puts it down to the incomprehensible laws that govern this entire dimension where she has been dumped, apparently, by some unknown mistake (committed by herself? By the universe? Who knows!).

She still wonders what Greg Talu might have tried to do, and how far he's gone. But she no longer thinks of calling him at the ministry, of him telling her in his rusty voice, "Sorry Lili, it was all I could do," or even worse, "Lili Danes? Have we met?"

Mother has launched a new attack now, channelling all her energy from weeping over her father's deportation into it. Lili's cause, unlike his, is still within the range of some restorative action.

These academics at institute and rectorate level are too cowardly, or just too small to change the facts. She's going to the Party's Central Committee; someone gave her a name and is going to put in a good word for her, so that the person behind that name will have been succinctly briefed ahead of the meeting. From up there, everything is achievable, changeable, restorable, with the right amount and quality of persuasion.

The Party took away; the Party can give back again.

If the admission matter has already become a familiar theme in her daily life, which has a clear chronology between complaints and appeals, there's something else that's a great deal more elusive, and therefore lies half buried under her radar.

She doesn't know exactly how it came to pass, but she

slept with Vlad. Her first.

It's not as if she meant to. More like, why not?

And she doesn't quite remember the specifics of how they landed in bed.

Much of what she's living is like that, actually. A nondescript nebula that erases all edges and holds her securely insulated from external stimuli. She's been walking on air like a sleepwalker these past few years, through school, through family routines, through dull, eventless teenagehood, always heading towards some sort of redemption, whether it's university admission or just the future.

Close your eyes, hang on tight, and the doc will make it right, goes one of Dr Baci's rhymes.

But now it seems she's kept her eyes closed while doing precisely what she wouldn't do with Gabriel, and which eventually broke her teenage love apart.

Mother may have been right worrying that Gabriel might want adult things from Lili. He had been so in love with her, and she with him, definitely; but he had wanted what men want, too. All in one package, the in-love thing, together with the other thing. Which she had feared and dreaded. She had turned it and tossed it in her head and in her heart, but she had never been able to close her eyes, hang on tight, and let it happen.

Or maybe she had closed her eyes and hung on tight ever since.

Lili had wanted to just hold hands and kiss. Gabriel was such a great kisser: their lips and tongues glided and melted together and started an irresistible heat in her body. And he was a sexy combination of tenderness and directness. He was the no-nonsense guy who could melt in an instant and allow himself to go emotional. He could tease her, and mock her, and play the grown-up guy dating the ignorant little teenage goose, telling her how to dress or how to shape her eyebrows, but then he would hold her cheeks in his palms and tell her he was crazy about her.

She just dated him, with no plan, no road map, no thoughts of the future. There was only the next date, or the last one on her mind.

"Will you be mine, Lili?" he asked.

"So you get bored of me?" she teased him. He laughed, as if he'd expected it.

"That's all up to you."

"And what should I do so you don't get bored of me?"

"This."

And he kissed her. Lovely answer. Not so satisfying, though.

She couldn't get over the panic that having sex aroused in her. The very notion. Packed with disapproval, with intimate fear and shame, with anxiety over what might happen as a result. Stories that she had been told and that she was telling herself.

That's all that men want, and oh, the length they go to get it... That S thing – shhhh! He lured her; he had his way with her and then he dumped her; he left her pregnant.

The expressions that people used about the S thing seemed to refer to things that were done to her. It was never "She had her way with *him*," not even "They had their way with each other."

Or maybe there was a way of saying that, but on a more institutionalized level: "They live with each other" (which did not necessarily mean sharing a flat, but having regular sex); even this expression was said with a bit of reproof, or at least suggesting messy adult things. It was also not in line with the Party guidelines on a moral life, which pressed for marriage and kids.

She did actually go to bed with him, literally, a few times, intending to give it a try, maybe she'd be ready to go all the way, but she pulled out just before the main action, repelled by the inherent brutality of the act itself. She was in love with Gabriel, but there was a repugnant part of his body that started to get in the way as soon as things got going.

Supposing she did go the whole way, after all – what would the universe be like afterwards?

Would everyone notice that she had done it? Maybe some radiance on her face? Or something on her body showing from under her swimsuit (that was silly, but how could she know?). That she no longer would be a girl, but a woman, was such a terrible, shameful thing, at her age, with her intellectual preoccupations, really, that was only for bad girls!

The other thing was, she would be totally addicted to Gabriel, as if belonging to him (she couldn't quote the source for this, but such a change would surely make her his slave). He on the other hand would be satisfied, and satisfaction soon dissolves into indifference. The scenario was obvious. Sleeping with him would be like taking a horrible pill that would turn her into a zombie and him into a free man. No way, even the thought of it gave her a shudder.

She started in a very wide circle, but pretty soon she decided to cut it short. His arm on her shoulders and his head bending to hers gave her courage.

"Look, Gabriel, now you're taking me to the bus stop and then we both go about our own business."

"What do you mean?"

"I mean we should put an end here."

"To what?"

"To our relationship."

He halted. They'd got to the bus stop and he looked at her, worried.

"Why?"

"Because I can't give you what you want."

She avoided his eyes, but when she finally looked up to him, he was stupefied and almost scared.

"Do you realise the nonsense you're saying? You'd rather do one stupid thing instead of another?" He was almost angry now. "And why can't you give me what I want, as you say?"

"Well – it would be too much."

"Too much for what?"

She hadn't expected to be questioned. Her own reasoning didn't go very far.

"I can't do such a thing!"

"You can't do SUCH A THING? What is it, *killing* someone?"

"Oh, stop this, it would change everything, me first of all, and I don't want that."

"What would it change?"

She sighed with resentment at all the questions.

"Well, for one thing I'd get too attached to you. And, I don't know, it's going to change everything and I'm scared of that."

The bus had come and they both got on. He whispered through his teeth once again, "You're talking nonsense," then gradually he came back to himself. But he held her arm with a firm grip. After a few minutes, he spoke again, self-control back: "Have you been thinking a lot about it?"

"Yes, a lot."

"Gosh, it's bad to be thinking so much – and on your own. Next time maybe we can do some thinking together."

When he got off, he said quickly, "Talk to you tomorrow, OK?"

Oh, no, she thought, he isn't going to let me get away with it!

They hid in dark entrances to apartment blocks passionately kissing and groping, only to rush out again when it got too much, or when they heard someone coming. She went to his place while his parents were out at the theatre, but left just as unspoiled as she had come; they argued about it and twisted it every possible way. Then, one day, Gabriel told her on the phone he had got tired of chasing.

He was dating someone else now.

Dark weeks and months followed, one of those tunnels where she closed her eyes, hung on tight and crossed through: shut off the dark, shut off the ghosts, just move on, whatever it takes, move on, towards no clear end, just an end of it. School and exam preparation had helped. Trudging through that routine was better than reminiscing.

Sometime later, Gabriel did call her again. They remained friends. In the hectic final year of school, she finally managed to forget him.

A year later she lands in bed with someone. Not caring to resist. To be fair, she had no reason to resist. She's no longer the little girl; having sex with her boyfriend as an eighteen-year-old is no longer that shameful deed. And then, she has no fear nor misgivings about Vlad. She's safe with him from the nightmarish prospect of becoming a slave, and his love for her is material, available any time. Sex with Vlad won't expel her from the list of good girls, but make her a confident woman.

Besides, she couldn't disappoint Vlad by saying no to something she has no reason to reject. They never fight. He's always sweet, always by her side. It's the least she can give in return.

True, Gabriel had said that making love was the best thing on earth.

She gives an inner shrug. He might have used that as a persuasion argument. It feels to her more like going all in, playing the game to its final act, for the sake of completion, for the sake of un-chinked harmony.

The other part of making love is the love aspect. Vlad and love?

No.

She might have been hoping to get there by doing the S thing, making love as in creating it. Isn't theirs a love story, and such a glamorous one, too? Shouldn't she, then, feel love, and enact it? If they do what lovers do, she'll catch up at some point. Vlad Baci holds the rare promise of a safe and happy life, so she can't give up without doing the work.

What's more, this love redeems everything that's gone so terribly wrong in her young life – family, home, social being – and creates a new Lili out of the past, flawed version.

As if that wasn't enough on her mind, Vlad has kept mentioning getting married.

"Excuse me?" she opened her eyes wide the first time. "We only met two months ago! What do you know about me? Why would you want to marry me?"

Upon which he set forth her qualities as if it was a shopping list. What nonsense! She didn't know anything about him either.

"Well, ask me!" Vlad retorted.

She remembered the so-called oracles they kept in lower sec. Large notebooks, where you asked questions like *what's your favourite film and why?, what is love?, are you in love?, who is your favourite actor / actress, how do you see yourself in five years?* You gave the oracle to the people you were interested in, first of all your best friends, but then also to your crush, to his or her friends, and then, to anyone else insignificant. The main goal was to feverishly read how compatible you were with your crush.

So did Vlad volunteer an oracle-type of interrogation? Would he really expect to get married based on that?

But her protests make no difference. Next time Vlad will mention it again, in passing, "If we get married we can...", or "When we are married – sorry, *if* we get married – we're going to...." to the extent that protesting has become pointless. Vlad has made up his mind that he wants to marry her, and that's it. He wants nobody else in this world. There.

The clarity of what makes sense or not is vanishing, therefore, with each date, which is every day, and which inevitably involves the Bacis, too, on the posh side of the city. Vanishing with it is that garage of her own, which she had mentioned to Val Nestor what feels a lifetime ago, where she can deposit at least her tired head, if not her dreams of a life lived at its truest.

Mother updates Lili on every new course of action on the admission battlefield. The range is not particularly broad: one main contact in the Party Central, with maybe one more in standby, careful not to make any blunder and cause power wars up there. Such wars are risky, you don't want to get caught in between.

Then, two or three further connections to that main contact, which could – and would, at the right time, one by one – be leveraged; and of course, finally, the tactic of waiting patiently in between humble follow-ups like a gentle shake of the connecting ropes. The exciting time of daily news and updates is gone, because there are no more informants to whisper about what is going on between the walls.

For Lili that means long blocks of time when nothing is happening, and she has got used to the barrenness of mere waiting. The school memories are distant now, as if it's been at least a year since she graduated. Autumn has set in, and Dana has started going to classes and telling her about this or that lecturer. Lili listens with an emptiness in her chest. Not that anything is hurting. She's just sitting on her raft, waiting for it to reach solid ground, so she might finally step out and go about her life. The solid ground keeps receding, however, from mid-August to early September, then to any time by mid-October at the latest, when classes are starting, following the grape picking or potato sorting work. But it's already late October and no delivery is in sight.

One late afternoon she's coming back from Dana's. It's dark and the streets are empty. Everyone seems to have fled within their homes. Tiny, dim lights are sprinkled here and there.

There's what looks like a roadworks trailer stationed on her street, like a dark lump melting in the night, but for the open door at the back, revealing a low voltage bulb hanging from a wire as an improvised lamp. She quickens her step, it's always better not to be loitering when workers are around. She's just passing by the back side of the trailer when her ears catch the peeping sound of radio transmissions. What are road workers doing, are they trying to listen to the Voice of America? she wonders briefly. But then, there's a male voice inside the trailer speaking in a hushed voice, and the peeps and hisses grow fainter as he speaks, then louder again.

She's hurrying now. Weird. Weird! Not just listening to, but also talking to the radio?

Wait – are these workers, or Madam Secu's civilians?

She gets home to find Mother transfigured. Lili can't tell if she's been crying, or if she's seen a terrifying ghost, or both. She dodges Lili's straight gaze. The radio sounds are still buzzing in Lili's ears and the air feels brittle and disquieting, as if some electric blast has taken place.

Lili acts on habit and backs off into her own room. Here the air is breathable, but the weirdness behind the door is causing that cringe to grip her heart. The old familiar cringe. What's going on, what's going on, a hushed voice is whispering and then shutting up in fright. Why's Mother upset? What made her cry, yet again? What calamity has taken place? Where's a bit of safety?

She picks up her book and lies down on her bed, the same habit of diving in the tunnel, eyes closed, just go through, soon it'll be gone and you can go back in the open, some light will be there. The print is racing before her eyes, at the same pace as the inner flutter that the cringe enforces.

She can't sit here like that. Mother may need something. She can't leave her on her own, to carry everything on her shoulders. Is it the Party Central and the admission case? Or is it the other thing—

She totters to the kitchen, the cringe gripping her throat tight, eyes set in a ghostly stare. Mother is washing something in the sink, something that has no shape and no relevance.

"Something's up?" Lili asks in a white voice, with a

white buzz in her heart.

Mother doesn't look up, which is always a bad sign. Her hands are rubbing something frantically and water is pouring and pouring from the tap.

"What is it?" Lili asks again, in a deeper, fainter voice, going a step further towards Mother, as if in a reflex to hug her and comfort her, but halting half-way, unsure Mother wants that hug, unsure her hug can make any difference in the face of what may have happened.

Mother swivels her head almost as if in fear, almost defensively, and now Lili sees again that sight she dreads: Mother's wet cheeks, her face red, the blue of her eyes overflowing with tears. Lili can't take that, it's the most appalling sight she has seen in her life, it's the spectre that switches on that cringe, that electric flutter in her chest, that stare, and the race down the tunnel. Run run run, shut off shut off shut off, where's the safe haven when Mother's eyes are melting, if Mother's collapsing!

Mother sniffs and starts speaking in a voice squeaky from crying, then she hears herself and attempts to make fun of it, but falls back right away into crying, she stops rubbing that thing in the sink and tilts her head back, eyes closed, eyes pressed tight, squeezing more floods of tears out, her face all crumpled in a grimace of intense pain. Lili stands there frozen, she has forgotten herself, she is only her eyes watching this scene, the rest is thin air or not even that; the rest is emptiness.

Mother drops the object in the sink in a gesture of surrender, shakes the water off her hands and presses the back of her palms into her eyes, and Lili hears a hiss from inside her mother's chest that forebodes a long sob, which she has heard before, she has heard it, oh yes, more than once, when she locked herself in her bedroom to stop hearing it.

But Mother changes her mind, pulls herself together, and only lets out a deep sigh; she's a mother and must spare Lili's feelings, she must not scare Lili too much, she's just a kid. Lili feels she's going to burst, seeing that Mother is still trying to protect her, at the height of her own pain; too much sacrifice, Mother shouldn't need to bear so much on her shoulders, if Lili could only make Mother happier, if only she could remove those tears, that grimace from Mother's face, from Mother's heart – Mother shouldn't be allowed to suffer anymore!

They both sit down and Mother is composing herself, a rueful smile blending with tears across her face.

"Someone's been here, my dearest. Someone from the prosecutor's office."

The prosecutor's office? Are they being indicted for their complaints against the admission results?

No. Something worse than that. Lili's only got small problems, she's just a young girl. It must be that other thing, the big dark one, again. That dark ghost Lili hates for what it does to them, for what it does to Mother.

"The two of us—" Mother articulates words with difficulty between sobs and sighs "—there's only the two of us left now—" and a new surge of tears floods forth. "We only have each other now, Lili!" she manages to utter and her voice gives in under the hoarseness caused by weeping.

Oh.

That.

So it's over.

Hang on tight now, for a terrible aftermath.

CHAPTER FOUR

Everything had stood still when she heard the news, but then things started to race by.

Phone calls Mother had to make notifying their nearest family, bravely, almost neutrally, frozen as it were, lest she should break down.

Phone calls from distant family, or connections, who had heard about it and could not believe it – some not even aware that Professor Danes had been arrested.

Phone calls from the Physics Institute to express condolences.

Phone calls from the theatre to express condolences.

Rhetorical questions – "Can I do anything to help?"

Sometimes, Lili happened to pick up the calls. She did not know how to say it. You can only say what you know, what you have encountered before. She did find some words eventually, but they had nothing to do with her father. With herself. With their past. Nor with the present.

And then people inevitably sounded so stricken and compassionate, when Lili only felt somewhat dazed. She wasn't about to break down, if that's what they were expecting. She was just a ghost hovering quietly about the house, lighter than air, whiter than fog, so Mother might not worry about her. Lili would have gladly imploded so she might occupy only negative space in this story, with no perceptions, just eyes closed, ears stoppered, jaw tight, and through with the funeral and its elaborate preparations.

Then aunts and uncles and cousins and many

others she had never known started thronging into their house, cooking the funeral meal, doing the house cleaning, counting the chairs and fetching more from the neighbours, rugs rolled up and furniture shoved aside to make room for the big chain of tables, uncountable amounts of pottery, cutlery, napkins, plastic cups and a huge cauldron to feed a platoon, all were pouring in, which was in a way welcome; there were people alive swarming about, voices, activity.

The Bacis' white Lada was busy carrying stuff and relatives, from authority offices to the cemetery and to other relatives to get even more stuff. Vlad was wearing a particularly tight rictus across his face now, tighter than his inborn one, and eyed Lili with concern and commiseration, offering professional help from specialists his father knew, or various vitamins and tranquillisers in the form of capsules or vials. That he was taking so much trouble for her went down on his tab, for sure. The tab lay somewhere on a shelf in her inner archive. Someday, everything would add up to something that would count. But today was not that day.

Today everything was immaterial, in all senses of the word. She was floating in a dreamy set, her only concern being Mother. Lili would have gladly worn armour and waved a spear to shoo away the Professor's ghost so that Mother might be mercifully, finally, allowed some space to be at peace.

Somewhere deep below the ghostly hovering lurched a sense of astonishment that her secret wish to have her father removed from their family life had bizarrely been granted. Death was a radical way she had never dared to articulate in her mind, but that must be the way things had chosen to happen, and now her only fear was that she might not be able to compensate and comfort Mother over her loss. Mother loved her, all right, but Lili suspected that she could never replace her father, no matter how close she and Mother got in their new-found solidarity.

More than that, she feared that her father's disappearance would bring only more hardship for Mother to cope with, including worries about money, tough household jobs, and the pressure to deliver in a man's stead. That was an undeserved prospect. Lili had only wanted Mother to have a lighter burden on her shoulders, but now the terrible blow could only leave her the hope that Mother would, given a bit of time, bounce back as she usually did, like the fighter she was, and then the two of them, one day not so far in the future, might actually start enjoying life.

Lili spent the night before the funeral at the Bacis'. Dr Baci himself had persuaded her to come over, on account of sparing her mother worry about her daughter on such a night.

The tradition had it that the house should be full of people, relatives or not, and keep vigil for the dead before his final journey. The deceased was not in the house – nobody knew where he was – but the tradition had to be kept, as there was not much else left to keep. The night would be spent sitting and maybe talking about him, candles would be kept burning, while in the background the final preparations for the funeral meal would be carried out quietly: all the stuffed cabbage rolls rolled by hand and placed in the huge cauldron, the koliva to be boiled and portioned out in the saucers, the bowls, or together with the other dishes on the plates, all to be given as alms after the service.

Lili meant to protest – she wasn't a kid, she was the only support her mother had left – but she also knew that Dr Baci was right. Mother would, indeed, worry about her, and she actually suspected that Mother herself had asked Vlad to take her away for the night. Better not to cause Mother any further trouble, just go along with her wishes, she decided.

She went to bed in Vlad's bedroom, while he slept in his study space in the basement. She had offered to go to sleep there instead, but everyone had maintained this was out of the question. They wouldn't let her be alone, not that night.

Vlad drove her to the cemetery the next day, where, in the chapel, there was a coffin lying on a shabby black sheet, surrounded by floral wreaths with various condolence messages written on the ribbons. It was astonishing how many people had sent flowers, including the Institute, the Rectorate, the publisher who had rejected the Professor's latest book, the Party office in the university, department colleagues, Mother's colleagues, and more she hadn't the time to identify.

The family was ordained to stand around the coffin during the service, and Vlad stood next to her. The chapel was freezing and draughty. The walls looked as if they were made of stone turned black from the smoke of the countless funeral candles that must have been burnt here, and the priest's chanting took shrill notes at times. The coffin was closed; it was just a wooden box with a ribbon folded around it, reading: *We will never be consoled – your Maria and Lili.*

The coffin was empty, everyone knew that. The body had not been found, and the prosecutor had preferred not to give pictorial descriptions of the circumstances of his passing away. Not that it mattered much at that moment; the coffin was there, and that was all that mattered.

She felt the lump that usually cringed in her chest move up, astonishingly, to her throat, and a gush of water welled up to her eyes. She couldn't make sense of what was going on in her body. Vlad's hand gripped hers more tightly yet, as if saying "Hang on in there, be brave," and Lili was brave; the water was dammed and sent back behind her eyes, and the lump was pushed down below awareness. The coffin was just an empty wooden box, this here was just a ritual, the floral wreaths a convention; one does that for funerals. The funeral was the only thing that continued to feel strange here, or not to feel like anything at all, as Lili couldn't allow herself to feel. She would not dwell on this cringe, she would not inhabit it, just as Father was not inhabiting that coffin, and Mother was not there either, tears on her face, staring into the void. Only the audience was there, watching an empty ritual unfold.

The amount of tears and of the colour black she could see all around her, including her own clothes, was getting unbearable. What were those black things doing there, what were they doing to her? She was like a shadow, like the ghost of herself, not for mourning, but for estrangement.

So that was the end of the family jokes replaying the old Yimmi Papa refrains ("Come, you're a lovely Papa, oh, you're such a clever Papa and such a good Papa, come Yimmi Papa just one more story, please, you know I love you Yimmi Papa…").

And it was the end of the moods swinging up and down in the house.

No more risky, politically clumsy blunders.

No more being bookish and scholarly.

It was the end of something bigger still, something that had felt like a given, something there, like the law of gravity, beyond rolling eyes and making faces, beyond sulking and pulling back, screaming and kicking, beyond not finding words to say what one meant, or even finding the real feeling to put in words – was it anger was it doubt was it fear was it insecurity was it judgement was it – come, show your face again, your real face, the one I know so well and love so dearly, what's going on with us, what are we doing to ourselves…

Something was hopefully going to end this service and the whole nightmare of accompanying the empty coffin to its grave, stopping the hearse at every crossroads in the cemetery for some more chanting and wailing dust to dust, to give the audience a renewed chance to break down in tears.

But when they stopped by the grave there came the blow.

Apart from the muddy hole that was gaping outrageously.

Lili suddenly opened her eyes to see the crowd. Behind the family, close or distant, faces familiar or barely known, behind the circumstantial friends or enemies, behind the clique around Bodu-Beran and other impostors, there was a compact crowd of young people holding a banner reading "We miss you, Professor!" Their eyes were set on Lili, or so she felt, but they were not commiserating with her. They were themselves in mourning. She almost had an impulse to reach out to comfort them. The sadness in their eyes, the banner they held in a compelling picture of despair, there was nothing left of being brave, of staying away from pain. It was all about looking pain in the face, being real about it and committing oneself to it. No ritual, no pose, no being nice.

The students were missing their Professor, their mentor, their model. Lili's father.

Father.

Lili felt her knees go lifeless for a second. If she should break down now, she would be held by those young people's solidarity. Dust to dust, pain to pain, then coming out again at the other end. She could let herself go, on the awareness of what the Professor – Father – had meant to his fellow humans, and she could take it from there. She could erase the details of the past, dismiss the faces around and all their good intentions, and grieve.

Vlad's arm held her tight, though, not letting her go. She cannot give in to it now.

Funerals are much worse than death itself; you need to be tough enough to survive and carry on. Life after the funeral will take you back, an item lost and found. The critical moment of collapsing will have been bridged over.

The weeks floated by. There came at one point an official letter from the Party Central, which brought no significant change. Things were to stay as they were, and keep floating by. All clues, connections, interventions, justice-be-done promises, ministers – archived as relics from another life.

November rolled past, whatever it may have meant to others – mid-term papers, university lectures advancing into the subject matter, freshers settling into their roles – but it was immaterial here, where Lili was.

The house had acquired an added sense of gloom. Various actions were undertaken: sorting clothes, books, and various personal effects to give away, commissioning a modest marble cross for the grave, formalities about records, pensions, certificates, property clearances over the house, contract closures and transfers. Hassles that only made life more desolating.

She was not sure which ordeal was greater, her failing to get the study place that she was entitled to, or the gloom at home. She spent most of her time in the same ghostly hovering that had been her element ever since the news of her father's death.

At times, she experienced flashes of awareness, realising how absurd her staying home for the year was.

She had done her bit and carried her mountain. But now she was living someone else's life.

Lili had no idea how the daytime could be filled. There was no studying to be done. Maybe there would never be. What was that thing called admission, again?

The house went through re-ordering, as if attempting to redefine itself in the new reality, so Lili, too, tidied up her desk and the shelves. She dropped her old school books, worksheets, and supplementary practice books in a cabinet that she had long used as a dumping site for outdated documents such as teenage diaries and oracle books. The episode had to be closed and left behind her. She had to gain distance and forget. For no specific purpose, just to keep herself safe from all that emotional muddle.

Dumped to dumped, past to past.

Everything else was thin air. The past had to be archived, otherwise it was weighing too heavy. Cut the strings, put it away, never go back there again.

Days came and went, and weeks were bundles of days. The Bacis helped her navigate that amorphous mass of time. Vlad was there every day, giving her a time-out, even a place-out. A few times a week they would go to the Bacis' and just kill time with a videotape.

Lili couldn't have said exactly what her time with Vlad was made up of, but she never wondered either. She took it for granted that he would come over in Dr Baci's white Lada, park it under her window and let himself in through the garden gate and then the house door. He would knock and come in with a smile over the rictus on his face, bending to kiss her, like a sweet husband.

He would start reporting on what was new, on whatever little events he'd experienced in his classes, on how his parents were doing, and whether his father or mother were on the night shift, what Mrs Doctor Baci had cooked the day before, whether there were plans to drive to the mountain cottage at weekend – and if not, maybe Vlad and Lili could, on their own? – and countless other items of information.

Driving to the mountains on a Saturday morning felt good, knowing that other people were still at work while instead, you were leaving the city with weekend gear: food supplies, hiking boots, music tapes and any other staple items and utensils that might be useful in the cottage.

The Bacis liked their comfort and were well-organised people. Dr Baci enjoyed tinkering around the house, so there was always a good supply of torches, fire matches, spare light bulbs, nails, pliers, spanners and saws around the house, for you to survive the weekend, no matter what may befall the house. Mrs Doctor Baci saw that the other type of supplies were always in stock, such as kitchenware and house cleaning products.

She spent her days numbed in a misty place of her own, but when they drove to the mountains, the cottage was a welcome, solid substitute for the ghostly place where she lived, which oozed with significance and dejection. Here, instead, was neutral ground: the objects were just objects, comfortingly real and tangible. No history.

The cottage also gave her a new role. She cooked – if only basics – what Mrs Doctor Baci had lovingly packed in the recycled shopping bag for them, which ranged from meat, rice, or pasta to salad ingredients, oil, and even home-made jam, eggs and bacon for breakfast. Nothing was ever missing. Vlad would do some minor tinkering job that the chief surgeon had entrusted him with, and was visibly thrilled to see the roles assigned: he, man; she, woman; house, their own. She smiled, mostly to herself, oh Vladyboy, you're cute, and went on filling the time with activity. Filling time felt good. Whatever it was, it made the days go by quicker and lighter.

Vlad had a double quality: he was a sweet guy and he adored her. She missed him when he was away, and closed her eyes when he took her in his arms, thankful for the touch, for the warmth of his body. Given some time to weather off the recent blows, she would be able to give him more than her thankfulness. She would reward his kindness and his loyalty, but for now, the best she could give him was a kiss back, a response to his embrace in bed at night, a tacit assent to the game of promised lovers.

Not that Vlad sensed anything missing. He was, by all signs, perfectly happy. She alone knew, or counted, the tab not to be full.

It didn't exactly help that certain little details popped up now and then.

"Honey, my mates got tickets to the match next Saturday, can I join them?"

"You're asking me for permission?"

"Well – yes, basically. I don't want you to be upset, us not being together on a Saturday, but we can also do something in the morning if you like—"

"Vlad! Come on!" Lili waved to him with big eyes. "You're kidding, right? I'm not your mama to give you permission, and I'm sure I'll survive a Saturday without us being together!"

She heard her words and her harsh tone. She only meant it straight enough to make him understand that he didn't need to put her on a pedestal, but it suddenly sounded as if it cut deeper than intended.

"I mean, it's so sweet of you, but of course you can go with your friends, what's wrong with it, please don't ask me again. If I want to meet with Dana I won't ask you either." Meeting Dana was, of course, just a hypothetical idea, which she mentioned only to make a point. They hadn't seen each other since the funeral. Dana was busy with her uni classes. Lili was busy as the lady of the cottage.

His loyalty and his good-boy reflexes sometimes made her feel uncomfortable. If anything, she wanted to be a woman, not a mom. Everything she knew or imagined about love was about two people gazing deep into each other's eyes, no ranks, pedestals or distance in between. She wanted the closeness, not the power. She wanted the passion, not the care-taking. The man, not mama's cute boy.

Unaffected by such concerns, they kept on sleeping with each other regularly. She felt no particular urge, but when they were sharing the bed at weekends, sex was a matter of course and a renewed statement that they were adults.

At least some claim to freedom was being granted. At least something was moving on.

She had no way of comparing, but she guessed that Vlad was a sweet sex partner. The act itself was – well, it was what it was. The mechanics of the ritual unfolded every time in the same way, mostly with him on top, occasionally switching with her; but it still aroused some sort of curiosity, or expectation, that this time, there might be a different thrill. At the end, turning on her side and letting herself fall deep into sleep. Vlad was doing it, so it had become clear that it was perfectly normal. She could call it a day.

Lili felt strangely grown up. Just out of school (ages ago, it felt), and now she was spending weekends in a mountain cottage with a guy, playing the young couple under the generous wing of the in-laws.

Had anything been going on about the university exams at all?

Apparently. Some indefinite time ago.

Now it was almost Christmas and Vlad was frantic about getting her a Christmas tree. He also kept telling how his mother was procuring supplies for the Christmas feast judiciously, and how Dr Baci had announced they were taking a vacation, going to Geneva over New Year's – and the kids were welcome to join, too. Dr Baci had got an invitation from an international surgeons' club, to be held early January in Geneva.

Geneva was, to her, a place on a map that would forever stay just there, on a map.

There was no money in their household and she couldn't picture herself there, as if an unthinkable leap into the screen, hopping into the film, would be required. But – what clothes to wear, how to move her hands, who to be? The Lili she knew was petrified in a state of inadequacy. For Geneva she would also need to have a passport and sign hundreds of application forms and written declarations that would never be approved in time – or maybe they would, for Dr Baci's sake? She suspected the surgeon didn't enjoy that high a privilege, after all.

Vlad mentioned the New Year's party repeatedly, in excited anticipation, as if he could see it with his mind's eye.

In fact, why couldn't they go? Money wasn't a problem, there's enough to go round!

"And don't you worry, Daddy's going to see that we get the visa clearance!" he asserted with conviction, looking her straight in the eyes.

His conviction started Lili's mind into producing occasional, but recurring pictures of themselves celebrating the New Year in a luxurious hotel in Geneva (any hotel in Geneva was bound to be luxurious). Against all odds, the year might get a cinematic end. Vlad, her treasure, her passport to a bountiful future, would make this, too, possible. Her picture-loving mind longed to return to its creative habit, but she quickly dismissed such fantasies.

"What are you doing for the New Year's?" she asked Dana on the phone.

"Susi and I are going skiing, a whole week at the Alpine Bliss, Susi's grandpa has arranged it, of course," Dana replied.

Susi? Of course, Dana's new best friend at university, whose grandpa used to be someone very big. Like Vlad's grandpa. An army general? A high-ranking Orthodox Church official? Wasn't it all the same? Lili didn't know whether she was jealous that Dana had found another best friend, that the two of them were at university, or whether she felt stranded altogether. She had little bandwidth for feelings and reflections.

Her day-to-day focus was just on getting through the day. Vlad stood out in that routine most, but she had mixed feelings about him. She was barely nineteen now, and being in love, perhaps even about to get engaged, including the perks of the Bacis' generosity, their car and their mountain cottage – it all should have felt a bit more intense, she thought. A bit more like her life was live.

Nothing was live at the moment, though. It was being filtered through various gates of a mind that had crashed in the gloom of her house, the emptiness of her days, the aftermath of recent events, the obscurity of her motives in being with Vlad.

That was anything but live. It was more like karaoke. She just kept moving her lips to the text of the music, getting more familiar with it, to the point where she was tempted to believe that it was the live thing.

The admission story was a tiny planet lost in the cosmic darkness. It was there all right, but Lili was here, caught in the mimicry of a normal life, because normalcy was soothing. That story could stay where it was, until the time came to check if it was worth going for it again.

Trying admission again was part of a script that was flawed, in her case, from its premise. Sitting the exams a second time, she would only reinforce its falsehood, by acting like someone who had failed the year before. But this wasn't who she was. All the times in the past she had rebelled by saying "this isn't me" had piled up, it seemed, into this major dilemma that left her no choice.

Was there another way to get back at the world for the injustice it had done her, and prove herself beyond any doubt, without enacting the "fail–try again" script?

Wasn't going to university to get an identity part of a script itself? Wasn't sitting those exams validating it?

There had to be another script. What could she choose instead of this fake matrix of her life?

Vlad was there as the one conceivable salvation. With him, she didn't need to prove anything. The prospects he offered belonged in a different paradigm: Lili would be the lucky woman, the comfortable wife and daughter-in-law, enjoying the harmony. Maybe that was her way forward, breaking the pattern of "trying again".

Every now and then she remembered how the Professor had refused to be part of the admission committees. There had been arguments at home, because it obviously caused him extra trouble at the Institute, where he already felt he was being marginalised. Mother kept emphasising that he should make himself as useful as possible and show how co-operative he was, if he wanted to expose the political agenda they held against him. It was the only way to prove that they were persecuting him. But the Professor would sulk and keep smoking cigarette after cigarette, and when Mother wouldn't stop pleading, he would burst out in protest and leave the room, banging the door behind himself.

Back then, Lili found it unreasonable and even reckless of him to be acting rebelliously, when he was the one complaining about being sabotaged. Of course he was, what could he expect? And what was the problem with marking admission papers – did he want to go on vacation earlier? In the days leading up to this year's crippled Christmas, the memory of this question visited her briefly, and now she had an answer of sorts. Marking admission papers had turned out to have always been a dubious business.

"See what I mean? That's what our life would be like," Vlad points out, arching his bushy eyebrows. His earnest face is both touching and remotely hilarious. "Forget about just Geneva – in general. Everything we have would be yours, too. My old ones love you, you're already like a daughter to them, and of course I love you, you know that, but just so you understand, you got everything, everything's at your feet, you only need to say the word. Dad could arrange for us to go on honeymoon somewhere nice in France, or Austria, and Mom, she'd help us too, you know, we wouldn't be like – well, on our own, you having to do household chores, no, you'd have your classes, just like me, but we'd all be a family together—"

"So there is some room left in this fantasy for my classes, I appreciate that," Lili counters, half teasing, half seeking reassurance.

Or maybe that's the condition the deal hinges on. "And what if I wasn't going to any classes? No university? What then? Would your parents still love me like a daughter?"

He stops breathing for a second and frowns in confusion.

"What do you mean, no university?"

"I don't know, we're just fantasising here, right?" Lili leans back, sensing a danger she hasn't yet considered. "I'm just wondering if they'd still love me like a daughter if I failed university again – and again, who knows?"

"Of course they would, what kind of question is that? Once a family, always a family, no matter what! You could also choose another course with less admission hassle and when you graduate you could just stay home, in fact, there would be no pressure for you to earn money. You could have all the time in the world to do what you like."

To do what she likes.

"When I graduate, Dad would be sure to get me a good post, we could move out and find a place of our own, you'd decorate it the way you want it—"

"Hold on a sec, Vlad," Lili shakes her head. "What's all this fantasising? All this 'Oh we would and we could and—'"

"That's the point, Lili." Vlad rises on his elbow and bends over to her. They're lying face to face on her bed, propping their heads on their hands, arms bent in triangles. "It's not a fantasy! It's right here, under your nose, you only have to reach out and it becomes reality, any moment! You can already get a taste of it, us, a family, our cottage in Busteni, meeting my friends. Wherever we go, you're my precious other half, haven't you noticed? I'd take care of you – I already take care of you, and your smile is my daily objective," he declares.

Lili bursts out laughing and lays her head on her arm. She's almost charmed by so much devotion, if only it didn't ring again like her sitting on a throne high up while her loyal servants are busy fulfilling her wishes. She would have everything at her feet, he says? All that submission and being taken care of, which feels so touching, involves remoteness and solitude. Instead of having anything at her feet, she'd much rather have a man to look up at.

"A life without big worries, what's wrong with that? Where nothing's too bad not to be made right again, and where we all love you."

"This whole conversation, Vlad, is so childish," Lili shakes her head, smiling. She resents her condescending manner, but somehow Vlad wrings it out of her every so often.

"Childish?" Vlad's eyes bulge out. "Why, because I love you and I'm putting everything I have at your feet?"

Her feet, again. Oh. "Yes, no, I know," Lili searches for the right words but doesn't know exactly what she's looking for. Vlad's persuasion is what she finds amusing. It's almost like her pleading with Yimmi Papa for another bedtime story, throwing in for ammunition all sorts of arguments and claims, the difference being she was asking for a story back then, while Vlad here is after a marriage.

There was nothing wrong with a life without big worries. If anything, just a bit uncanny. The uncanniest of all being, she had no real feelings, only thankfulness, and the hope of a straw. Vlad held a grand promise of an unconditional arrangement for life.

But was it unconditional, or merely single-minded? He had no idea who she really was, Lili felt, because his lenses possibly didn't reach that deep. She couldn't fathom what his love amounted to, what substance it was made up of, and what the pledge was.

Gabriel's love had been tangible. He wanted her, and kept his hand on her hair, shoulder, hand, arm, or thigh every second they were together. He often teased her, or held her cheeks, touched by something he might have recognised in her, and sometimes rolled his eyes when she was too silly. He called her pied puffin, at times with great fondness, other times with an erotic thrill, other times still with sarcasm. She knew where she was with him, and what brought about each nuance. His eyes were alive, piercing her with the intensity of each emotion, which responded to some part of herself.

Vlad, by contrast, wore his unperturbed gaiety and candour. His fondness of her was self-generated and required no fuel from her side; it must have been switched on last summer in that resort, by some trigger she couldn't imagine, and carried on by itself within constant parameters that nothing, apparently, could interfere with.

He was over there with his love and his promised possessions, while she was over here (where, exactly?) with her bottled up inner world and a collection of promises.

Vlad's promise was simple: Take my hand, and you will have everything at your feet.

Gabriel had said: Be my woman, and we'll both discover love, the most rewarding thing on earth.

Zooming out, Val Nestor had made a promise, too: Carry your mountain and it will set you free. And Gregory Talu had promised to see that justice was done.

It was just Father who, after breaking his original promises, had made threats instead: Abandon your mind, and you'll be lost.

And what of those promises? At least Father had gone on record breaking them. Gabriel had changed course on his quest for love, Nestor's mountain had come up with an error, while Gregory Talu had said nice words on a summer evening under the starry sky.

Was Vlad's promise any safer?

She might as well become a hairdresser. Hairdressers made good money and you didn't need to have your intelligence measured for that. No exams and no claims. Blending in, an average person with no special ring to their name. One only needed to do some work in life.

Forget complexities and reasoning.

Of course there was no Geneva for New Year's. Not even the Bacis went.

Lili asked, surprised, "Oh, you're not going to Geneva for the New Year's?"

Dr Baci's eyebrows twitched instantly, his turn to be surprised, and replied quickly, "Geneva? No, we're going to Busteni!"

Vlad mumbled an explanation that she couldn't make out, but it didn't matter. She shrugged inwardly and made a quick mental note that she needn't have reviewed her wardrobe just in case she'd be swept off to Geneva against her rational will to stay home.

She made yet another mental note, stretching back in time, of Vlad having mentioned plans more than once that never came to anything in the end.

They had been invited to Ema Dragu's birthday, sometime in late October; this was the daughter of the so-called Court Bard, the poet who chanted odes to the beloved leader and his wife. Yet, the day came and passed, and when questioned, Vlad muttered something that Lili took for a message to drop the matter, which she was happy to do, not being particularly keen on the clique of last summer.

Then, Paul Stănescu, the son of the National Public Prosecutor, had set up a celebration for his girlfriend. He was in a relationship with the female protagonist of last year's movie about school leavers, which Lili still remembered from the times when she was singing the title song with Dana and a few other girls along the vaulted halls of their school. The actress had just put out her latest single. Lili didn't think much of the single, nor of the starlet's singing talents; still, it would be cool to get to see her in person at a party. Except that no party materialised in the end, which at the time she assumed had been cancelled.

But now, it looked as if there was a pattern. Vlad would repeatedly tell a glamorous story or announce an upcoming event with growing excitement, but things fell flat just before it took place.

The memories of last summer, although archived, were still within recalling range; she might have revisited those snippets where Vlad would be chattering, his pals would be laughing, but the conversation would be flowing on past Vlad's contributions. Were they truly his pals? Lili was more than aware that they lived in his neighbourhood, as he kept mentioning, but had they ever visited each other even once in all these months?

If Vlad didn't truly belong in the fancy clique, that was fine. She hadn't belonged in the party fellowship either. They had that much in common, then: both longing to join in, neither really making it. He seemed to be several steps ahead of her, though, towards that belonging they both wanted, or maybe those steps were towards a big lie?

So, no Geneva. Just an improvised get-together with Vlad's medicine mates, in a shabby flat on the ninth floor of a working-class apartment building, at the other end of the city. Well. It could be worse: staying home, for example. There would be some music, and something going on.

Vlad took care of the logistics, carrying the music equipment and the colour TV in his parents' white Lada the day before New Year's Eve, as the Bacis would be driving to Busteni the next morning and depriving Vlad of the car. If he couldn't get Geneva, he would get at least this party right, and would sweat hard at it, so everyone could see he was the heart and soul of it.

His generosity sharing his goodies, Lili suspected, had something to do with a role he was keen to play. Among his VIP clique, he might have been the funny busybody, but with his chums in the normal world, he seemed to be the helpful giver. She could imagine Vlad saying, "Somebody's gotta do this, and that'll be me because I'm lucky to have the means."

She's helping to unload and carry paraphernalia from the car into the flat.

"Did you pack the whole living room, Vladyboy?" one of the guys asks, picking up a box overflowing with cables. "Is this Mr Doctor's toolkit?" He winks at Lili.

"Of course not!" Vlad replies, slightly flattered. "Just wasn't sure what you have, easier to pack all the stuff in one go. New Year's only once a year, they say, so we don't want to miss anything, do we?"

"And what's in here?" another guy asks.

"There? Oh, erm—" Vlad is trying to rummage inside with one hand, while holding a large carton on his chest.

"Oh, come on, stop it, just asked, no need to bother," the guy turns away. "We'll see upstairs when we unpack."

"Santa Claus is coming to town," one of them chants.

"Vlad Baci is coming to the neighbourhood! Let's give him a warm welcome, people!"

"Shhh – you nuts, man? They'll take us for dangerous elements, shouting things in the street – but hey, no worries, Vlad here – and Lili, of course, his one and only! – will be testifying for us when we're in custody."

"What you don't say, actually it'll be the honourable Dr Baci himself, you're kidding me!"

"Sure, but that's because it'll be Vlad here that will call up his mom and dad, won't he? Won't you, Vlad? What else did you pack in here, man, why's it so heavy?"

"I told you I grabbed everything just in case. Oh, it must be a pot of my mom's winter salad, she made plenty of it and put some aside for us, it's her fav—"

"The winter salad! Yayyy, Mom's supercalifragilistic salad – what's in it, other than potatoes and pickles? Truffles?"

"Truffles? What's that?"

"Shut up, stupid! Erm, imported olives?"

"Olives are imported by definition, guys!"

"Hey, don't digress, please, I want to know what could be in this precious winter salad that Mrs Doctor Baci took the trouble to make with her very own hands, for our delight on New Year's Eve!"

"There's vegetable stuff," Vlad provides clarification, "and veal, of course."

"Veal, of course!"

"Of course!"

"The winter salad always has veal, didn't you know, sucker?"

"No, actually, it doesn't," Vlad corrects, "but we do have tons of veal in the freezer, so—"

"Tons of veal, man, tons of veal! Vladyboy, did you lock the door when you left, so no one breaks in for the treasure? Lili, did you watch him do it? I know he's walking on clouds, in love as he is, and thank goodness he's got you—"

"Of course he's got her, it's her he's in love with, man, gosh—"

"Yep, I know that, but what I meant is thank goodness they're together, and taking good care of each other, right, Lili? You take good care of Vladyboy, don't you?"

"Of course we take good care of each other, that's what love is all about, you know that?" Vlad cuts in.

"Oh, that's what love is all about, Vlad knows, guys. Sit down and take notes, y'all, will you."

"Yeah, yeah, you carry on with your teasing, but he who laughs at the end laughs better, hey guys?"

"And you laugh at the end, Vlad, is that what you're saying?"

"Of course!"

Vlad is busy untangling the cables. They all wait for him to go on and explain.

"OK, so Vlad laughs last, who laughs first here? Anyone?"

"Me!"

"No, you sit down and keep taking notes, as I said, cos what Vlad has to share with us today is precious wisdom. But why do you laugh last, Vladydaddy, you're not going to heaven I hope?"

"He is in heaven already, in the seventh, remember? Walking on clouds, holding hands with Lili here? Ring any bells, hello?"

"Sure, sure, though Lili here seems quite deft at walking on earth, doesn't she, and she's not laughing at all, neither first nor last. Lili, do you laugh with Vlad?"

"At, about, for, despite—"

"Oh, come on, guys, cut the nonsense and give me a

hand here," Vlad says. "We laugh last because we do have love after all, not like you. Paul Stănescu – you know, the Public Prosecutor's son, my neighbour—" Vlad prompts the guys' memory.

"Yes, we know who Paul Stănescu is, Vlad."

"Your neighbour."

"The Public Prosecutor's son, of course!"

"Yes, sure, great, so he's with Maya Stefan – you know, the film star?"

"We know Maya, too, Vlad!"

"Is she also your neighbour?"

"No, stupid, but she may well become, if she moves in with Paul, right Vlad?"

"I doubt that, actually," Vlad points out knowingly. "They're moving in together, but not with Paul's mom and dad—"

"Oh, what a shame, so then Paul will no longer be your neighbour, Vlad, will he?"

"Shut up, man, just let Vlad enlighten us what's going on with Paul and what love did to him, and why Paul and Vlad – and Lili, of course – and Maya! – why they all laugh last!"

"We all laugh last because we know something you don't, guys, no offence. It's that when you truly love someone, you take good care of them. Lili knows," Vlad adds with a tender smile to her. "And Paul, too – you know he threw a party just to celebrate Maya's new single?"

"No, you didn't tell us, Vlad, something wrong with you?"

"He's in love. That's one other thing that love does to people, they get out of the habit of updating their mates."

Lili felt uneasy when they met Vlad's pals. She saw that he

was constantly being made fun of, or that he was being funny himself, either way without him realising.

His gregarious cheerfulness was nice, and put him in the spotlight. But he seemed almost too keen on the spotlight, almost unable to stop begging for pats on the shoulder. Vlad was the one blindfolded in the hide and seek, running in all directions with arms stretched out, giggling and squealing with the excitement of the game, while Lili and the others were standing on the side, exchanging knowing looks.

Lili would have been capable of handling this insight on her own, telling herself she was just being a tad mean, and that Vlad was such a sweet guy. That the others were noticing, though, was harder to ignore. It meant that she was not being mean. That was the real Vlad.

Even worse, the mates' jokes seemed to be a long shot at herself, daring her to lay her cards on the table, as in: Who are you really, going out with Vlad, although you're not like him? Being the one who was looking on, seeing the comic in his behaviour, strangely reinforced the wise mama role Vlad often cast her in. The others, inevitably, also saw the no-nonsense woman in her.

Was she becoming one? The lily in her – was it turning into a sturdy sunflower?

There were few motives to account for her duplicity, but that was a path she wouldn't explore in her thoughts for now. It led to another version of Lili that she would vehemently deny.

She felt that the teasing pressed her to take a stand. Should she step in and defend him? This would mean acknowledging that she saw their game, and ultimately, Vlad's comical figure. She would persist in complicity with his chums. She was fond of Vlad and treasured his candour, but if that meant stepping in for him against his buddies, it was obviously the wrong love.

Alternatively, if she kept quiet, wouldn't she be letting him down? It was only right to stand by him, unconditionally, as he stood by her. True: she would have been happy to stand by her man. But a little boy?

Until answers were available, the interim solution was to dismiss the complicity of the jokes, and stay away from the guys altogether.

This was an ironical twist: one of the first things that had attracted her to Vlad was the unspoken promise that she would become part of a circle of people, and this way, sink in normalcy.

Whereas now, that circle was reduced to Vlad and his parents, because the rest either she preferred to avoid, or did not exist (and may never have existed beyond Vlad's gossipy chatter and name dropping).

New Year's, with all the awkwardness of unmet expectations, was, thankfully, just a day and a night, and soon over. Lili was relieved, but now an ocean of emptiness waited ahead.

She took up knitting. A long, A-shaped skirt, using a thin type of wool.

In school she had done quite poorly in crafts, whether knitting, sewing, stitching, or crocheting. She hated activities that required minute attention to detail, and crafts did just that. Her work was always hanging loose at one end, creased, stained from sweaty hands, or the little stitches were irregular and wiggly. She still got decent marks, which made her feel uneasy, because she found her work a mess.

But now knitting seemed to have found its perfect usefulness, at the right time. The endless repetitiveness of knitting stitch after stitch, row after row, did Lili good, as it slowly but tangibly built up towards a final outcome. She would need to focus on each stitch and row, counting and measuring to make sure the A-shape was emerging, symmetrical at both ends. More specifically, she had to keep adding stitches every other row, from a hundred and eighty to three hundred and forty and seven hundred and sixty-nine, keeping counting.

It was a task to sink herself into, time measured only by rows and stitches, and by the size of the slowly growing knit work.

Mother would cry out, “My goodness, it makes me sick just looking at it, so many stitches in one row, how can you do it?”

Lili would just shrug, her hands drawing the thread around her needles, unstoppable, impassive, relentless.

“How many stitches have you got now?”

“Nine hundred and seventy-two.”

Vlad would come and go each day, Mother would pop in to check on her, the sun would go down early afternoon and the electric light would be switched on, meal times would go by, sleep intervals too, and the skirt kept growing, taking shape, if very slowly. Vlad sometimes picked her up to go to his place, and she would take the knitting with her, at first timidly, wondering what the Bacis would think of her, but soon confident enough to carry the knitting and the needles in a plastic bag as a steady accessory wherever they went. She learnt how to watch videos while knitting at the same time, provided she made clear marks of how many stitches she needed to add, and when.

She saw *Flashdance* and got absorbed for a while in the story of the girl who fails at first, then succeeds in the end. But she kept knitting. Then there was *Back to the Future* where the escape into a different life resonated with her – so her knitting slowed down for a while, but then got frantic with the excitement of the idea. Michael Jackson was a challenge to watch while knitting, but it was good that it was just short clips. Queen’s *I Want to Break Free* made her put the knitting gear aside and dance along to it mentally. That song definitely hit a nerve.

The Bacis would enjoy having her over, watching their videos, because, as they say, the more the merrier, or, in the Bacis’ rhyming slang, one-two, fun and groove, three-four, show me more.

Mrs Doctor Baci would sometimes cast vaguely odd glances at Lili's knitting, which Lili could not exactly assign to curiosity, dislike, or amusement.

But it was all just another detail in the film she was watching like a fly on the wall, on the set where her life was unfolding.

There was surely life after knitting.

There came the long weeks of exams and assessments for university students. Dana was in over her head studying, panicking about requirements and the time needed to cram all the stuff in. Lili listened on the phone without any cue for a reply. She knew nothing of what it might feel like. What was clear was that Dana didn't have time, for the next five to six weeks, even for a chat on the phone.

Vlad would only come by for an hour or so in the evening, when he would sigh and yammer about the hard time he'd had that day reading, or about the eccentricities of the professor whose exam was coming up.

She had her knit-in-progress instead. Luckily, with no deadlines and no assessments attached. The slightly wiry, yet soft touch of the wool kept her senses alive, and the buttery white of the endless mesh of stitches flowing over her lap gave a palpable sense of achievement. She was in the middle of something. The days had a purpose.

There was a downside to knitting, built in precisely to its repetitiveness.

It allowed her thoughts to start wandering, and, left on their own, they wandered down alleys that were not always cheerful. The replay of the summer was the most toxic, and caused her to shake her head every now and then, as if shooing away a bothersome insect.

As long as her father had been in the labour camp, her inner predicament over admission grades, committees and appeals had been safely private. But since his passing, the thought that he might be getting wind of the whole matter from wherever he was now, gazing right into her mind, was giving Lili a hard time.

It was no longer just her terrible bad luck; now she found herself at times feeling ashamed telling herself that Yimmi Papa's clever girl had failed so miserably an exam that should have been a mere formality, precisely in the subject in which Yimmi Papa had been the expert.

Shame had been with her all along, facing the other people, the Bacis, Dana, her former school teachers, her neighbours, whoever she happened to bump into and was friendly enough to ask how she was doing.

But at some point, she had got over the shame of facing the others. Possibly at the point where Yimmi Papa had been deposed in a grave, a point at which the rest of the world had suddenly become a hushed non-entity, and the admission story, just thin air. About the same time, they had received the final negative answer from the Party Central, so she had had to tidy up her alienated home, and acknowledge that she was there to stay.

She had got herself comfortably numb, as a band was saying in a depressing song, and had disposed of mental calendars.

But if there was even a slim chance that Yimmi Papa might be figuring out, from where he was now, what had been going on – that was too much to handle. Lili would have to bear the imagined criticism, sadness, bitterness, or anger that Father might be looking on with, and she would have to face her own childhood image gone awry with failure. So here she was, getting into an emotional muddle, where knitting could only rescue her by helping her to suppress her feelings, and work another stitch.

A rational voice was spelling out a message in response: *Yimmi Papa would never blame it on you, but would be taking on the whole world on your account*; this wasn't making things easier, however.

It was enough to start picturing Father getting even

more reckless than he had been when alive, inadequate and self-damaging like a pathetic Quixote, holding a book in his arms, dressed in a Professor's robe, defying the statues and yelling insults for the sake of his daughter.

And picturing Lili herself, her own part to act? Love and gratitude that were due for his unstoppable sacrifice, overwhelmed, however, by shame and fear of the consequences, turning against him in anger, "What the hell are you doing, keep your damn principles under control and forget your nutty scientist's philosophy of ethics, freedom and cult of the individual, you pitiful, spiteful big mouth!"

She was hoping that there was no life after death, or if there was, that her father had other stuff to do up there, instead of paying attention here.

Mother's phrase, "It makes me sick to just look at it," horrified by the thick folds of her knitting, started to stick in Lili's mind after a while; by empathy, it seemed, she was starting to get a fleeting wave of nausea, too.

At first she put it down to the emotional muddle that was rocking her time and again, but if the knitting enabled her to move on past the muddle, the wool itself seemed to be doing something else to her. A smell, that wiry touch, maybe the buttery-milky colour, and so much of it all over the place, as if about to swallow her up. She tried putting the work down, standing up and leaving the room for a few minutes. A glass of water sometimes helped. She would resume, holding her breath the moment she picked up the work, to avoid any whiff reaching her nostrils. If she resumed her breathing just after that first moment, she was good to go.

Soon however, the slight nausea became regular, whenever she took up the work, or even just caught sight of it, lying in overflowing folds on the chair. The wool's milky colour seemed to press a button that instantly evoked its smell, and the sickness would bob up in her throat.

She took a break from knitting. A pity, though, as she was already through with the first half of the skirt. She had worked through the endless rows of two thousand and forty-nine stitches, and then neatly bound them off, one by one.

She told herself that now, with the first half over, lying folded in the plastic bag with the rest of the gear, the danger was that she might give it up, before bringing herself to start again from a hundred and eighty stitches. So she held her breath, bravely picked up the knitting needles and cast on stitches for the second half of the skirt. Once on, there was a pressure of continuity which would make sure she carried on and on and on again, stitching her way through the woolly loops.

The funny thing was that she was also experiencing the nausea, if briefly, at times when she was not knitting at all. Walking in the park with Vlad, or watching his video cassettes a dozenth time, or just lying in bed going to sleep. The wool was doing things to her, obviously.

Or maybe she was just getting sick of the sensible constitutionals with Vlad, watching the same videos, and waking up to the routine that she had set up in the past months.

Waking up to the cold house in particular, to the desolate bathroom with broken tiles and freezing pipes.

Waking up at all, as if it was no waking up, but just switching between levels of dreaminess.

The Bacis' family-cosiness was getting tiny chinks, too. Dr Baci was jovial as ever, but she was sensing a sort of falsehood, as if the surgeon's jokes and rhymes were a tape being replayed, while he was somewhere else, in a "will be back soon" way. Mrs Doctor Baci was more real, and her smiles were limited. Lili got the brief impression at times that she had something on her mind that she would have liked to say aloud, which she only withheld at the last second.

She noticed now that she and Vlad were spending time at his place more often when his parents were not there. She was vaguely relieved not to have to join in the convenient joviality, which used to be a way of removing herself to a safe place. Such self-removal was necessary twenty-four hours a day, but it had become exhausting.

No wonder, then, that her body was getting sick of it too, sending out a body's typical signals of saturation.

But the next thing that caught her attention and pulled her into the here and now was the realisation that her period was late, which had never happened before. At first she thought there was nothing wrong. But it was one week late now. The realisation stirred a wave of nausea distinct from the one she had been experiencing lately, more like panic in the bowels, and dizziness, as if standing on a cloud-high brink.

No, it can't be, please just don't let it be from that stupid night!

The night sometime mid-January, when Vlad's kisses had felt sticky and unpleasant, yes, almost nauseating, anticipating this sickness now. It was the first time that the thing had repelled and jerked her from snug indifference into vivid disgust. And now, the cherry on the cake (how nauseating!), precisely that night should have such lasting effects.

What she couldn't understand was that her period had been normal, later in January. It was now mid-February, and she had avoided intimacy with Vlad ever since, as if some underlying wave of nausea had gripped long before she had become aware of it.

"Vlad, we need to talk."

They're sitting on her bed, facing each other, legs crossed.

"Yes. Sure. I'm all ears."

She knows the straight words, but they make her feel

sick. So technical and dry. But there's no other way, she needs to hang in there, close her eyes, and get through it.

Just not too loud, in case there are still prying ears.

"My period is late."

It's out.

His eyes open wide in shock. "What? You sure? How can that be?" His whisper brushes along the border to screaming.

How could that be, other than from sleeping with each other like long-seasoned spouses?

"But it's been a while – I was actually kinda missing it – what a shit!" Vlad exclaims in panic.

Lili keeps quiet. Is he going to need emotional support? She feels no ability to provide it.

"Well, actually, I thought you're the medical student, and I should ask you how that can be—"

"Yeah, right, the immaculate conception should be out of the question, shouldn't it?" Vlad tries some humour, but the rictus across his face makes it look like sarcasm. Lili is aware she's going red and very, very hot.

"OK, it won't help analysing the causes, but what are we going to do?" she asks bluntly.

"Hell, I don't know!" Vlad grumbles, staring at the ground, his dark eyebrows knitted together. "Dad told me to stay away from such trouble, and if I ever mess up, it's my problem, I shouldn't even tell him!"

Great. Medical student, son of doctors, has no idea and no solutions for this fact of life. The virtuous surgeon doesn't want trouble with the Party, losing his job and going to jail for mediating an abortion for his son's girlfriend. Funny rhymes and cordial dinners are, after all, conditional.

"So your dad's out of the question. How about your mates? Would they know any remedy?" The oh, so many friends he has. The medicine guys should know. The fancy clique should have the connections.

"How am I supposed to even ask? What if one of them reports me?" Vlad looks at her almost imploringly.

Pathetic.

He stands up and strides back and forth. They avoid eye contact, each immersed in problem-solving, or self-pity.

"No, it's too risky, I can't ask anyone," Vlad bursts unexpectedly after a few minutes. "What about you, don't you know anyone you can trust and who might have an idea?"

Lili can't believe her ears. Should she ask Dana, or the other study-hard girls from high school? They'll definitely know what illegal pills can be taken to terminate unwanted pregnancy, or be able to direct her straight to a specialist, sure! Her vast circle of well-off, socially and politically privileged friends, kids of Party officials and the like, there will be someone, nonsense, any one of them will help!

Piece of cake.

Gabriel. Wait, hold on. Breathe in, deeply.

Gabriel? No way!

How would that be!

Gabriel would know. His dad, not a surgeon but a pilot (also privileged, and not willing to lose a job to go to jail), had told him, father-to-son, "If you ever get in trouble about a girl, my son, come to me, don't do any nonsense on your own, it's too risky!"

Gabriel would know, even without going to ask his father. Because Gabriel knows. And Gabriel can. He was always a guy you could trust to take care of things.

But she never went to bed with him, and she should now ask him about a remedy? So she put up all that fuss back then about not being ready to become a woman, and now she should go and ask for help, not being ready to become a mother? Worst of all, do it because her boyfriend won't?

She knows Gabriel will help. He still cares about her and will do her the favour of passing on a tip. Hopefully, he won't drop a sarcastic word, although he's so good at it.

Even without words, just one brief look in his eyes, for a split second, and she'd be done in, killed by the shared awareness of how miserable things have become.

When did it start?

"If you really can't ask anyone, then I guess I could only ask Gabriel, although I'd really, really hate to have to!"

"Gabriel! Oh, that's getting better and better, so now we're asking the ex for advice," Vlad counters.

"Feel free to pick someone else," Lili retorts coldly. What a loser. She had no idea what a wimp this guy was, after all. All of them, a bunch of fakes and wimps, with their family rhymes and have-it-all.

Her ex. When did she ever get so old as to fight over exes and pregnancy? What happened to grades, and the laws of physics – what happened to John and his Woman?

She'll ask Gabriel, and will bear the brunt of the awkward conversation. Bearing the brunt is what she's become expert at.

"I'm coming with you when you meet him," Vlad replies, as if threatening.

"Why, worried?"

"You bet, worried. You're my fiancée, forgotten? Do you think I'm gonna let you meet your ex to ask for advice on an abortion for my baby?"

His baby. Some traces of dignity.

Or just insecurity.

His fiancée. Did she ever consent?

Well, for all she cares, he might as well join her, all right. This way, she might actually be spared Gabriel's sarcasm. Vlad being on the scene will hopefully keep the conversation factual.

Gabriel the engineer – and the ex – can teach Vlad the medical student what to do about his girlfriend's condition.

Gabriel shows up with a faint smile in the corner of his mouth. Lili knows that smile. It's the kind of greeting as in "What have you been up to, pied puffin?" that he would sometimes tease her with. He keeps it wordless this time, however.

"Hi, Gabriel. Gabriel, Vlad, Vlad, Gabriel." Huh, that much is done.

Gabriel shakes hands with Vlad. He's behaving. No playing pranks the way she knows him, and as she suspects he's thinking all the while.

They're standing in University Square, the heart of the city, people thronging past them at a crowded bus stop.

"OK, so the thing is—" Lili starts off, but then wonders if she should let Vlad take over and handle it. Vlad, however, is looking sideways, his swarthy face and pallid complexion even greyer against the grey of the street and the passers-by, all immersed in the cold desolating early March. The colour videos on his colour TV are a memory of a different story.

She fetches a sigh and goes ahead. Nothing else helps.

"So, as I said on the phone, I – we – there's a problem, and I'm hoping you know something that can help."

Gabriel is gazing at her intently.

"You need a certain remedy," he says under his breath, but distinctly.

She opens her eyes wide. "How did you know?"

If there was someone listening in on the phone line when she called Gabriel, then the secret's out, and they can expect the Public Prosecutor to bust her any time.

"Of course I knew, you said on the phone you have a problem." Gabriel lets his old half-ironical smile show up on his thin lips for a moment. "I know what kind of problem it could be. So is that it, then? OK, I've got something for you, right here," and he carefully takes out a small envelope with something in it.

Vlad grabs it and this way dashes back into the picture.

"What is it?" he asks, professionally scrutinising the contents of the envelope. Now's his chance to prove himself.

Gabriel turns his head as if just then noticing him.

"It's called – Ergomet," he pronounces the name in a whisper. "They give it when you've had a spontaneous abortion, or after a controlled abortion—"

"—to help eliminate placenta retention and prevent infection," Vlad interrupts, nodding in recognition and approval of the medicine.

There are four vials in the envelope.

"Shhhh, whoa, no need to go public here," Gabriel pulls the reins short on Vlad's professional enthusiasm, casting cautious glances around.

"It's originally used for veterinary purposes – cows and such," Gabriel adds pointedly.

Good joke, thanks, Lili nods silently.

"OK, so how does she take it?" Vlad asks.

"You can swallow the content, but they say it's more effective as a shot," Gabriel explains.

"Injected where?" Vlad keeps questioning for professional accuracy.

"In the nose," Gabriel replies. There's a moment's confused silence, before he scoffs and lets the joke out. "A normal injection, where else?"

"So subcutaneous, I see. It could have also been intravenous," Vlad nods expertly.

"Yeah, sure," Gabriel says and turns back to her. "You take two or three the first day, and hot baths might give it an extra push, and then you should get some more vials, for a few days, a week at most. You'll need a prescription to get them, but I guess that shouldn't be a problem, should it," he says, dropping his voice, making it clear he's not meaning it as a question, but as a statement.

"Sure, of course, prescriptions are no problem," Vlad

hastens to reassure him. Gabriel ignores him. Lili, too.

"Do you know—" Lili starts, then hesitates. But the silence Gabriel is keeping is pushing her to go on. "—what it means if my belly has turned hard, it's not really growing yet, it's still early, but it's harder than usual."

"Whoa, whoa," Gabriel opens his eyes wider, "you're in deep shit, I'm afraid, Lili. It means you're past the eighth week, in which case you need to hurry. This thing here," and he gestures to the envelope now in Vlad's pocket, "is only good up to week ten, so if it doesn't work in the next week or so, you've got to get on to the next level, and I can't help any further."

"Eighth week, how can that be," Lili whispers. She recalls how intrigued she had been about the calendar. She trusts Gabriel to know what he's talking about, but she just needs to get some sort of explanation. "I only missed one period, now, in February," and she feels herself blushing as she says it. Mentioning her period to a guy, just like that, in the street, with the Ergomet for cows just acquired – all these technicalities, oh, she hates medicine!

"Pfff, Lili, really, you had no idea? Gosh!" Gabriel shakes his head and turns away, looking at the street, then back to her. "You can get your period even when you're pregnant, didn't you know that? No? You neither?" and he turns to Vlad.

Vlad stares back at Gabriel with vacant eyes, the rictus on his lips frozen.

"We get gynaecology in year four."

Gabriel sighs. "Oh, well."

"What, oh well, what is one supposed to do?" Lili protests.

"What is one supposed to do?" Gabriel echoes her protest, in a tone that threatens to become reproving. "Take care, that's what one's supposed to do."

"We did take care!" Lili retorts. Fighting furiously against the need to keep whispering is becoming frustrating.

"Oh, yes, how?" Gabriel dares her.

"We counted the days," Lili replies offhandedly, defying him.

"Counting the days, great," Gabriel echoes her again, ironically.

"What else can one do to take care, what do you expect?"

"Well, there are other ways to take care, yes, in case you didn't know, but I'm not here to lecture you on that. Next time you'd better read the instructions before use."

"Which instructions? How do you mean that?"

Gabriel stays silent, looking straight into her eyes.

"Come on, pied puffin," he lets their old pet name fall, "I don't want to be mean to you, forget it, OK? I'm just a bit worried, that's all."

She feels tears well up into her eyes, but won't let them come out.

"But what else were we supposed to do, Gabriel?"

Gabriel rolls his eyes, meaning he can't explain properly.

"Well, we're adults, aren't we? If we go to bed with someone, that is. And one simply needs to talk to good friends and ask cautiously around, and there's information under the table of course, just like Ergomet, under the table, you know, no prescription. There are magazines, there are people you know outside who can tell, who can send things —"

Outside! That's what he means, of course, if people are outside, outside of this country, where not even questions are allowed, let alone answers, and let alone decisions, if people are outside, in West Germany, or in the States, of course they know it all and can do it all! And Gabriel's father being a pilot, this week in Abu Dhabi, next week in Paris, of course he knows stuff and can get things even here, under the table, because he has the right connections, other people who are constantly outside, and trade in forbidden information, condoms, or who knows what!

But how was she supposed to know, nobody can expect that from her! She has no idea about pregnancy weeks, about what things like Ergomet might be needed for, what else there is to avoid pregnancy apart from the funny plastic things she has heard about, but never seen one or heard anyone claim they're using.

Sex she has discovered to be a rhythmic movement, but she had read about it in a tiny book called *Vita Sexualis* on her father's bookshelves, where a detailed, textbook description is provided. Well, it's obvious that with Vlad's advent in her life she has tried it out for herself, and it is indeed a rhythmic movement back and forth, back and forth. And a still somewhat disconcerting sensation when the male partner's crotch opens up to get on top of her.

But she never thought there would be a whole subject matter attached to it, too. Like, what alternatives there are to avoid consequences, and what the process is, once it gets started. At school, they'd only learnt the scientific terms, anything else was hearsay with a hand laid over the mouth in fear, shame or bashing gossip.

Gabriel knows all that, he's done his homework. Equipped for real life, even in the scarcity of this country. Good for him. Vlad is not equipped, because his father is afraid for his job, and he's not equipped also because his friends are not the kind of friends he'd ask if a criminal case were involved. And he's not equipped because although he's twenty-three, Lili is his first "real" girlfriend. Like a virgin, to quote Madonna.

Gabriel gazes at her intently, with a look which is unmistakably earnest as he whispers:

"Please do take care, pied puffin. This is no trifle. If this stuff doesn't work, go take the real solution, quick, but no amateurish fiddling, I'm begging you. This can be life and death and they'll let you bleed out if you get to the hospital and won't tell who helped you. And if you do tell, and they manage to patch you up again, you go to jail, do you get me?"

Lili's eyes are hooked on Gabriel's, listening as if mesmerised. This cannot be real.

"I know this is not the kind of story you would be in," Gabriel resumes after a moment, as if reading deep into her mind. There is not a shadow of reproach in his voice, although a voice in Lili's head is briefly, just briefly, allowing itself to laugh sarcastically: *This isn't you, right? That's what you get for going to bed with a faceless stranger who just happens to be popping in after you didn't do it with the one you were in love with – where the heck are you, anybody home?*

"And maybe you've been through a lot lately," Gabriel carries on, in an even deeper tone, "but you've just got to pull yourself together and take good care of your life."

Vlad is lively on the way back to Lili's place. He seems to have got a fresh wave of inspiration and optimism and feels empowered, a solution in an envelope in his pocket.

"Lili dear, everything's going to be just fine, I'm sure," he promises her.

Ergomet tastes horrible, she discovers when they get home. She won't wait until Vlad pilfers a syringe from his mom's kit. The yellowish liquid in the vial combines sweetness with a pungency that is typical of medicines, which turns her bowels inside out.

She dismisses Vlad by giving him a mission, to get a syringe, because she needs to be alone. His helplessness became so obvious to her at the University Square. She needs to do some thinking, and counting.

The counting inevitably brings her back to that last night of sex with Vlad that repelled her, sometime in mid-January.

Why didn't she just stay away from having sex, if she didn't actually want it? That – that is surely a legitimate question, but one without an answer. No idea why she did it. She had felt nothing, so opposition couldn't well up in her either. One thing had led to another, for instance parents being away, and Vlad's tenderness building up, so what was there for her to do?

To give a No to an unfolding process, you need a reason. In Vlad's unfolding prelude she had felt nothing but what the sensors of her nervous system picked up: a taste in her mouth, a touch on her skin, a pressure on her chest, a coming and going between her legs. Maybe, yes, she acknowledges now, a story of family harmony enveloping the act itself.

And if Ergomet only helps for another week or so – what is the next option?

There is no next option she can think of. Gabriel urged her to take good care of herself, but her map is blank.

People to talk to? No chance.

Mother – she must never even suspect what is going on; her love for Lili must not be burdened by such an ugly story. Lili must keep up the good, little innocent girl act.

She had already added a burden to Mother's ordeal, with the admission and the appeals. Not just the emotional mix of pain, anger, helplessness, or the amount of strength invested in rebelling; but also the financial straits. As a result of failing admission and following Father's passing, they had lost any entitlement to welfare support for Lili, which would be granted as long as she was under twenty-five and on a study programme. Otherwise, Father State assumed that Lili's place was in a factory earning her own bread and margarine.

Then who? Dana? Out of the question. Even just to share the secret with, to let it all out: Lili is past the need to share. This is not the usual teenage yammer – hasn't been ever since last summer. But letting this secret out would only feel as if she were putting that knot in her belly out in the world, with all the risks involved in it being seen. Lili can't go about shocking the people in her life with news that she herself can barely comprehend.

So now, what is there for her to do? Pull herself

together, as Gabriel had said. Meaning what? She can only hope that the Ergomet will work, and if not, that Vlad will somehow sort it out. She must hang in there.

Vlad gets back the next morning with a syringe kit. He takes off his coat and places the plastic bag on her desk with quick, purposeful movements like a doctor on a patient visit. There. Now she's being taken care of. He gives her the shot almost dexterously, and she's thankful for not having to swallow that thing again. There is one more vial, which he says he'll give her later today, instead of tomorrow, to push for a stronger effect.

In the course of the day, she starts feeling faint period pains, which she only now realises are what is medically called "contractions". So this is what giving birth will be like, she thinks, when she's grown up many years from now, just fifty times stronger?

Her nausea takes on a new tone: a sweetish phlegm in her throat tasting faintly like Ergomet. By the same reflex of the past weeks, she now can't bear to have the knitting with the creamy white in sight. She shoves it back into its bag, crumples the bag to stop any smell coming out and tucks it deep into her wardrobe, on the bottom shelf. Out of sight, out of smell, out of mind, hopefully.

She's taking a hot bath while Mother's not home, and she minds every spasm in her arteries, the heat building up in her body, her thoughts with the Ergomet flowing down the blood vessels, causing some unrest somewhere in her womb, and she's waiting and waiting, hopeful, laying a swath of cotton wool in her panties, almost feeling moisture coming out. She goes to bed letting her body and Ergomet do their joint work.

She asks Vlad what Gabriel might have meant about not fiddling with it amateurishly. Vlad vaguely explains something about inserting things "inside" and "working them" to get "that thing out" – but she feels a convulsive shudder and can't follow up to find out more. She knows, or thinks she does, that it's forbidden by law, but nobody talks about what exactly it is that's forbidden.

CHAPTER FIVE

The bottom line is that once pregnant, you have to have the baby, and Father State will take care of you, even without the biological father, so that you can take care of the baby.

Another shudder.

Lili had always been an orderly girl: never troubling neighbours by breaking windows with a ball, never getting into conflicts, mingling with the wrong kids, and least of all, displaying poor conduct in school. She had always toed a line that had never needed to be explicitly drawn for her; she had been the good girl, good Yimmi Papa's girl, good teachers' girl, good friends' parents' girl, the good girl of the neighbourhood, doing her homework without supervision, getting good marks without coercion.

An all-time good girl – now this: messing around with a boy, and coming home with a big belly, like the cases that were whispered and gossiped about, when the lass hadn't been a good girl, but messed with no-no things. Everyone knows that boys always have this on their minds. All they ever want is to "stick their willy into your slit," as an old woman in the neighbourhood revealed to Lili years ago, tapping her between the legs and then raising her pointer finger, for the lesson to be remembered more vividly. Orderly girls have to watch out and not let themselves get fooled.

No wonder she's in deep trouble now, having to sneak under the radar and sink deeper and deeper into promiscuity. A nauseating wave of shame causes her bowels to wince (the same bowels that are hugging that growth, caught in the roll-out of a snowball process that is threatening to force itself into sight and demand acknowledgement).

All this motherhood is alienating. She has a mother to look after, to look up to; what's this thing growing inside of her, thrusting her into being a mother herself?

She knows there is a life after this. If not Vlad, the forever giver, the Father State will provide, in its own way. The legitimate square metres of living space; a nursery place for the baby after the three months of maternity leave; priority getting loans through the employee scheme, along with many other possible priorities, whenever it might be helpful to mention she's a mother: a handshake, "Congratulations, Lili Danes, for doing your duty to the motherland," alongside whispers she'd got pregnant right after leaving school.

A list of entitlements she never asked for. A heroine she abhors.

Vlad and the Bacis don't even feature in that film. A voice in her head sometimes attempts to point out, rationally, that she and Vlad could simply get married, as the talk has been they will anyway for a while. She would officially belong in that second home, no need to worry about what Father State has to offer, about whispers of promiscuity. And she would catch up on university and whatever else later. Vlad and the Bacis are the best able to take care of her and make things right.

But she dismisses that scenario before it can fully take shape in her mind. All this taking care that love allegedly is all about; Vlad would forever honey her, and she would fondly mother him in return. It makes her sick to think of it, hauling up the pregnancy nausea from her guts.

It might be its relentless growing and growing, into a different life than what she has chosen for herself.

Or at least thought she had.

What of all this did she choose? The line on the lists, her father's disappearance? Vlad's care-taking? Well, actually, she did choose this. Or no, not the care-taking, but love. A promise of love.

And what is she going to choose when this belly

problem is sorted out?

The summer will be coming, inevitably, and it will again be a matter of choice; is she going to sit for university admission the second time? And if yes, physics again, or just anything that will get her in, since not much matters in the wake of this devastating year?

Or is she going to just learn a craft, with haircutting only one of the many choices when choices don't really matter? Will she waive any demands from life, at least for the next thirty years?

Until next summer, she is caught in the incomprehensible claws of Father-State and Mother-Land. What reason is so strong for the two to force pregnancies to their completion? All she knows is that they are both quartered on some battle front of madness.

Lili remembers the stages from Motherland Scout to Young Communist, moving on to the ranks of adulthood. In this suspended year of her life, she's no longer a Young Communist, because she's no longer in school, and she's not a Communist Student either. She's too young and unattached to any structure to be a Party Member. She's off the grid, but still living within it, for all she can tell, hearing the patriotic songs on the radio, the TV news on record crops and exceeding targets in the industrial units. A general mobilisation is buzzing day and night, a sense of urgency as if preceding a war, blended with an enthusiasm next to beatitude about the progress made towards victory.

Where are they heading, exactly, and what's the feverish race all about? If only that was clearer. Because that seems to be the explanation as to why all pregnancies must be brought to fruition. The motherland needs all babies. The motherland needs all women to do their birth-giving duty. And Father State sees that you toe the line. Takes care of you, but locks you up and removes your parents if you don't.

So it's her turn now to become the compliant soldier? Did it take all this year to get her down on her knees and wrench from her a disavowal of her absurd, self-centred fantasies? *This isn't me, this isn't me*, a voice switches between wailing and yelling inside her, but who is Lili Danes?

What was it again: Raskolnikov walking through disaster, carrying his own meaning?

One day in early April, when Mother asks her to sit down, with a weary smile, she freezes. How did she find out?

"Honey," Mother starts in what sounds like a carefully considered tone, and sighs, as if she's going to address delicate matters. Lili's eyes are glued to Mother's face in suspended panic. "Look, I know that this is going to be a bit unpleasant," Mother goes on with compassionate eyes.

Lili's bowels are about to rebel and shoot up their nausea again, pregnancy or not.

"But I do want to tell you that I'm by your side, as you know so well. I just feel I need to tell you that, you know, well, it's already April—"

Is Mother counting the weeks and the months, too?

"—and, you know, I talked to your tutors the other day, and they'd be happy to start classes with you again, especially as they're so sure there's not much work to do, you having done all this so well, last year—"

What's she talking about? Tutors, classes, work?

"I'm sorry, look, Lili, I know you might ask why I've been active behind your back, but I just wanted to keep you from another disappointment in case you wanted to resume studying but the tutors weren't available, so I thought I'd ask them first. It's all about a bit of revision and some basic training to get back in shape, as I said, it's just three months away, the exam—"

The exam?

Mother can't be worrying about admission!

Lili can start breathing again. The world is safe. The snowball is still rolling, but this is solely something between herself and the snowball to be sorted out.

"All right, I'll do it, Mom, no worries," she says nonchalantly.

"I know it's been such a long way, honey, all this year, well, actually only seven or eight months, that is, but you have so little left to go, you'll be fine, you'll see," Mother bends forward and pats her on the knees. "You and I," and Mother winks at her knowingly, "we're both brave marathon runners, remember?"

Lili smiles as if remembering, but she's confused. Remember? Marathon runners?

"Oh, come, honey, you don't remember?" Mother opens her blue eyes wide, with a sunny smile on her face. "Well, yes, actually it may be that I was only telling the story to your father," Mother realises.

She gives a fresh laugh, in the way of an introduction to the story she's obviously about to tell, and stands up to make herself some coffee. Lili wishes she'd get straight to the point and leave the theatrical tricks aside, now that she's been made curious to hear a story.

"So, come on, what marathon?"

Mother laughs again in response.

"That is a hell of a story, my dear," Mother emphasises the words and looks at her over her shoulder, while she's placing the coffee pot on the bluish flame of the oven. "I can't believe you never knew it, because that tells a lot about your own mother."

Mother stays focused on the coffee operations, as if preparing the act. Lili is getting fidgety. How long until she finally hears what it's all about?

"It was on our tour in France," Mother finally begins, as soon as the coffee has swollen and she has taken down the pot and placed it in the sink to cool down. "Must have been '79."

Mother takes a mug and the pot, covered, to the table and sits down again. Now.

"We had a free morning, with a rehearsal at five pm, followed by a performance, in a village called Villepreux. I said I'd like to go and see Versailles before, as it was on the way there, and everyone, when they heard, said yes, me too, me too! So we talked to the driver and agreed to start in the morning and drop us in Versailles. So we all get on the bus, you remember our old Setra, right, of course you do, the good old Setra that took us all across Europe, through all those wonderful places..."

Mother's voice trails off in nostalgia. Lili keeps quiet, letting Mother's emotion fill the room. Mother's tours meant lots of chocolate, mesmerising soap flavours, boots or overcoats that yelled out made in the West, and hours of story-telling in Father's tiny study.

"Well, so, we all get on the bus early morning from our hotel and head on to Versailles. Our guarding angel is with us, of course, he can't let us fool around as we please, and besides, he's also keen on Versailles, or whatever it is that can be got while we're touring the infamous decadent Occident."

"Your guardian angel?" Lili interrupts shyly.

Mother laughs. Lili is not sure if she's really amused, or if the laughter is a disguise for anything between anger, disgust, revolt, helplessness or the like.

"Yes, dear, our guardian angel, Ilarion Walter, our Party Secretary at the theatre."

"Oh, yes, I keep hearing this name, is he a good actor?"

"He's not an actor." Mother stops significantly.

Lili keeps quiet because she's not sure she's getting it.

"He's our Party Secretary," Mother explains with an allusive smile. "He is there to look after us, lest we get naughty."

"But what does he do the whole time? If he's not an actor, fine, you're not an actress either, but you organise things there, their performances, the rehearsals, it's clear what you do," Lili protests.

"He doesn't do anything, in that sense of the word, Lili,

he's the Party's consignee in our economic unit, and he does – well, no idea, writes reports, collects information, I don't even want to know – but in any case, he's always there, when we have meetings, when we go on tour, when we rehearse, he must be everywhere and know everything, and so he was on our bus heading to Versailles that day, too.

"When we get to Versailles, it must have been about ten, I stand up to get off the bus, and then all of a sudden nobody really 'feels like it really', you know: lazy, not wanting the strain of walking for hours around a big place, all in a foreign language, whatever, all of a sudden it looks like I'm the only one getting off here." Mother pours herself the coffee. "But then I realise, hey, I'm the only one, how am I going to get to Villepreux if you're all leaving now, obviously, on the Setra? To which Ilarion Walter replies a bit peevishly, 'Well, there are trains and buses, you'll be fine,' and then right away he turns to the driver and tells him 'OK, let's go!' So he literally presses me to get off, and I see the bus door closing and off they go.

"I say to myself, fine, let me enjoy the morning in this place, and make the most of it. I spent about four hours in Versailles, which was fantastic, Lili, unimaginable, really, for us, coming from our little country even more so... But my feet were killing me at about two p.m. when I get to the train station in Trianon. I still had three hours to go, so I wasn't worried. It had been such a lovely half-day, what could go wrong? Now it was time for work.

"So here I am in Trianon, checking trains and buses, and it becomes clear that all of them only run from five p.m., or early morning." Mother pauses, and gazes at Lili with significance, eyebrows raised.

"Oh, shit," Lili whispers.

"Oh, yes, Lili, oh, shit... now you must know I've never been on good terms with Ilarion Walter, back in the old days even less. You know me, I can keep my mouth shut and be prudent, but that guy was hysterical and often totally out of line. So we were mostly civil to each other, but it was clear to him that I wasn't to be fooled, especially in the party committee meetings."

"You?" Lili opens her eyes wide. Mother was the one who had always reproved Father for being reckless and saying too much of what he thought.

"Well, yes, me," Mother smiles, almost flattered. "Right, I never actually said anything of what I really think, but I didn't clap hands either, which in itself is a message that goes out there.

"So the moment I'm standing in Trianon finding no means to get to Villepreux, I realise that Ilarion Walter must have wanted me to get into deep shit, maybe even fail to turn up in Villepreux, which of course would have meant that I'd be banned from touring the West next time, what, forever! Because there's always traps and tricks to make you become undesirable; they can't wait to be able to tell you that you can no longer travel in the West, because you messed things up, because of yourself, that is, not because of the Party's policy.

"I check a tourist map displayed there, and estimate that it's about twenty kilometres to Villepreux. I check my watch: it's two fifteen. I just have to be there in two and a half hours. My only chance is to walk all the way."

"Walk?" Lili gasps.

"What else?" Mother shrugs. "I take the road, and start off."

"But were there no cars that you could have stopped to take you at least part of the way?" Lili asks.

"Hitchhiking? In the West? Huh," Mother gives a sarcastic scoff. "You're joking. That would have been a crystal clear reason to be banned from tours in the West! Don't you realise, honey, getting into a car with a Westerner! Who would have been able to know what we'd talked about, whether we had made some secret arrangement, some high treason, betraying our little country in order to stay there? There are two things a mortal can do in our socialist country, both having to do with movement: you can *run away*, you know what that means," and Mother pauses with significance, "or you can choose *to stay*, when you are travelling for work, you know. Rock bands, or athletes, or others who are fortunate enough, like me, to get through the wall of the Eastern Pact and land on the other side, will be tempted to stay."

Lili nods. Yes, she's heard the infamous, fearful words. In school they had studied, in early years, patriotic poems and stories, and one of the epic poems told of a hero in a World War I battle, whose words were now carved in a stone monument: *No crossing here.* The hero had defended the Romanian army's position at the cost of her life. But later in school, on the school corridors during breaks, she had heard a joke whispered around: the monument's plaque had been replaced and it now said: *No crossing here. Try the Danube!*

Apparently they swim across to the Serbs – and then get lost to the West.

Mother takes a deep sip of her coffee, with a faint gurgle, before raising her eyes again to Lili and resuming the story.

"So I just started off, in big strides, you can imagine. What was maybe most terrifying for me at that time was the thought that I didn't know the way and I might run even later. Cars passed by and I could see the drivers' long necks looking at me in the rear mirrors, most likely wondering who this crazy woman was, and what she was doing on a deserted country road.

"I just strode on and on, getting into a sort of automatic pace, 'Just stick to the pace,' I told myself like a captain ordering their squad, 'stick to the pace no matter what, forget about knives in the chest, forget about strain in the thighs and pain in the calves.' My sandals were flapping loosely against my soles and round my ankles, but that was the least significant fact in the whole world, except they were putting extra strain on my legs.

"At one junction, it must have been at least three quarters of an hour into the marathon, I came across an elderly lady who was coming out of a graveyard. She looked at me startled, and I opened my mouth and gasping, I asked if she knew how far Villepreux was. Her eyes almost bulged when she heard that, and she said something like at least twenty kilometres, which made me panic. I must have taken a wrong turn somewhere, I thought. It was only later, when I was telling the story to your father, that he said I must have heard twenty instead of twelve.

Anyway, I carried on with my marathon, panting in even more panic, but I could sense the limit that I had reached pushing my body. Everything was hurting, but I just stubbornly shut the pain off in my mind, and only looked straight ahead, down the road, hectically searching for road signs, never minding my inside, just the outside. Getting to Villepreux was all that occupied my mind.

"I did find a road sign after some time, pointing to Villepreux on a footpath winding away off the road, but not saying how far. I saw the road sign, and rushing past it I checked my watch: it was five past four. Just about forty minutes to go, but I had no idea how far I was, how long it would still take me. I decided – although that was hardly decision making, as there was no thinking going on in my head – but I just took the footpath without deliberating. I assumed it would be shorter than the regular road.

"What I didn't know was that it would take me through bushes, where I suddenly got chills down my spine not knowing if I was safe, and not knowing if it really was the right way. Losing the path here, what with bushes and grass and maybe scarce signs, would be the last thing I needed. I realised I was going uphill, because my calves were contracting even more, and my breath turned into a chaotic gasp. With every bend in the path I kept hoping the view would open suddenly, and the bushes would clear away, and I'd see the village in the valley at my feet.

"This did happen, yes, after all, after a time that felt like ages. I can no longer remember anything but the frantic rush, as if I'd been a robot, as if I'd been running on autopilot, just go-go-go, keep moving your feet and drop the rest, drop the thoughts about fears, worries, drop the counting, drop the pain, drop the landscape, drop the sunshine, drop France, drop who you are, drop everything, stay away from it all, just so you can cope with this, and afterwards you can get back.

"So I did go round a bend and all of a sudden the view opened and I could see a village down there and my heart pounced with the unbearable hope that it just had to be Villepreux. I nearly stumbled downhill and took the first asphalt street, following the signs to the centre. That's where their cultural centre had to be, where we were rehearsing and performing later that evening. That's where I had to be on time, because that was my job; the technical director must be there to ensure that everyone's on time and all preparations are made for things to run smoothly, so I couldn't possibly be late, not even just spot on the minute! I had to be there at least fifteen minutes early.

"I checked my watch and it was twenty to five, so I'd been jogging for two and a half hours, no idea how many kilometres, it might have been ten or it might have been fifty for all I knew, for what my body felt. I spotted our Setra from the distance, and thanked goodness for it. I went up that street and there they all were, standing in front of the building, smoking, talking in subdued voices, and when Ilarion Walter saw me, his jaw dropped and his face went yellow, and then I knew he had done it on purpose. He'd wanted me to arrive late or not to show up at all, but here I was, I must have looked purple, the set director chucked her cigarette away and dashed over to me and grabbed my elbows. That's when I felt I'd go weak, you know; all of a sudden, the tension was gone, you know that feeling, don't you, you can allow yourself to fall, to feel, and then you do fall, you collapse, now it was okay to collapse.

"I made it to the bathroom, and she splashed my face with cold water and I started crying hysterically, no tears, just sobs, almost like not getting air into my lungs. She fetched me some coffee and everyone was looking on appalled."

"But they must have been aware," Lili speculates. "That was why they suddenly didn't want to visit Versailles, so you were left alone."

Mother stops short and looks at Lili dumbstruck. Then she waves the hypothesis away with a shake of her head. It would be too much to suspect all of them in one story.

"Whatever, it doesn't matter now. It's just an old story. But since then, Ilarion Walter often calls me Mrs Villepreux, or the Marathonist. I guess it taught him a lesson, too. He calls me that with something like respect: who would mess with me after such a thing, ha ha," Mother laughs theatrically.

Lili looks down at the floor. That is who her Mother is. The warrior, the fighter, the woman who never gives in. Lili must get her act together and pull everything through. Forget the pains, and worries, and fears, forget the grey daily routine, ignore the strain, and the anger, and the disgust, get away from it all – this is the secret of being strong, this is what she has to do if she wants to master it and come out the other end, delivered.

Weeks passed by, unperturbed by Ergomet. If there was one thing Lili was relieved about, it was that she didn't have to lay eyes on the disgusting yellowy potion again. Vlad was now in charge, whatever that meant. There just had to be something. Something to do to terminate this pull into a different, alien reality.

In the meantime, she was allowed to lie with her eyes stuck to the ceiling, floating somewhere in a dazed space of her own, because she had to be brave and hang in tight. Now and then, she was back keeping track of the time, which instantly caused a flush of panic: another week gone by, the twelfth, the thirteenth, the fourteenth.

This time last year she had counted the weeks towards the end of school.

Her father's arrest, the final months of the final school year, the admission, the appeals and the back-and-forth with the Party Central gatekeepers, her father's funeral, even the recent dilemma about what she might have to wear in Geneva for New Year's – she was now dislocated from all of that. Strangely, it felt familiar, as if she had long been living in dislocation.

Maybe the growth inside her body was a disturbing wrench that she had to hold out and overcome, by holding onto the numbness. Panic was replaced by a renewed immersion into emptiness.

And her belly was swelling all this time, a bit visible now, when she was taking a shower. She had always been quick in the shower, because of the cold bathroom; now there was an added rush, because of the unmediated exposure to her body. She had to get through with it as fast as possible, close her eyes, lock herself away and push through.

Whatever you do, don't realise what is happening, or you'll go nuts, and that won't be of any help. Look away, hide your belly, and wait for the delivery. Vlad had better know what he's doing.

It was late April and, apart from the trees blooming, there was nothing new. Lili had started her long tram and metro journeys across the city to her tutoring sessions. Unlike the year before, she now almost enjoyed it, having no other structure in her daily routine. She would leave home earlier on purpose, and briefly deliberate which route to take that day; she would often take the long way to the teacher's place.

She avoided changing if she could, although the trip took longer detours in such cases; but on the upside, it was easier to find a seat, and then she'd lose herself in blankness, staring out the window or into the emptiness, not caring about the time.

Time was immaterial. At least in this life. The life of studying and tutoring, the life of the old Lili.

In the other life, time was threatening enough.

Her waist had started getting fuller, although it was still fairly slim, considering the months. She must be just into the fourth month now. Her abdomen was the shape of a small melon. Round, and hard.

On the upside, the nausea was gone. She had resumed knitting, and was doing it even more feverishly than before, with a renewed sense of purpose, which was finishing the skirt in order to wear it. Soon she would be proud of her work.

Vlad's face had grown swarthier and skinnier than usual, and a certain gloom hovered between them when they met. They met less often now. He did call every day, but he only came over to her place every other day or so. Now she also had to study, it went. Dates and going out? No mood for that. Lili was thankful, as it meant that she could handle her numbness on her own, without being exposed to the tension of their thoughts circling around the same topic.

During one of her classes, she starts feeling the need to pee, but the teacher keeps talking and talking. She finds it impossible to interrupt her only to ask to use the toilet. *Come on, you'll be fine and pee when the lesson's over*, she tells herself. She's good at holding it in. But the sting in her bladder grows louder and louder, and becomes a pressuring net, clasping her belly and threatening to burst. The teacher keeps talking, while she needs to take notes, but finds it excruciating to focus on the content and steer her attention off her belly, practising the well-learnt lesson of ignoring a pain in order to survive it.

The pressure is getting impossible to ignore, it almost feels like it's screaming in her face, *GET UP AND USE THE DAMN TOILET*, but how can she interrupt the teacher's elaborate explanations of the laws of thermodynamics, only to ask to pee?

She checks her watch secretly, but to her despair,

every time she does so, only a few minutes have elapsed. The session draws to an end, but the teacher goes further on her rant, as Lili knows she often does. She's being kind and generous, the old lady, by not being strict about keeping time; but today, she wishes the teacher would stop, and kick her out. There are occasional stabs now in her womb and at times, a wave of cold sweat like panic washes over her body, at the imminence of no longer being able to hold her bladder.

The teacher takes a momentary pause, contemplating the tree blossom outside, with a dreamy smile on her face. Lili seizes the chance and, painfully blushing, she asks with a tremor in her voice:

"Excuse me, could I possibly use the loo?" Like a primary school kid. All about the body functions, what about using the brain, Lili?

"Sure you can, Lili, go ahead," the teacher smiles at her.

Was it that easy?

Lili almost stumbles along the short corridor to the bathroom, squeezing her thighs desperately, now that she has to move her legs. She wrangles her stockings and underwear down and crashes onto the stool, staring in the void. The last fraction of a second before the warm liquid gushes out, releasing her belly.

God it's such a relief.

Did that painful pressure have anything to do with the occupant of her abdomen, she wonders? (Yes, of course, Vlad confirms the next time they meet.)

On her way back home, she gets on the tram, ready for the first half-hour leg of her journey, and clasps a handle, standing near a young man who is seated. The young man raises his eyes to her, and immediately springs off and gives his seat up to her.

Her first impulse is to thank him but reassure him she's fine. She's not old or sick.

But then the rush of the young man's gesture strikes her full in the face.

She's wearing a bell-shaped dress, which she thought would conceal the little melon she's carrying, but apparently, because of its shape, the dress is doing just the opposite. She looks like any woman wearing a bell-shaped dress: pregnant.

She makes no protest, but sits down into a black hole.

Getting off the tram, she buttons up her jacket and sticks her hands deep in the pockets to mask her waist better. With her head bent, she rushes through the rest of the journey home, and scurries past Mother straight to her room so as to get changed quickly. And never catch sight of it again.

CHAPTER SIX

So this is where it has come to. The clarity strikes spot on.

She's a pregnant woman.

No more mitigating that fact. A man has given his seat to her on the tram. The truth is out there and she must acknowledge it in here, too.

She's almost half way through the pregnancy and soon she'll need special clothes.

Shudder.

But shudders are not enough. She needs something that creates an outcome. A tangible one. At least as tangible as the melon she carries. Quick.

She has allowed herself to slip into abandonment. She has taken that idleness for a refuge; now she sees that the idleness hasn't been idle, but worked against her like clockwork.

She has relied on shadows outside – Vlad – to deliver her from the growth inside her. And inside herself, she has defected to a faraway country, leaving a will be right back sign behind her, without any commitment.

But the melon kept growing nonetheless, a baggage testifying to the natural course of things, this side of her defection. A baggage revealing the fine line between true choices and the why-not non-choices, with their boomerang consequences.

What now? A blank map.

There are no blank maps. It just takes a lens that's powerful enough to reveal the tiniest dots. There's always something there. Physics knows that. Never absolute void.

She's been through the list: Dana – blank.

Mother's out of the question.

Dana—?

—?

—Val Nestor?

Insane.

Still.

Nestor's earnest advice sessions.

His unfrozen language.

His switching on the radio for privacy.

Nestor's caring. Caring enough to get angry and hurtful to her.

Nestor hopefully won't judge her too harshly.

Although he was quite judgmental and preachy about her not carrying her mountain.

(Now she's carrying something else.

Say it!

A pregnancy.)

But then, he'd also ask about her love life. Crossing teacher borders nonchalantly.

Oh, the hell that might be unleashed! The thrashing and kicking.

But he would care enough to tell her what's what.

And there's no time or space left now to worry about extra pain: she must go through it regardless. Yes, it'll hurt. But maybe it'll open up a path, too.

Vlad. His gloom. His fading out of her daily routine. A shadow. Too late to wait for him to come true.

It's past midnight.

Tomorrow she's going to school to find Nestor.

She wonders again, for the tenth time, how Mother doesn't seem to have noticed anything. She meets Lili's eyes with the same tenderness Lili takes as a sign of blissful ignorance.

Mother carries on, of course, hovering about the house, in the aloofness which she opposes to life's adversities, whether it's the loss of her husband, or the task of making ends meet and managing the household. Making a fire and tending to the pitiful gas stove which keeps getting clogged, trimming the bushes in the garden and carrying the mounds of twigs out in the street and setting them on fire, tidying up the cellar and dragging fifty-kilo containers for wine making, now useless and long unused – all of which are tasks that the Professor would have done with his strong arms and good understanding of physical laws.

And then, the rest of the routine tasks, such as queuing for milk or butter, not to mention chicken offcuts for soup, or rare delicacies like bananas or coffee. All of this, on half the money that used to come in.

Lili knows that Mother is on a marathon day in, day out, no Villepreux behind a hill, but an aimless, perpetual strain, which is probably preventing her from seeing Lili's bulge at the waist, or even conceive of the possibility.

Father, thankfully, isn't around. He would have seen it. Father did not remove himself. That was actually his problem: he was incapable of handling pain and strain, and kept shaking everyone into acknowledgement.

Lili remembers a circus act that had been on TV quite a few times. A Chinese performer placed a plate on top of a tall, elastic steely rod, and flipped the plate into spinning. The secret was, of course, the right impulse at the right speed given to the rod, to rotate the plate, and then the plate's weight would keep the spinning going. He'd place one plate on one rod, then go to the next rod and place a plate on it, too, then hurry back to the first to refresh the rod's vibration, and then the third, the fourth, and so on. At the peak of the act, there would be at least ten rods spinning plates, and the guy would dash nimbly from one to another, giving the rod a renewed impulse if the spinning threatened to die down. The aim was not to let any plate drop on the floor.

It seems to Lili now that she's doing the same. And Mother, too. Dashing from one rod to another to keep it going, to keep the plates on top, no dropping on the floor, no shards, no letting down, no stopping, because stopping would mean breaking down, while the perpetual movement ensures survival.

Exams, household, grief, worry, unwanted snowballs – to keep them going, they have to stay safely away from breakdown.

It was only Father that had not mastered that. He had allowed all his plates to drop on the floor, one after another. He wasn't good at handling problems, by any common standard. In the Chinese performer's place, he would have stopped the act, engaged with the public, questioned the reasons and evaluated the set, crying out "fake," or "absurd," instead of running the show.

He hadn't found a place to get away to, the will-be-back-soon way that everyone else had mastered; the place that enabled them to weather off whatever challenge, and hang in there. He had been trapped in the perception of the present moment.

Nestor asked her to meet on the fairground in their park. He would be there with his wife and baby daughter, and would leave the two together to talk to Lili.

He's meeting her with a grim face. Then, just before hugging her, he puts on his naughty grin.

She has primed herself for his thrashing and kicking, for shock and reproof, but she'll close her eyes and hang in there until the storm is gone. There's no getting back now.

"So here we are again, old faces, long time, huh?"

She nods with a tight-lipped smile. It's a bit like a step back to faces of the past, instead of having moved on with her life.

"How are you, Lili?"

"Good."

"Good," he echoes ironically. "That's why we're here, right? Because you're good."

They start walking aimlessly, just to do something with themselves until the real conversation topic reveals itself.

"We've lost touch with you, Lili."

"We?"

"Dana. And myself. But of course, I didn't exactly expect you to call on a former teacher just to chat about life. But Dana did, and she's been a bit worried about you."

"Worried? She's – busy! Busy going to classes, busy cramming for exams, busy going skiing with her fancy new friend, the granddaughter of—"

"I know whose granddaughter she is. Yes, she's busy, but maybe you wouldn't notice how busy she is if you were going to classes, too."

"Yes, well, it wasn't my choice."

"No, of course not. That was the most stupid thing to happen. Still can't really wrap my head around it. But I mean, maybe she's not as busy as you think. Maybe it just feels that way to you. And maybe in fact she's still out there, thinking of you, and would be happy to see you."

"Sure. Well, she might have made it clearer to me. I never got the message."

"Right, well, the two of you must sort it out by yourselves, I'm not saying anything more about it."

That's new: Nestor stepping back behind the line.

"But I wonder why you think it matters whose granddaughter Dana's friend is. You surely don't suspect that's the reason Dana likes her?"

"I don't care why Dana likes her."

"If you didn't, you wouldn't mention it."

"Well, maybe I do, a bit. But does it make any difference?"

"Have you told Dana what bothers you?"

"I thought you'd leave this for the two of us to sort out."

"Yes. But you don't seem to be interested in sorting it out. You prefer to lock yourself in your bubble together with your sulk."

Oh, no, here he goes again with his preposterous reproaches.

"Lock myself away? With my sulk? What am I supposed to do? I just try to carry on with my life the only way I can find, one day at a time. What else is there to do? Thrashing and kicking around so the world goes back to suiting me?" The gravel crunches under their feet. "It never suited me in the first place," she adds in a low voice.

"Nothing wrong about thrashing and kicking, Lili, you know?"

"Sure, for people like you, who can afford it."

"What makes you think I can afford it, but you can't?"

"You're a teacher. That gives you an advantage."

Nestor scoffs.

"And who else can afford it, then, in your world?"

She shrugs.

"Well – anyone who has a say, I suppose. Otherwise, what's the point of making a fuss?"

Father had a say as a family head, but he deluded himself he had any say against the whole world.

"So, if I'm following your reasoning, if you don't have a say, you don't make a fuss. Which raises two questions: what do you mean by fuss, and what is it you don't have a say in, Lili, right now?"

"What?" That's getting too messed up and beside the

whole point of them being there.

Although, she has felt for so long she has lost any say in what comes and goes in her young life.

"Okay. To make it short, you do have a say in whatever doesn't suit you. My goodness, Lili! It's incredible how uncomfortable you are, deep down, with yourself, ironically, as it's that hidden self that's so special."

"Special, me? Other than fetching school prizes in maths and physics, what's so special about me?"

"That, too. But you'd be just an ambitious little beaver if it wasn't for this precious combination of a sharp mind and vivid imagination. Not many people have that range, believe me."

Sure, now he's telling her to mind her imagination. Last year he was all about staying focused.

"But – that's also the rub," he carries on. "You stand by and watch the spectacle, never fooled by flippant gloss or empty promises, you place demands on life and choose to dream about stuff you truly believe in, but then, what do you do? You try to blend in. Because you won't let the others notice how remarkable you are. You'd rather be common. That's what drives me mad about you, you know, Lili? I've been trying hard to get you to make a fuss for once, but you just won't budge.

"Why do you think I bullied you all those years? You think I'm cruel, I'm nuts, or what? You're a very bright young woman, Lili, but hey, where's your voice? All the years you wished you weren't the nerd; the party fellowship, remember them? Why did you never open your mouth and let us hear what you had to say for goodness' sake, then the clique would sure have wanted to have you along, they were also looking your way and waiting to hear from you. Where were you?"

"Where was I?" she yells. "I was carrying my bloody mountain, that's where I was, trudging along and hanging tight in there, that's where I was, because that's what I was taught to do, right? Wasn't this what you hammered on about, that I wasn't doing my bit and wasn't fetching the highest grades, doing justice to my brilliance?"

He's speechless for a moment, with a heavy gaze in his dark eyes. Is he realising he might have shot amiss?

"You really thought that was what the mountain was all about? I kept goading you, teasing you, all in the hope of getting you to scream and kick a bit, to stand up for yourself, even at the risk, yes, of standing out. If that's who you are, then let yourself stand out, for hell's sake! Instead of wavering like a ghost around yourself, get in, see what's inside, and start from there. Let us hear what Lili Danes might have to say, speaking out her mind, letting out her anger, her sadness. Her grief."

The crunch of the gravel has stopped, as they're standing still, facing each other. Crows glide over their heads with drawn-out caws.

"Carry your mountain doesn't mean labouring like a slave, Lili. I meant it as – be who you are! And then the rest comes along, whatever you want: grades, romance – life. But you've got to be there for it to find you."

"So here I am, now! I guess. But – I'm not alone."

"No, of course you're not alone! Dana, and myself, I'm here today, right? We're—"

She shakes her head but doesn't find the words to correct his understanding of what she has just said. He stops short, his eyes piercing her for the other meaning.

The gravel is almost overgrown with new grass.

He grabs her elbow and starts towards the roller coaster.

"Come with me!" he mutters.

There's an urgency in his stride, squeezing her arm, that puts her in a state of alarm. What's going on?

He pays for two tickets. The roller coaster is running idle, no one on the fairground so early in the day.

"I'm not going," she says, digging her heels in.

"Yes, you are," he replies without turning back to look

at her. He keeps pulling her elbow.

"I'm not going! Never!"

Never a roller coaster! She doesn't need to be flung through the air by a crazy contraption to be having fun. Even more preposterously, to feel alive.

"No! I'm not going!"

But Nestor drags her relentlessly and shoves her into a car. He straps her up with deft movements, and then hops on the seat behind her.

How could this be happening to her, she asks herself in a daze?

The car starts rolling. Just hang on there, get ready for hell!

The ride takes a few light years of plunging and soaring, pulling and hurtling, vistas and tunnels. Her insides are being shaken and tossed in a daredevil orbit that keeps her strapped in.

The straps that keep her safe, that protection that also hinders her and ties her to this insane car she doesn't want to be in, holds her captive where falling might be death but also freedom, life being live and not self-removal, no flight, no defection.

And yet she can't help rolling and rolling in the car, on the rails, the pre-designed trail she'd always known she'd never take, and yet here she is, implacably rolling with the system, instead of jumping or pulling some emergency brake and yelling 'I want out' of this insane race – however did she let herself be nudged into it?

Nestor springs out of the car and reaches out his hand to her, but she's still sitting with the strap across her chest and the steel bar against her stomach.

He releases her and helps her out.

She totters along the wooden platform and down the stairs, back on steadfast ground.

And then rage surges into her throat. Or despair.

"I'm here for you, Lili, talk to me!"

"You're not here, nobody fucking is, I want out, just out, I can't go on, this can't go on, Val, it can't go on!"

The fairground is vacant. A wife is watching her baby on the caterpillar ride many yards away.

Lili stands in front of the teachers' room the next day. It's just rung for the break. She can hear Nestor's voice somewhere down the corridor, over the din, shouting a biting remark to some unfortunate silly teenager. Then he shows up from round the corner, striding to the staff room. He eyes her with a slight frown and barely acknowledges her on his way in.

Lili waits, uncertain whether he's coming out again for her, or he's just ignoring her.

She waits the entire break. It rings again, and teachers start streaming out of the staff room calling out some final remarks over their shoulders to colleagues inside.

Is this it, then? Nestor's promise. His mountains and riddles and teachings. She was such a fool to tell him and then to be standing here like an awkward statue of speechlessness.

He opens the door but steps back as if he's forgotten something. She can hear his shrill laugh. She closes her eyes for a brief moment, pursing her lips: she'll never have anything to do with this guy again.

He emerges in the door frame again, with the leftover grin of his conversation. He starts down the corridor heading for his class and only casually brushes past her. He's holding something in his fist that he places in her hand before she can make sense of what's happening. The next moment he's vanished round the corner. In her hand there's a crumpled piece of paper with a phone number. No name.

The nameless man has confirmed, and one sunny afternoon, Lili and Vlad go to his place. She has the address, but on getting there, it's not clear which house exactly it is. There's a number on a fence to the street, but the house is a compound with several entrances. It looks reassuringly common, painted in light green, with bushes growing wild in the front garden. None of the Bacis' tidiness.

They keep sitting in the car to make up their minds which door to pick. Lili's bowels are threatening to rebel again. But it's gone too far already to turn back.

"Damn, we shouldn't look as if we're searching! We'd better get out of the car and go straight, as if visiting a friend. Try our luck."

Vlad heaves a deep sigh and pulls the door handle to get out.

"Let's go and see," he whispers.

They ring at the door closest to the street.

The guy opens the door and lets them in on a very cordial note, shaking hands with Vlad and welcoming them with a loud baritone voice. He has a paunch, and a white, puffy face. Vaguely resembling a full moon. Placid, watery eyes. Neither young, nor old. Vivacious and smart.

Doesn't he actually look just like a secret police guy, Lili wonders for a second, holding her breath. Not the coarse one, but the slick, savvy and versatile specimen, almost charming if it wasn't for the frozen face, seemingly open to enjoying life, a glass of wine, and a good conversation "between you and me," someone you feel you could trust to be able to help you, someone who knows every trick in the book.

Is this guy a doctor at all, by the way?

He lets them into a living room with scarce furniture, only the basics, and floorboards that look just as worn as in her own house. The windows are conveniently covered by semi-transparent blinds.

"Right, here we are," he says. "Take a seat, please."

They sit down silently. It's now all up to this slick guy.

"So, tell me, what's the situation? How far into it?"

"Well," Vlad takes a deep breath starting off, "we suspect it was late January."

"Oh," the guy raises an eyebrow. "Nearly four full months, now mid-May," he thinks aloud.

"Can it still be helped?" Vlad enquires in a mouse-tiny voice.

The guy crosses his legs under his paunch before answering.

"Yes, my method works up until four and half months, past which, at least theoretically, the foetus can survive if it's being expelled."

Lili feels fluffy dizziness and the rumour of a nausea building up somewhere deep inside.

"So theoretically, past that moment, doing anything to expel it counts as murder, quite a different league, you know. But what took you so long?" he enquires, no reproach to hear in his professional voice.

Vlad waves his head as if ducking a blow and mumbles something about Ergomet.

"I see. So Ergomet didn't work. It must have been too late for it, too. It's difficult to know so soon for it to be effective. And then there's the next remedy, the intervention that is usually done, but at this stage now, no one could do it, it would be butchery and the mother would be in serious danger. Plus you would need specialist equipment for during, and after."

Right. That's illuminating to hear. So what are they here for?

"My method, however, is different, in two very important ways. One, it poses absolutely no risk to her mother. The other, even if there is any complication afterwards, when you get to the hospital there is no trace of any intervention. It all looks natural."

He stands up and takes a peek behind the blinds, out the window. Is he expecting to see someone out there? He gets back to them, sits down and leans forward, putting his elbows on his knees.

"The thing is as follows. You know that the foetus is lying in a fluid in the placenta—"

"The amniotic fluid," Vlad whispers like a brave school boy.

"The amniotic fluid, that's right. When the time comes for the baby to be born, the amniotic bag bursts, and the fluid is let out. This is the surest sign the baby is coming. That's because the baby is no longer inside a liquid bubble, but in direct contact with the uterus muscles. Like any muscle, the uterus will shortly reject the foreign body, expelling it. That is what we call giving birth.

"What I do is, in a very simple intervention, I pierce the membrane of the amniotic sac and let the fluid leak out. In a time window of about six hours to five days, the birth process will get started. It's a miniature birth, of course, because there's no baby, but a foetus only half as large. The intervention takes a few minutes, doesn't hurt at all, and causes no wounds on the uterus walls. In the event of a post-op complication, you go to the hospital and they can only see a natural abortion. The body itself has triggered it, and there is no cause to be investigated in such cases. They just happen naturally."

Silence.

"So everyone is happy and covered," the guy concludes, with a sly smile.

"That's brilliant," Vlad proclaims.

"The only thing, of course," the guy goes on, "is you need to plan a bit what you are going to do when the pain sets in. This is, as I said, a miniature birth, so you might want to go away somewhere. It can be smooth and nearly painless, like menstrual discomfort, only a wee bit stronger, and be over in an hour, or it can take up to eighteen hours and get a bit unpleasant."

"No problem," Vlad replies enthusiastically, "my parents have got a mountain cottage, we can go there and say we wanted a short break."

To Lili these are insignificant details. The only thing that matters is that there's delivery in sight.

They agree that the intervention will be carried out at Lili's place. It's much safer than at Vlad's, by being far from the surveillance in the privileged district.

Vlad drives Lili back home in a state of euphoria. They've finally found a solution to the problem. And such a convenient one, too.

Lili stares out the window, past the buildings of the city that she knows so well. At last. The bulge will go away, its consequences, either real or imagined, dissolved.

One sunny afternoon in the last week of May, Vlad drives the guy to Lili's place. Mother is having a rehearsal at the theatre.

She watches them get out of the car, Vlad most likely telling some joke with his usual grin on his face, keen to be funny. The rucksack the guy seizes from the back seat looks shabby, which possibly is his clever tactic of avoiding a professional appearance. Is he a doctor at all? Lili wonders again fleetingly, as if that mattered now. She doesn't even remember his name. In their conversations, Vlad and herself have only used a conspiratorial label: "the guy".

Very smart. If they should be under surveillance, someone repeatedly called "the guy" would raise no suspicions at all.

But the ball has started rolling now anyway. Unless someone's going to burst into her house and catch them at it, there's no going back.

There has been none all along.

It's only a matter of timing: will they be ready here before Mother comes home? Will the resulting process be over in a time window during which she can be away from home? In time to still get to do some studying before the exams?

The exams. That predicament of ages ago has slid down on the agenda.

The two guys come in. The one she knows so well is being quite voluble, although she can sense a certain trepidation in his voice. Maybe chattering is his way of hanging in there, while hers is silence with a stare. The other one is slick and efficient, as she would expect him to be.

She lets them into her bedroom, which is the brightest room in the house. In front of the windows the tall fence is overgrown with ivy, conveniently protecting them from indiscreet peeks from the street. The two men drag her desk to the middle of the room, and ask her to place blankets on it, so she can lie down on them. The specialist requires a large bowl to be placed at her feet. Vlad leaves the room without hesitation and fetches the white plastic mixing bowl where Father used to pour two kilos of flour and knead the Christmas bread, and let it grow to twice its size.

The guy takes out his instruments from the shabby rucksack: there are some rods and other, smaller tools, but she looks away quickly. Vlad places her chair opposite the desk and then tells her she can undress the bottom part of her body.

Has she used the toilet already? Yes, she has. Both small and big? Yes.

"Good. You can climb on top of the desk now. Lie down, Vlad holding your head if necessary. Come forward, closer to me, yes, that's good. Now relax, relax your muscles girl, nothing's gonna hurt, I promise you."

Pain will be nothing anyway. That part of her body has been getting weirder and weirder, from the time when she first undressed in Vlad's bedroom for their first time but felt nothing, to the rhythmical back-and-forth that she identified as the routine of intercourse, to those rods now fumbling for something inside her, spoons pressing the edges, no sorry, the labia to gape out wide, all along no feeling no pain no tickle just the faint awareness of something going on. That has been the only sensation all this time, something is going on, on the outskirts of her body. Her body that is just a vessel anyway, which has now rebelled while she has been away so she can hang in tight (the will-be-back-soon way), and in her absence, the body has done its work and has been threatening to take control.

But now things are getting mended with the rods and the other instruments whose names and uses she doesn't want to know.

All of a sudden, a splash gushes out of her body, into Father's large mixing bowl. No more kneading Christmas bread. That splash, as if she hadn't been able to hold the pee – can it get any filthier than that, can her body do any more repulsive stuff?

"Easy, girl, don't worry, that's normal, that's just what we wanted, isn't it, now the fluid is out and your problem is solved. You're a virgin again. Well, almost, in a few days, but it's on the way, nothing can stop it now."

Above her, Vlad is holding her head but watching intently, he's been watching the whole operation like a diligent medical student. He helps her sit up and climb down from the improvised gynaecological chair that used to be her study desk. She picks up her clothes and puts them back on. The guy goes briefly to the bathroom to rinse his instruments, then gets back and places them neatly into his shabby rucksack. His full-moon face bears the same, unperturbed, satisfied look. The satisfaction of a job well done. Vlad whispers to her that he's driving him downtown and will come back straight away. She raises her eyes to him wonderingly: why come back? She's got work to do for the tutoring session tomorrow. He seems slightly startled, but gives way. "Fine, sure. Take care of yourself. I'll call you later." He quickly re-arranges the desk and the chair in their original setup. The guy turns to them for one last communication.

When the pains start, they need to monitor their frequency. They usually begin at around ten minutes, then the interval gradually gets shorter and shorter. When it's about one minute, it's almost there. How long it takes, no one can tell. But they should have painkillers at hand, at best injectable, those are more effective. And then, after the foetus is out, they need to wait for the placenta to come out, too. If it's not out within the hour, they must go to the hospital. Oh, and one more thing. They can say at the hospital either they knew about the pregnancy and were expecting the baby, or they had no idea. But they must decide now what they say if it should come to it. Best to decide now, before things start getting crazy.

Lili and Vlad nod mechanically. Yes, they will.

Then the two guys leave, get into the car, and the white Lada rattles away.

And then: clean off the traces. The Christmas bread bowl washed up, dried and put away in the pantry. The blankets, folded and tucked back in the storage under the bed. Air the stuffy room. Erase every little remnant of what has been going on, whether it's an object left lying around, a smell, a furniture setup, or the colour of the fluid left behind in the bathroom sink – so that the world may get back to its pristine state and turn the episode into a mere glitch in the quantum field.

The guy was right, strangely: now she's Mother's girl again.

And how will life go on from here?

Oh, yes. Admission. Studying. Wasn't it Mother's wish that she got back on track? It's almost June, in six weeks' time the exams will be starting. She has been studying, and diligently attending the tutoring sessions, but that feels as if it has been but a dream. Now at last her mind is free to get back to what used to be important.

Lili takes out her worksheets and notebooks from the bookcase and drops them back where they belong: on the desk. The desk is herewith also restored to its original function. She sits down and delves in. Mother could be back any moment now.

The only tiny thing, like a minuscule hairpin, still hanging over her, is the expectation of what is still to pass before her life can truly move on.

After the intervention on Wednesday, she carries on with her exam reading but counting hours and days. Should they drive to the Bacis' mountain cottage, as Vlad offered?

Vlad has offered many things that turned out later to be rubbish, or not meant to be taken seriously. What will happen if the going gets tough: will they race from the mountains back to the city, to go to the hospital?

She monitors every single little cramp she can detect in her womb, to see if she can identify any pattern. She has no idea where she should go if the pains set in. Vlad reassures her that she will get the painkillers first, for the first couple of hours, which will give them time to see what is to be done.

Thursday, Friday and most of Saturday pass uneventfully. Saturday afternoon they take a long walk in the park opposite the Bacis'. The parents are away for the evening, but their car is home.

After the walk around the same places, past the same benches, round the same lake, they get back to the familiar flat. Vlad plays a movie on the VCR and she stares through the screen.

And then it comes. A contraction similar to menstrual pain, but holding for about half a minute. She checks her watch. Vlad's eyes are glued to the screen. She pretends she's watching too, responding to Vlad's comments about the film, but inside of herself she's alert.

And there it comes again. Stronger, and just as long. It's been twenty-two minutes.

"Vlad?" she whispers.

"Hmm?" he replies absent-mindedly.

"It's coming," Lili says.

"Huh? What?" Vlad realises a few seconds later. "You sure?"

Lili nods. "It's the second one, after twenty-two minutes," she says.

"OK, let's wait and see if we've got a pattern," Vlad tells her.

By the end of the film the spells have got so painful that Vlad gives her a first painkiller shot. They come at just about eighteen minutes.

"So it may take the whole night," Vlad says. "I'll give you a double shot before I take you home, all right? And I'll also give you something to help you sleep."

She has no idea, and nobody does, whether she'll make it through the night, or if she'll wake up screaming with pain, and then Mother will be by her bedside. But she's got no time for silly little girl fears. Vlad reassures her too, before she gets out of his car, that things will be fine tomorrow morning, and she should call him when she needs him.

Lili gets a deep sleep through the night. Thankfully, the pains have subsided when she wakes up next morning. A voice in her head is wailing, "What if it's stopped altogether?" She goes to the bathroom, washes her face, then goes to the kitchen for breakfast. Mother is in a rush, leaving for a performance at ten.

It's nine fifteen. She fries two eggs and, on her last morsel, she feels a powerful claw in her womb. Swallowing is suddenly an almost impossible operation. So there it is, the pain. Refreshed, amplified to full intensity. Her head drops on the table, and she's gasping for air. Soon the gasp turns into a roar of pain.

When it's gone, she staggers up from the chair and to the telephone.

"Vlad, hi, come, hurry up, it's coming, oh goooood!" her sentence trails off in a scream, as she's unable to stand on her feet but she's bending over and leaning against the wall, then letting herself slide down along the wall, like a splatted fruit slipping to the floor. She eases her bottom on the floor, her legs spread apart, the phone receiver hanging down from the shelf by its cable. Vlad must be going crazy hearing all this, so she must pull herself together. The pain recedes again, and she knows she must use the lull to stand up, hang up the phone and go to her room to lie down on her bed. The pains must be every two minutes or so. Can the neighbours hear her screams?

She only manages to trudge along the corridor to the far end, where her bedroom is, very slowly, maintaining her balance with her hands on the wall on the right, and the furniture on the left. Her head is spinning as if the pain has knocked her over. Such wrath, such spiteful blows!

She opens the door and steps into the room, but then the claw comes back and grips her body mercilessly. She staggers to the bed, but doesn't quite make it; she can only lean against it and ease herself again to the floor. She lets her head drop backwards onto the bed; no amount of strength is left to hold any body part straight, and she's lying there like a dead leaf, except for the claw inside that is the most powerful sensation she has ever experienced. Her screams are no screams, but roars soaring up from her innermost, as if the vibration of her vocal chords spreading throughout her limbs might overcome the grip of the claw.

There is nothingness beyond the grip and the struggle for air, for survival.

Vlad opens the door and rushes to her, and then leaves the room again. She has no words, she hears nothing, she's only that pain. He comes back with the same large mixing bowl for the Christmas bread. She somehow guesses, unable to make sense of what he says, that he wants her to lift her bottom from the floor so he can shove the bowl underneath. She cannot move, moving hurts, all the muscles hurt even without moving, where can she find the strength to bear even more than that claw! She's only a dead leaf in the grip of the pain.

When the blow recedes next time, Vlad lifts her bottom half-way and then she lifts it an infinite way upwards, just enough to let the bowl go through and when she lets herself fall again, she's half lying on the bed, half sitting in the bowl and her breath is only a roar, the breathing the roaring is exhausting as if the pain was not enough –

— and all of a sudden she feels a large lump like a ball rolling outside of her body on its own, something huge like nothing else ever within her, it's rolling and opening her labia and gliding out, like an asteroid on its orbit, and it's rolled past, it's gone, in its wake a tail of debris and fluid and the pain is gone like a jinn that's been sucked away, letting go of her body, leaving her drained, almost dead, floating in a pool of shock and senselessness.

It's twelve and Mother's voice calls out from the corridor "I'm baaack honeeey!"

Lili is reading a book in her bed. She has, almost incredibly, been able to take a shower, Vlad helping her to the bathroom, and apart from a softness in her drained body, she's back to reality.

Mother pops her head in, "How are you honey, oh, you're such a good girl, sitting and reading, what a cosy Sunday time over there where you are!" and then closes the door just as abruptly, going to the bathroom to wash her hands and then get lunch ready.

Lucky Mother doesn't always pay attention, but goes on about her life without truly being there, running her marathon and focusing on getting there, instead of the pain.

Vlad had grabbed the lump in newspaper sheets and driven off as soon as it was clear that it was safe to leave Lili alone again. The placenta had thankfully been ejected in the same go.

He disposed of the parcel somewhere in a field on the city outskirts.

Lili looks out the window at the green lime tree across the street. She has given birth, between nine fifteen and eleven thirty, conveniently suiting Mother's timetable at the theatre. The foreign body, the lump of fears and shame and helplessness has been disposed of and is out of this world.

CHAPTER SEVEN

Back into the world, into her world, whatever it used to be.

It used to be far from snug, but it gives her a certain feeling of snugness now. Back to the things she knows how to do and she can exert some control over: studying, for example.

She's rediscovering every detail of her daily routine, recognising the earmarked pages in the books, re-tracing the winding path through her notes to recapture the meaning of the lesson when she had taken them down.

She remembers how, last year, she had listed the chapters she needed to cover each day, counting on a seven-hour study slot, except when she had her private classes. This year she feels this is too tight. She needs to dive in, back into the equations, integers, strings, and forces; but not the checklist way. She has asked the teacher to only timetable sessions every other week. She needs to focus now; input or guidance is no longer critical. Whatever had to be learned, must have been learned, otherwise it's too late anyway. Now she must have the compact time to revise and review from a vantage point, to connect one formula to a variety of equation models, and she must exercise her mind until it gets so fit that any test is only, truly, just a test.

She doesn't take the long way round the city any more. She's running to catch the bus, and she doesn't mind the crowd on it. Taking the shortest route saves her about three quarters of an hour compared to the time she spent in spring, when time was immaterial. It's not as if there was any rush, but the landscape of her day is acquiring contours, opening new avenues for her to steer along.

It's a new feeling, steering. It reminds her, although she doesn't always formulate it in her mind, that, thankfully, there is nothing standing in her way anymore, sucking up her strength, blowing away her focus.

But even this, her focus: she no longer thinks of the admission results. Her mind is hungry for exertion, and she's ready to give her all. What may or may not come out of it is a long way ahead and out of range.

Her knitting, with the needles stuck in, is lying in a plastic bag at the bottom of a drawer.

She notices faces, clouds, smells of flowers that gypsy florists offer with a stretched out hand and a light-hearted bid. The building site for the new metro line is making progress, as she now notices that the detour the bus needs to take has become shorter. The market stalls stink, but she enjoys the sight of the season's fresh potatoes, strawberries and zucchini. There's richness of colour, shapes, textures, and anticipated taste; she decides on the spot to use a few of her coins and get a small cabbage, a tender green-yellow with tousled young leaves, and a dill bundle.

She misses Dana. Can it be that they last saw each other at her father's funeral?

Dana has repeatedly asked her to meet, but she's found an excuse each time.

She couldn't have looked Dana in the eyes, knowing that there was no way she could be open with her. Gabriel had almost begged her to talk to absolutely no one – "the fewer people know, the better, trust me, it's better for you and it's better for them, in all respects" – and he was right, of course. What was the point in placing that huge burden on Dana's shoulders? Dana was just a kid who'd got admitted to uni straight after school, and like a lucky girl, she'd met nice people there and was taking fun weekends in the mountains; who was Lili to come to her with such a horrifying secret, and what would Dana have thought of her? Their friendship, thin as it has become in the past year, would have been shaken forever.

Besides, she realises, she didn't even want to talk all this time. What was there to chatter about? That she was knitting endless stitch rows at home, instead of reading for term exams? That it had come to the point where cold and hunger, though as biting as ever, no longer played much of a role? And lately, that she had been trapped in an unwanted pregnancy that was threatening to change her into a total stranger?

How much can a nineteen-year-old be expected to shut off in order to be brave and hang in tight?

Dana would have noticed her waist, for sure. Maybe she wouldn't have thought of it precisely; just like Mother, looking at her but not seeing her, trusting Lili to the point of self-delusion. But there was still the risk Dana might suspect something was wrong and corner her with questions.

Now, however, she and Dana might try to see if they can find things to chat about as in the old days. She recalls their bi-weekly treats downtown and the choice between pizza on the main boulevard and profiterole ice-cream next to the concert hall. They would chat and gossip and yammer about maths or chemistry, and about classmates and their tasteless jokes. Sometimes, guy talk – what he said, what she said. Then they would take a tour of the two or three shops in the area that might have something nice, either that pair of black velvet shoes, or some necklace from the artists' outlet shop.

She knows Dana's bound to be busy again, with her term exams, but Lili's got hers, too, now; no more humility, or feeling left out. She's perfectly entitled to ask her friend out, even if only to check if they're still friends.

Dana is wearing a new one from her store of bold outfits: fashionable baggy trousers a striking sky-blue and a yellow dotted blouse with square shoulders. She almost seems to be yelling "I'm a grownup, you'd better watch out!"

Lili hugs Dana hello, secretly smiling at her imagination going on a spin.

"I'm so happy you called, you've no idea," Dana says when they're sitting down on a bench in the park. There's the familiar mixture of earnestness and playful chiming in her voice.

"Yeah, so am I," Lili replies with a smile. It might be the same bench where she had explained to Dana last August about the admission muddle. It's June now: the exams are implausibly near.

"How's—"

"How's—"

They burst into laughter. A few mamas sitting around the playground turn their heads.

"Yes, well," Dana hits it off in her old wailing tones, "it's cramming, cramming, cramming, what can I say. It's been a tough year, Lili, I can tell you, really tough!"

Really tough. Lili smiles as she glances back over her own past year.

"Why so tough? I bet you got good grades—"

"Yeah, well, they're passable, not too bad, but—"

"—and you had great holidays, I suppose, skiing and mountaineering and all that. Was that passable, too?"

"Yeah, true, that was nice. Susi's a spoiled girl, oh my goodness, sometimes she drives me mad – me! You can imagine, Lili, you know how fussy I can be—"

"Oh, Miss Fussy Young Lady, we certainly know her very well!"

"—yes, well, you don't know fussiness if you haven't met Susi, mind you! But she's a nice girl nonetheless," she adds as a counterpoint. Dana contemplates the playground nearby with a thoughtful smile on her angular face. "She takes down carbon copies of lecture notes if I skip the class when I'm having one of my nightmarish migraines, and she calls me every day, and she asks for advice whatever ghost of a trouble's at the horizon. You can't really imagine what could become trouble for Susi, she's such a worrier. She gets migraines, too. And moods – worse than mine, can you believe that, Lili?"

"So she's taking good care of you, I gather?" Lili asks, half irony, half tenderness.

"Well," Dana's voice goes on a curvy tune, "we're more like two mimosas between ailments and panic attacks." They laugh out again, to the surprise of the mothers and grandpas nearby. "Almost as close as the two of us used to be, when it comes to checking in with each other's insomnia or what's up on the guys' front. You about Gabriel, me about those hopeless flames. No guys now on the horizon, in case you were going to ask!"

"Oh, I was going to ask, indeed," Lili chuckles. But she wasn't, actually, because she's not in the mood to talk about her own, anti-romance.

"But," Dana carries on, "Susi doesn't read Hemingway. Not even for my sake, as you did, Lili," she adds with a melancholy smile, turning towards her. "But I guess you can't have everything, can you. She's an amiable mate, through the challenges of daily living. But she's nothing like you, and what we used to be together."

Lili nods, looking down, feeling tears welling up.

"How's Vlad?" Dana resumes with a naughty smile, opening the girl-to-girl conversation.

Yes, how's Vlad. How's their romance. These are the questions.

She has no clear memory of his face on that fateful Sunday, she only knows he was around, doing things. He must have been relieved afterwards. His joviality soon returned, as did his eagerness to make plans.

"We could get married by Christmas, sweetheart, and I'm pretty sure Daddy could arrange a honeymoon in Greece. Imagine!" She'd smile and turn her eyes to look out the window, or go back to her book.

"He's a nice guy," she thinks aloud, "although – a bit helpless."

She gazes around, from the park bench where they're sitting. All that space, it feels good to be able to breathe.

"His parents are getting impatient, you know, with the admission coming. They're now somehow worried that it's all going to come out soon, that is, their brilliant son's girlfriend has only been stalling them for a year, and now they're withdrawing all their joviality."

Dana is gazing at her intently, but Lili relishes another moment of watching the birds in the treetop. What she's about to tell Dana seems to be amusing her.

"But why is it now that they're worried? They've had the whole year."

"Precisely," Lili laughs. "No idea. Maybe the tension's getting the better of them. Well, things might have been going on in the background without me knowing it. Or maybe I didn't want to know it. The thing is, Vlad has proposed to me a bit more formally."

"What? Goodness, and you're only saying this now?" Dana exclaims, putting her hand to her mouth in excitement.

Lili laughs knowingly. She knows what comes next.

"Yes, he did. He came over on a Sunday, Mother was at the theatre, and he went down on his knees and all—" That was a different Sunday.

"Wow, I can't believe that!" Dana squeals.

Lili nods. It feels good to talk about exciting things, for a change.

Between sentences and conversation turns, she's trying to parse the story she's about to share with Dana. How much of it is shareable at all? Vlad has returned to his old self (which she, thankfully, hasn't), chattering and hugging her hello-goodbye, now and then leaving a platonic, fleeting kiss on her lips. There's the shadow of last summer's romance, or whatever it was, hovering between them, and they seem to act it out faithfully: his extensive cheerfulness, her quiet smile. Lili senses at times a question at the back of her mind, whether his proposal – and her own acquiescence – is nothing but the impulse to hold on to that early story, and relief at the dissolution of their recent ordeal. Are she and Vlad in sync for once – he's thankful she was so brave, while she's thankful he stuck around?

She hasn't pondered these questions yet. She's immersed, again, in her studying routine, and is retracing, one baby step at a time, her old joy at the summer breeze, the fragrances of jasmine and lime trees, at the crickets chirping at night.

"Yes, but – hold on, there's more. So—"

"And what did you say, Lili, I take it you said yes, then?"

Is it the girls' excitement hearing about a proposal, or is there a shadow of concern in Dana's voice? Never mind, the story goes on, and it's not so much about a proposal.

"What I said – well, hard to believe, but I said okay, let's see—"

"Okay, let's see? What kind of an answer is that?"

Lili halts.

"A sort of an answer. A temporary one. Look, I know, I did say yes, in a way, but more like, yes but…"

"But—?"

"But – let's talk about it after the exams. I mean, I'm kinda open to it, now that it's been almost a year, why not, it'd be easy living while I'm doing my own thing, but it's just that I've got other things to focus on right now, so let's deal with it when the summer's over.

"Anyway, I went on as if everything was the same, didn't tell Mother a thing, but he couldn't keep his mouth shut and told his parents about it. The result is, he wanted us to go to the seaside right after my exams, but his father said not on my money. So that means of course no seaside."

"What? But Vlad's twenty-four!" Dana opens her eyes wide in disbelief, or in anger.

Lili nods. "That's the point. I said, look, going to the seaside was not my idea. If you want to go with me, can't you find a solution?" Poor Vlad. Cornered again for solutions.

Although, to be fair, being twenty-four has not much to do with having your own money. It's not as if he can quit med school to get a job so they can go to the seaside.

"And?" Dana enquires impatiently.

Lili fetches a deep sigh and shrugs. "Apparently he can't."

"The hell he can't! He's a coward, that's what he is! He could ask his friends."

Lili smiles. Another thing she recognises: Dana's old habit of dropping tough labels with passion and fierceness.

Does it hurt to hear it? Not really; it's not the first time Vlad's acted like that – and that's another thing she recognises from the past. The recent past, especially.

"Sure he is. Papa's little boy. Everyone's little boy, for that matter. Talking lots but good for nothing, as the poet says."

She feels her heart squeeze with remote guilt at the sound of her words. Sweet silly Vlad, she shouldn't talk about him like that.

Dana is waiting for more; she looks as if she's bursting with what she'd like to say, but still only just managing to withhold it. Lili tilts her head.

"But he's a good boy, at that. And he's around. Caring." Lili knows how big a difference caring can make. Vlad's been the only one to care, all this year, when Dana was busy exchanging migraine tips with Susi, Val Nestor busy with his teaching, everyone else busy with their lives.

There's a muffled sound from Dana.

"Yeah, I know," Lili acknowledges, "you'll be all protest, I suppose, but it's not that straightforward, you know? Vlad's sweet, considerate, and in a way, reliable. He might not be good at solving problems, but he's there."

"So you'll be solving the problems, Lili, and he'll be there looking up to you with grateful eyes, wagging his tail?"

Lili frowns. That's a bit mean, even for Dana.

"Vlad sounds like a choice *I* could make, Lili, not you. I'm the one who always held forth that I only need a good old-fashioned safe life, with a reasonable job and a loyal husband, in a decent flat. You were all about Raskolnikov and Lennon. What happened to John? Where's the Lili I know?"

John. Where he is now, he doesn't care about Lili Danes, so he thankfully can't mock her childish dreams of saving his life so they can fall in love, that love written in the stars. Would he mock, or would his voice turn warm and kind? Telling her – what? *It's like starting over*? No. That's what Gabriel played on the phone instead of hello when she picked up, ages ago, when he wanted them to get back together. Starting over – isn't that a childish dream, too? Is that ever possible?

Not even with Vlad. They haven't even got close to mimicking a prelude to sex since the madness began. They totter carefully, as if tied by some tacit mutual agreement, and steer away from the muddle of who wants what, what it feels like, what consequences must be considered. They're instinctively seeking a simple, foolproof way to be just companions, kind and loyal to each other.

"Oh, come on, Dana, let's not be silly here. School's over, and life's butted in, at least for me, in case you forget, you being busy taking lecture notes in tandem with Susi."

Dana swallows hard, her eyes darkening but still set on Lili's face.

"No one can help what happened last year, Lili. If anyone could, I'd be the first to volunteer, trust me. But I'll just say, remember Val's scale of values? We weren't sure what he meant. Maybe it's time to think again."

Val Nestor and his preposterous verdicts?

Although: Val will always be special. He was there, too, caring, Lili remembers.

Maybe Vlad is not the only one, after all.

"What is that supposed to mean, that bloody scale of values again?" she counters.

"Maybe you don't get it, Lili," Dana sounds like she's pleading, "but I keep wondering: why are you putting up with all this? You're not even in love with this papa and mama's little boy, so why don't you tell them to go to hell with their villa and army general and ministry hospital and all! Look at me!" Dana grabs Lili's shoulders. "Look at me, Lili! I'm begging you to think about why you're taking this!"

Lili smiles and lets her head down in amusement.

"Look at me, Lili, don't look away," Dana shakes her shoulders. "Lili! Vlad's a silly well-meaning guy, but you're a star! There's your scale of values!"

Lili lets out a short burst of laughter. Sure, a Hollywood —

"You're a star!" Dana repeats emphatically. "And what panics me is that you seem to think I'm being dramatic again. I'm begging you to let it sink in. There's no one so clever and beautiful that I know. No one!" she adds with fierceness.

Lili ponders for a moment. So the other friend, the prodigal granddaughter, Susi, isn't—

"I'm not that beautiful, how come you—"

"Oh, Lili, sometimes you drive people crazy, you know that?" Dana lets go of Lili's shoulders to slap her own thighs with impatience.

"And that, I suppose, is part of my being beautiful, right?" Lili counters with a wink.

Dana shakes her head, upset.

"You just don't get it."

"Yeah, I suppose I do, in a way. My way. You and Nestor are my biggest fans, you both seem to have this strong belief that I'm so special, so brilliant, so—"

The more they give her the star thing, the more she wants to back off and run away.

"And that's why you're stuck in this incongruous match," Dana cuts in. "For as long as it takes you to understand. If you weren't so blind, you'd see you don't belong in this. You'd never have got involved in the first place, admission failure or not."

There's a thud in Lili's heart. She examines the pebbles at their feet. Is Dana implying that she might have chosen Vlad to get under the cover of normalcy, and blend in?

She sits herself on a chair in front of her mirror, lower body naked, legs wide apart, to see what's there.

She has needed to tell herself more than once that there's nobody watching, so she can go ahead.

Legs are tight together at first, won't open. Nobody peeks down there! Except for that sort of doctor. (Shudder.) Not even Vlad. He used to fumble in the dark, by trial and error, here it is, no, it's not, there, in you go. All under the duvet.

He would know from his anatomy classes, some chart of lines and curves with the accurate terminology in the legend.

Now that that doctor, *the guy*, has not just peeked, but investigated soundly, and worked his instruments down there, maybe it's time she takes a look, too. It's her own, after all.

Will there be anything different to see in the wake of what happened? She has no idea. There's no before and after she can compare.

She pushes her knees apart while keeping her eyes on the mirror.

If anyone was watching now—

But no one is. Go on.

There's a punch in her guts. Is this a wound?

So red. So – fleshy and raw. In the dark shade of the

frizzy hair, soft flesh, red and wet, like a deep cut that needs stitching, sewing up together side to side, to make the wound close and heal.

Any scars? The lines, the flapping wings, the hanging parts? She couldn't ask Vlad. He'd take it professionally, and she doesn't need another professional looking at that part of her body.

Gabriel would be game. With a big laugh, he'd say, "Let old uncle take a careful look down there," and would bend down with an earnest mimic. She would tickle under his gentle touch, but she'd shiver with pleasure, too. And soon, his playfulness would turn into earnest passion.

She walks her fingers along the red flesh, afraid at first it might hurt, but slowly drawing circles with a budding confidence. It doesn't hurt. If anything, it tickles. It—

It's real. Like touching a throbbing heart. No protective skin in between, no other shell. Her inside, on the outside.

If there's a spot where Lili Danes is at her most real, this is it. A touching stone of sorts.

It doesn't always tickle. Sometimes, she remembers, it feels like rubbing flesh against abrasive paper. When she didn't particularly want Vlad to be going at it. When it was just a casual pastime and her mind was elsewhere.

Maybe it only wants the things it wants, and the casual choices don't stand a chance. Unless she looks away.

But then, you can hardly go about life with this visceral approach. That's why they say you need to think with your head, not with your genitals. There's a reason why this deep flesh is covered by its wings, and over them there are layers of clothing and discretion. You have to do things you may not like, and hold out dark times against your choice of comfort.

Would it have got to be the same with Gabriel? If they'd done it, again and again. Would there have been moments of doing it with her mind elsewhere?

No, surely not. His parents didn't have a weekend

house, so it was a lot more difficult to organise time alone at his place. And when the occasion came up, the choice would have been hers, whether to go or not.

The choice is of course, hers. Always. Even with Vlad all over.

Gabriel asked her to meet last autumn, soon after she got back from the mountain resort. He called, and when she picked up, she heard a click, and then John's voice: *Our life together is so precious, together, we have grown, although our love is still special, let's take a chance and—*

It had been – what, a year and a half? – since they'd parted. He sounded warm and playful on the phone. Almost his old self. She said sure, let's meet.

There was no reason on the spot to say no.

It was the time when she should have started going to classes. September. Vlad was buzzing around her, all good intentions.

She went and met him in the central gardens, of an evening. Almost like in the old days. His eyes glistened through his glasses. They hugged and laughed again. They walked. He got hold of her hand, but she withdrew it the first chance she got. It was taking her on a dizzying ride back in time, and she had no range for such experiments.

He asked no questions about exams. He'd sensed something wrong on the phone and was putting a blanket on it now. Maybe he wanted to make her feel comfortable. Maybe he wanted to tell her it made no difference to him. The pied puffin was what did.

She went along, laughing and warming to him. That ease. A touch of their hands switching an unmistakable truth on. Or maybe not so much any longer.

They stopped and faced each other. He took something out of his bag.

"This is for you, pied puffin!"

She opened her eyes wide. Gabriel had never made her gifts, whether Christmas or birthdays.

She put out a hesitant hand and took the thin package. It was a delicate necklace, thin like the wings of a dragonfly. She'd never seen anything finer.

"My goodness, Gabriel! What's wrong with you? I mean – what's the occasion?"

"None," he said with that electric smile of his. "Just that you know me. Or that I know you."

She fumbled with the little thing to get it open. He helped her. When it was on, she couldn't see it anymore, but she kept her hand on it, at the base of her neck.

He was the same, yes. Real. As if he'd never been gone.

But she was behind a thin glass.

"It's just amazing, pied puffin. I thought of you again and again all this time. And now just like back then, I touch you and I go nuts. Don't you?" he asked, bending his head to search for her eyes.

Did she? Nothing echoed.

"No, actually – I don't," she had said. That going nuts had faded away.

"I mean," she added, "it feels so good to be here with you again, Gabriel."

"Sure," he nodded. "Let's go and see if they still have pizza."

He turned around and headed off. She followed and caught up with him, walking side by side, the park around them a mere invisible backdrop.

When did she forget him, she wonders now. She hadn't even realised she'd forgotten him, except during that conversation.

At some point she had lost the connection to something inside of her that had been true and real. It must have been while she was focusing on hanging tight.

After they'd said goodbye that night, she put that episode to rest on the shelves of her archives, and carried on handing herself out to Vlad like a thank-you gift.

But she can still get the next best thing, Vlad's secure attachment, when exams are over and the Bacis revert to their old joviality. There's a still available future that she can picture with her mind's eye, not scene by scene, like her emotionally draining teenage fantasies, but in a lump, a soft protective shell like a second skin, a little mountain to push on along the way.

And the reflection in the mirror? How does that wound, that raw flesh fit into this film?

At the last tutoring session in June, the teacher keeps her after the lesson for a private conversation. It's the same teacher she'd had, only a few months ago, when she'd felt that stabbing urgency to use the toilet.

"Lili dear, I just wanted to give you some other kind of homework."

She lights up a cigarette, stands up from her desk and goes over to the couch, gesturing for Lili to join her. This is not about the study syllabus, Lili understands.

"I just want you to think about something. I know how much this admission means to everyone, and particularly to you, and to your mother. Especially after what happened last year. So I just thought you might want to consider an option. You know that the admission to mathematics is much easier, with fewer candidates per place. And the programme includes an option later to specialise in astrophysics. Some young people prefer to go into mathematics instead of physics. The classes are held in the city centre at University Square, whereas the Physics Institute is over where the devil built its den, so to speak, and you need two hours just to get there."

The teacher pauses. Lili nods. Yes, she's aware of that choice, which some young people go for. It has crossed her mind, too, if only casually, and she dismissed it like a bothersome insect.

"I know, yes, you're right," she whispers.

"So I appreciate it's a tough choice, but I just wanted to raise it with you. Have you considered it at all?"

Lili shakes her head. The teacher's words have made it more real that she might fail again, by opening the avenue for a plan B.

"Right, I thought so," the teacher draws again from her cigarette. "The thing is, you know, I've been doing some thinking too, on your account, and to me it looks as follows," and with this she sits up and puts out the cigarette. She turns to Lili.

"You know my dear, I think your dilemma should start from the question, What would hurt less? Getting admitted to mathematics with a grade that would have put you in for physics too, or failing at physics with a grade that would have been enough for mathematics?"

Lili keeps quiet. "In other words," she murmurs a few moments later, "is the admission result itself more important than studying physics?"

The teacher tilts her head to one side then to the other, as if weighing Lili's words. "You may also see it that way," she concedes with a smile.

But it's not just that, Lili ponders on the bus back home. What is striking about the way the teacher formulated the dilemma was what would hurt less. Usually you look at options in terms of what would feel better. Was the teacher implying that there was some amount of pain whatever we choose?

What about that hanging in there that everyone advises, to stay away from pain?

What if there is no way of ruling out pain, not by planning, not by equations, and – now she sees it – not even by closing your eyes and hanging tight? She has done just that and become an expert at it, shutting thoughts off, until she had almost crushed her vital signs.

It took those months of soaring outside of her body

day by day, and then the horrifying pain that Sunday coming alive again when her body screamed and clenched, but then released. That deep, wound-like flesh had bled and let it all out and then healed as if the trial had never been.

In the aftermath, feeling her way back into her days' routine. Even, yes, feeling her way back into her science, not studying, not ticking chapters off, but delving in.

So this is what it's come to: a choice of the safer bet. Of course, her hypothesis – no, assumption, because she never questioned it – has been that she will get admitted to physics. There's no dilemma if you consider that one possibility alone. That's how her mind's been wired all along.

Single-minded, or empty-minded, just rolling, rolling, rolling on, like an asteroid on its orbit, mindless of itself, but just as unstoppable.

But if she's to stop this race and get off the roller coaster, as she has done lately, she can see the complexity of the teacher's dilemma. No, it's not a dilemma, but a muddle. Both ways feel wrong. Opting for getting admitted at all costs? Sounds unlike herself – but then, the prospect of taking another blow if she fails feels unbearable at this point. She and Mother could really do with a breakthrough.

Lying in bed that night, her eyes glued to the ceiling, she resumes her contemplation.

Asteroids clash and stars collapse – accidents and disasters are part of the physics she so keenly explores. A system's stability can always be hit by an external cause, driven by a force unpredictable from within the system itself.

She had rubbed her elbows sore working through problems, and assumed that her application guaranteed the one logical (and moral?) consequence of skating through the exams. But in this, she had disregarded the essence of the subject she was studying so hard: the inherent probability scale of any possible futures, and the multitude of causalities. How could she be so blind? Last year's failure hadn't been her doing, yes; but that wasn't a flaw in the universal laws. Behind doors in the Physics Institute, another causality had been at work, bringing two professors to a discreet arrangement.

Nothing was flawed. It just needed another go, another toss of the probability dice.

And if external disaster should crop up again, she would need to search deep within herself to find out if she wanted to keep tossing the dice again, or if it made more sense to change the game.

This habit of putting everything into equations just because her mind is shaped by science must stop. She must know there are limitations to it, as there's no numerical value for fears and struggles to enable calculation.

Although, Father did lecture on the Uncertainty Principle at the dinner table. Beyond the rule of classical physics, an observer cannot calculate both speed and position of those enigmatic, infinitesimal particles: just one, at the cost of losing the other.

Which means a sub-atomic uncertainty is woven into the fabric of this universe, proved by equations and laws. The physicists know they cannot know. "No mysticism, only quantum mechanics," Father used to say.

She's been oversimplifying her equations and reasoning, taking the world in Newtonian terms, which is precisely what Father used to blame the system bitterly for. He had argued again and again that the deepest answers could only be found where physics went beyond the range of the measurable, and attempted to account for the unaccountable.

There are no limitations, therefore: physics can, in fact, embrace it all in its equations. But not through school-level calculus. Not by chopping the reality into tangible chunks and assuming that our struggle will necessarily yield the desired outcome.

Still – how does it help her solve this dilemma now?

For one thing, the run-up to the exams is less feverish than it was last time, which may channel deeper resources of focus and clarity on the day of the challenge. And in the event of failure, it will help her come to terms with it, maybe even derive a new direction to pursue.

But a particular vision, whether Newtonian or Einsteinian, doesn't exactly make the decision for her. The equations won't provide an answer, only a description.

She wishes she could return to the state of Papa's clever girl. Basking in the sunshine of his love and knowledge, immersed in a nourishing fluid like a primordial soup. Some untraceable external cause had drained that fluid away, removing her father until, much later, his absence had been buried on a frosty November day, leaving her like a foreign body, surface rubbing against surface, edge against edge, inevitably expelled, out and out.

Beyond Newton or Einstein, there's a choice calling for her attention.

She must choose the pain she could live with, the fear she could stick by, the failure she could speak out.

The teacher's right. What would hurt less?

She has to remember what it was all for, or about. That used to be one of the things that made her feel different from the crowd: her goal was studying physics, not being admitted to university.

Or was it? Hadn't she placed all her hopes of being delivered from the alienating mundane on simply passing an entrance exam?

People get married so as to get a flat, join the Party just to be on the safe side, choose a university subject so as to secure a decent ride through life: she had promised herself she'd stay away from that. No hollow choices, instrumental in getting something else. She would build herself that garage by making meaningful choices.

Does it still feel that way?

The consequences of the one decision could be reversible later in life, but those of the other, not.

She glides into sleep, drawn by one thought only.

She needs to come home.

She needs to enrol for the exam, again. The same building as last year, the same clerk taking the official photo for her candidate ID.

She comes home and flips her candidate folder open to go through the documents, the photo slipping out and catching her eye. She opens the bookcase compartment where she stores paper, notebooks, worksheets and all the debris of a studying routine. She spots the thin folder of last year's registration, picks it out from under the pile, and places it on the desk alongside the folder she has just brought home.

The old photo slips out, too. She looks at both pictures of herself, dazed.

Last year: wavy hair hanging shoulder-length, eyes slightly raised above the camera, with what now looks like a transported smile towards sunny horizons.

This year: hair pulled tight towards the back in a bun, eyes straight into the camera, jaw tight. Facing the challenge. Earnest acknowledgement, the shadow of some fear, maybe traces of defiance. Papa's clever girl. A couple of aeons older – no, just altered by experience.

She likes herself better here, now. She looks cooler, with the self-confidence that the earnest defiance implies. When the fear is gone, the smile will be more real, more present, more powerful. Less self-delusional.

The shrill doorbell rings.

Someone to read the electric meter?

She drops the photos and looks out the window. She can't see anyone standing at the gate.

She leaves her room and heads for the main door. She pulls it open, and in front of her stands none other than Mrs Baci.

"Hello, Lili, excuse me, I couldn't hear any bell ringing, so I thought it's not working, and the gate wasn't locked, so I —"

"You can't hear the bell from outside," Lili replies with the standard explanation.

Mrs Baci is a strange apparition in the frame of her house door. How does she know where she lives? She doesn't remember filling in any visitor form at the Bacis'.

"I was in the neighbourhood, with some paperwork at the clinic here," Mrs Baci explains, tilting her head towards the old hospital on the hill. "I hope you don't mind me stopping by."

"No, not at all, please come in."

Mrs Baci nods and steps over the threshold, but halts as soon as Lili has closed the door behind her. They're standing in the small cubicle of the entrance hall. Shoes are sprawling around their feet, and the vacant wardrobe with its dusty mirror is their only witness. The electric meter is purring on the opposite wall, between the heads of the two women, level with their ears.

"I won't be long, Lili, thank you, I just had something very short to say to you."

What could it be that Mrs Doctor came all the way here for? She's done her studying like a good girl. The exams are the day after tomorrow. There's nothing that Vlad's mother could possibly take issue with.

Mrs Baci is acting in a way that's new, but she can't tell exactly what it is. Concern? Irritation? Embarrassment?

"I'll be very short, I don't want to keep you. I know you've got the exams."

Acknowledgement taken. And now?

There's been no fight or anything dramatic between her and Vlad.

There are no new immediate plans about driving to the seaside, not even to old Busteni for that matter. Nothing new on the wedding front. She's been pouring cold water over

Vlad's enthusiasm, by ignoring his scheming and changing the subject. Not that she does it deliberately; it simply feels as if the time isn't right yet for the topic.

So she can't be held responsible for Vlad's exaltation.

An exaltation that is of little consequence anyway, Vlad being Vlad. His exaltation always requires someone else's endorsement.

Mrs Baci inhales and with an unconscious nod, she goes ahead.

"Listen, I'm missing my gold necklace, and I've been looking for it everywhere, I can assure you, everywhere. It's a special piece, that is, it's not the gold itself, but it's got some special sentimental value, I'm sure you'll understand."

No, she doesn't quite.

"I know how much Vlad loves you. He's a dear boy. He's got such a big heart. But—"

So there is a but, after all, to Vlad's big heart? It's not everything, is it?

"—but he can be a bit naive sometimes, in his innocence."

What has Vlad done? In the name of loving his darling Lili.

A gold necklace, lost, Vlad, big heart, naive. What exactly is the gap here?

She realises suddenly that she can ask the question aloud. Missing this turn might look like she's being hostile.

Whereas – she hasn't got the faintest idea what this is all about. In all honesty.

"I'm sorry, Mrs Baci, but – I don't quite understand—"

Mrs Baci purses her lips and nods, as if she expected this.

So it's not working, being puzzled in all honesty.

"Look, Lili, I'll be straight, no good wasting your time, I'm sure you've got studying to do. If Vlad has given you the necklace as a gift, I'd like to have it back."

She feels her eyelids pressing against the eye sockets. She must blink.

Mrs Baci will think she's putting on an act. The slapstick gag, eyes wide open in bewilderment. Who could fall for it? Is there a chuckle with the hand against the mouth coming next? A peal of unrestrained laughter, even?

Mrs Baci is not the woman to fall for things so cheap.

"Excuse me, I—" she manages to stutter.

"He can gift you other things in the future, if he wants to. His father's keeping him on a short leash right now with the pocket money, but I'm sure this won't last. As I said, this is an object I care about. A lot. I mean, I'd be willing to buy it back from you, just – Vlad must never know. You can tell him you lost it. It would be our secret. Please, Lili, I hope you understand how delicate my situation is."

Blink and breathe, Lili. There's a freezing silence.

She looks down to get away from Mrs Baci's drilling gaze and to pull her thoughts together. She must be able to say something, otherwise Mrs Baci will go away madder at her than she already is. She'll think Lili's a bad girl who can't be reasoned with.

Hold on: Mrs Baci's is the delicate situation? She suddenly realises what's going on.

Standing here for the first time, in the Danes' doorway. Making assumptions about Lili's role in a domestic drama of a lost necklace. Offering money for it. But Vlad must never know, it goes.

"You think Vlad took the necklace without telling you and gave it to me? Secretly?"

Mrs Baci nods, raising an eyebrow. There you go, she seems to be saying.

"Did he say that?" Has Vlad gone totally bunkers? Did he take it to sell it and get money for the seaside? Is he so desperate that he's acting like a ten-year-old?

Mrs Baci exhales with impatience.

"I asked him several times, Lili, and he denies it, but – as I said, I've searched for it everywhere. It's missing from my jewellery box. It only makes sense that—"

"But this isn't like Vlad at all! He doesn't sneak, and – and he never gifted me things. I never—"

This isn't about Vlad. No use sticking out for him.

This is about her.

It's all the same who Vlad really is, or not, to Mrs Baci. He's her son. What she's here for has to do with who she thinks Lili is.

"I'm sorry, Mrs Baci," Lili suddenly recollects herself. As she raises her head from her searching stare, she feels how her shoulders straighten up. "But I can't help you. I haven't got any necklace or any other object from your house. Wish I could help. Maybe next time."

What's she saying? Next time?

"I mean, next time if I can help at all, I'll be very glad to."

There is no next time, Lili knows.

Mrs Baci purses her lips again and swivels around. She yanks the door handle, which gives Lili a start.

But she's going to say this, nonetheless.

"I'm sure you'll find it in the end, Mrs Baci. As the saying goes – don't worry, tell a story, while Loretta drives a lorry."

CHAPTER EIGHT

The exam days come and go, just like last year. She's getting the practice of it, she notices with certain self-irony.

The queue in the morning to get past the ID check and be admitted inside the building, the oil paint on the walls, along the corridors, the hushed rumour of the young people heading for the exam rooms, waiting for the final ID check, the checks of their documents once they're seated, the regulations being read out, the petrified breathless silence while the questions are being written in chalk on the blackboard, the start and end time being entered, the 'go' moment, the scribbling, the tip of the pen leaning against the front teeth pondering, the rigorous approach to each task to allow no room for errors creeping in, the repeated checks, the short spells of looking out the window in between for a moment's switch-off, only to be more alert on the next and final check, the handing out of the paper and leaving the room with the feeling that that was it, facts have been accomplished, I did my part.

And then the wait, at least two weeks.

Vlad has been around. Picking her up after the exams, kindly asking how it went.

Although they now have plenty of time on their hands, they still only meet every other day, without knowing what to do with themselves, nor why exactly they're seeing each other. Certain things must have been said at the Bacis'. He looks at her with dark eyes, where some indefinite pool of sadness seems to be lying, and some words he is holding back. Or he can't even find.

In the tropical July night she lies awake, feeling suspended between an emptiness behind and an unknown ahead.

Her body is sweating in the warm bedsheets.

Mrs Baci's shadow in the doorway has been haunting her. Something that had been purring on in the background, like the electric meter during that conversation, has now blown up in her face. She has been, in the past months, made to talk about menstruation, pregnancy weeks, and now about gold necklaces to be bought back.

Where's the Lili I know? Dana asked a while back. Yes, where is she – but who was she in the first place? Lili wishes she knew. The past year has created someone new, just as the Party propaganda goes on about the New Citizen.

Where she only saw a linear path from school to university to the blurry future, there's now a tangle of trails. Studying physics still belongs in the picture, but is no longer the one gate to freedom. It's more like an asset she must collect to round up her credentials. Father might have been wrong, after all; the choice is not just what to study and who to get married to. Apart from the home in your vocation, there's still another path to walk into a decent life, and that is *Don't worry, tell a story, while Loretta drives a lorry.*

That garage of her own, to weather off life's adversities? A family that has already provided all the answers and built a weatherproof bubble. Home revamped, family reshuffled, love re-imagined. The profession, but a pastime for daily mental employment.

She sees that new Lili budding up in her, like an embryo growing into a discernible human shape. It might feel like a stranger now, but it could gradually become her nature. Her mind glides from picture to picture, a Lili confidently settled in her fiancée role, hugging and kissing Vlad as she comes home, a wedding that combines wealth with understatement, a flat with quality furnishings in a central neighbourhood, a reliable daily routine between work and relaxation, all out under the sun, tidy, inconspicuous, fitting.

Vlad? Companionship. Taking care of. Mutual appreciation. Smooth decision-making. Occasional intimacy, no more and no less than a content, settled-down couple.

Contentment, yes.

And yet, since Mrs Baci's visit she has known something that she cannot quite account for.

She has kept away from assessments this whole year, because assessments press on for decisions, but Nestor's scale of values keeps popping up in her mind these days. Some conclusion is at hand, but still dangling, waiting for her to acknowledge it.

Her mental pictures of that content Lili Baci make up a film that is infinitely more realistic than her old fantasies about John, but are just as unreal. In fact, the Lili looking up into John's eyes was so real that the Lili in the flesh would sob in her bed. Lili Baci does nothing to her flesh.

Although again, that might be a good sign. That flesh, that raw wound might be better off and healing into a scar by being left alone.

But wouldn't the lily flower in her wither then?

She decided recently that she wanted to study physics more than simply being admitted to university. Was that choice about much more than just a study programme?

And now, does she want the cosiness that love provides more than love itself? Does she want the smooth domestic life that a family creates more than the true family?

She knows she's large enough to accommodate this budding Lili Baci, even-tempered, wise, in charge. It's up to her to let that mind film become her way of being.

But she won't let the embryo grow and take over. Not because of some noble principle, some abstract sense of honour, Winnetou-like. What was it again that Nestor said? She has to be there when life starts happening: career, romance, opportunities. What if she moves out of her world into the Bacis' weatherproof bubble, and she's not there when life comes visiting?

She senses for the first time what Nestor's scale of values might have been about. But the tangle of trails ahead of her makes it clear: this is not some first degree equation curve plotting a linear scale of who's superior to whom. It's not even about her being a star, in Dana's words, or not. What she's missing is not a scale of values, but a compass, a meaning she could be carrying in herself through dilemmas like an unstoppable Raskolnikov. If only she possessed that meaning. But she's still groping.

All she has found so far is something raw inside of her that tingles alive or hurts like sandpaper on unprotected skin.

All she knows is that she'll never be able to look Mrs Baci in the eye without remembering the rift opened by their conversation against the dull purr of the electric meter. She may wish to choose contentment over fulfilment, but contentment is no longer on the table in the aftermath of that showdown.

That marrying Vlad is now out of the question is clear.

But was it ever really in question?

It looks like it was, at least on a conversational level.

She's left Vlad on his own with his fantasising, while she switched off and delayed indefinitely. She told Dana about his proposal merely as an aside, without taking the trouble to share her real thoughts on it. She even hinted at it to Mother, who chuckled but kept her eyes wide open in disbelief.

She might have even told herself that she might marry Vlad, dismissing any potential objections with an inner *why not?*

It has taken Mrs Baci speaking her mind for a little truth to come back through.

Just as it took a terrifying roller coaster for Lili to speak up and ask Nestor for help a few months ago.

What went wrong? Lili asks herself, staring at the ceiling.

When did things start leading the way in her place?

Wasn't she the one so adamant about doing things that felt true?

Wasn't she the one who'd thrashed and kicked when Mother pressed her to ask for Bodu-Beran's autograph, claiming that wasn't her?

Wasn't she the one who'd stepped back from the party-making of the high school fellowships?

Wasn't she the one who wouldn't be Yimmi Papa's clever girl anymore? Who wouldn't be a star – because that wasn't her either, she claimed.

Instead, she'd ended up mothering a third-year medicine guy. Getting pregnant like a silly goose on top of that.

It looks as if life has been visiting already, but she wasn't there all this year.

And the consequences?

She's allowed ambivalence to sneak in.

Have I been using Vlad? the question suddenly pops in her mind. She crumples within herself at the horror of it. She knows she never had such thoughts, but it now strikes her that she might have acted as if she had.

She's allowed an ambivalence to dwell between her heart and her actions, not by design, but by listlessness. She's put her heart on half-mode, and that half-heartedness might be read as purpose.

That's why his chums provoked her by making fun of him.

That's why his parents have been watching her, keen to ascertain who it is they're handing their boy over to. Mrs Baci, above all, pushing her into the ropes on the hush-hush, mother to girlfriend.

Was she ever, even for a moment, attracted by Vlad's so-called eligibility?

It certainly felt good to be chosen by a guy who ticked all boxes. Almost all.

But she'd never been interested in owning expensive things. Vlad's high-society circles left her indifferent.

She was just a quiet video tape viewer. Maybe knitting along.

Maybe she was touched by Vlad's loyalty and wanted to reward him by gifting herself to him. Was she supposed to set things straight right away? There was so much going on the whole time, was it so wrong that she'd taken that ease and affection and leaned on it?

No, not that.

But at some point, she had been cast in a role that wasn't herself. That cool, scheming girl, the clever one who gave the steer from the shadows, while letting Vlad horse around in his silly childishness. She had let all those people believe she'd opted in: Vlad first of all, his chums, the Bacis, Dana, Mother, even herself – whereas she had only chosen not to choose.

It didn't take Mrs Baci spelling out her suspicions, just as it didn't take the roller coaster, for Lili to cry out her fears. What it really took was for something inside her to curl up tight and tense, turn her body into a ticking clock, and in the process, the lie she believed into rubbish.

It's not about a mountain or a grain of sand either, she suddenly realises. It's about the carrying.

Great or small is relative. From the inside, all challenges are equal. But the carrying is what matters, that's what Nestor meant on the fairground. Toiling away with a blank mind doesn't count, but committing yourself in truth.

It feels as if she hasn't inhabited her life for ages.

She hasn't been carrying anything. Only toiling away with a blank mind, putting off choices and course corrections. At times because the carrying felt too heavy, at others because she was afraid to scream.

Now she sees that Mother is the marathon runner, the unfailing Madame Villepreux, the warrior who wrestles with the pain by shoving the pain away.

And Father? Yimmi Papa was there, alive and awake, his wound out there for all to see. He must have been stuck with his mountain and the draining effort to push it on.

People all around are more or less successful at removing themselves to a place of their own, from where they might be strong enough to keep going over here. Lili's faint voice of intuition whispers that that place is only emptiness, a dis-place. She's been there.

A tight-lipped smile, a clap of hands, a consenting recital of a propaganda phrase, while all along queuing for chicken offcuts, shivering in their homes, squeezing themselves onto buses with blank eyes, shunning the TV news and skipping straight to the crossword puzzles in the papers, ignoring fake street workers who are whispering into their walkie-talkies: how else could one survive, if not by shutting one's eyes, removing oneself, so one can carry on with the daily routine, with the socialist competition, carry on standing in a queue for a little more survival to hold them yet another day?

Yimmi Papa hadn't learnt that skill. He had screamed and yelled and slammed doors until the house walls were shaking, and bawled at the Party empty talk, and tossed and flailed and thrashed about, and yelled all over again in rage and helplessness, seeing that he was being shut out for not being capable of empty talk himself. Until one day he was grabbed and removed, with a hollow ritual in a graveyard to finish it all off. He wasn't even in his coffin.

She always thought she must be better at it than he was. To keep safe, you must relinquish any hero status, she believed. But now she sees there must be another way than self-removal.

She'll work that out in time. For now, just for a short

while, she can breathe deep, and allow herself to be alive.

She has her body back, the body that has been screaming and flailing and thrashing about in her place.

She's made fresh choices as to who she wants to be, and what she wants to dream about in her fantasies.

Mother is going to be fine, without Lili mothering her.

Father is not coming back from his grave, but that abundance of love, that can be traced back. Maybe even retrieved. Some day. Some way.

This will be a version of her future that can never be, but which she wants to release, out of her mind, into the ether. It's also a version of Vlad's future that will never be, which is what cautions her to take extra care.

She cannot live out each version that offers itself; she can only commit herself to one, choice after choice, time and again. But what she can do is be that Lili for a few mysterious moments in her mind, as a ritual of honouring and leaving the unfulfilled version behind. In the past, she would enact a scenario driven by the yearning for it to become reality; now, she enacts it for a gracious closure.

Although this past year she hasn't been able to lean into her film-making imagination, except for odd, disparate pictures that would pop up in her mind uninvited, she'll close her eyes now and make Vlad a hero. It's what she can gift him at this watershed point.

* * *

Lili Danes is special.

She practically owns the National Astronomic Observatory on the city outskirts, from where she studies Saturn's rings. She's the one turning off the lights, late at night, when she goes, and she holds the keys to unlock the next morning. When the weather is optimal and Saturn at its closest to Earth, she spends the nights there.

She's been in occasional correspondence with NASA about a space shuttle which is to travel through the solar system. For two years she has taught at the university in Toulouse, during which time she was approached by Stanford. She saw her application for the US visa through all the political and bureaucratic channels, waited year after year, until the gates had to give in and let her out. She was on the next plane to Los Angeles, and only returned three years later.

(Did she return, though?

Yes, otherwise how would she… Anyway, go on.)

Lili Danes is special in many other ways. The lily in her is slim and undulating in the laid-back clothes she wears, as if her message to the world is: "I'm beautiful, but I don't need to shout it out. My world is my home, and you may see me if you've got the right eyes." *(A touch of Cora Balș, assured at responding to the world.)* She's still got her girlish look, but a mature woman's spellbinding, vaguely melancholic smile.

She knows life. Some of it. She knows love, and she knows loss of it. She has seen the world. She has been handed trophies she never coveted. She's done her own thing, and life has been generous. She's caught all the trains on her journey.

But now, at thirty-five *(half a lifetime away, nearly midlife)*, she yearns to settle down and touch base, dreams fulfilled. She's missing a companion hugging her before she heads out to the observatory. Her mate for life.

And she remembers.

Vlad coming through the door after his classes, bending to kiss her and asking, "How are you, honey?" Vlad constantly on the lookout in case something might be wrong with her. Vlad parading her as his fiancée. Vlad's unwavering determination to stick with her. Never questioning her intentions, motifs, priorities. Never questioning their compatibility. Vlad going, "Your happiness is my command, your smile is my daily target."

She knows no one else, after all these years, capable of such innocence and dedication.

Would he still have her, to love and to hold?

Would his heart be warming to her again? Would she be still capable of awakening that enthusiasm, that chattering merriness?

She spends long weeks tossing and turning this impulse inside of her. He'd turn her out. Or he'd simply say a bitter "No," with dark eyes. Or – "Hold on." He'd have a happy life by now, wife and kids and all. What business does Lili Danes have calling at Doctor Vlad Baci's Paradise Home?

But in the end, against the lashing of her ruthless reason, she walks one day to the hospital where she has discovered his name among the medical team.

He'd be a… Wait, what is it he'd prefer to specialise in? Radiology, or orthopaedics? The past months she's heard him mentioning gynaecology, with a thin shade of unease.

He'd be a gynaecologist. An obstetrician. Listed up there in the front hall.

As she walks up from the tram stop, she sees a tall, slender man hurrying out through a side door, striding towards the parking lot. His grey raincoat, rippling in the wind with dark pools of light, is flapping and trailing behind, as if part of him is waving to show her the way.

Her breathing is constrained, but she follows. Is this really Vlad? Like her, approaching middle age, turned responsible adult, what have the years done to him, added on his shoulders, thickened in his heart, and what have they erased?

Is he a care-taking papa? Has he discarded youthful love like a childhood teddy bear, like snapshots of a silly, unknowing younger self whose photo lies safely pressed under the pile?

There's only one way of knowing.

She hurries to catch up. Just a few steps behind, she calls, her voice strangled.

"Vlad?"

The man swivels around, intending to keep rolling smoothly on his way, but an invisible brake seems to take hold of him, his legs suddenly jolting. On his third step, he comes to a standstill.

"Vlad," she repeats. "It's Lili. Lili Danes. Remember me?"

He stares at her as if he's seeing a ghost. She gradually recognises him. The rictus on his lips is grooved in deeper, but is no longer conspicuous, framed as it is by other lines and furrows. His dark eyes are even darker now, unspoken yearnings lying deep. His raincoat hints at a manly body that must have grown over the years out of the skinny, loose frame of the young bloke.

He's – almost – handsome. As handsome as Vlad could ever get. An upright, capable, self-reliant man.

"How's life, Lili?" she hears his voice, deep, saying her name as if they'd never said goodbye.

"Life's good to me, Vlad. Is it good to you, too?" her feeble voice ventures across the space between them.

He is still for a moment, then nods once or twice, his eyes set on her. She feels small, an awkward little girl, coveting a secret treasure that this man might hold but not be willing to share with her.

"What are you doing here, a medical check? Is everything all right?"

What she's doing here is silly. Romantic. But silly still. Running after a man who's hurrying about his life. Does she have any right to stop him on his way?

"Is there something I can do for you?" he attempts again. His voice is composed. He won't care.

"I was passing by—" Preposterous. Who'd be passing by a hospital? But the words are out now. "And I thought I saw you… I wasn't sure, after all this time… Anyway, wanted to say hi, see how it goes…"

He lets her go quiet. Where's his chatter?

"It was nice seeing you, Lili. You're looking good. Take care," he says, swivelling back to his path.

That can't be it. Or maybe that's precisely it.

"Vlad!"

He keeps going a few strides until he comes to a halt again and turns around.

"I thought maybe... you must be in a hurry now, but some other time maybe? Sit down a bit and just... you know, have a chat?"

He looks away with a concentrated frown between his jagged eyebrows.

Although – she's not sure she'd want to have a chat if he's got a wife and kids waiting at home. Of course he'd have them. Not everyone chases far-off planets into middle age, like her.

"Seven p.m. tomorrow at the Fiesta?" she hears him saying.

"Great, yes, perfect, Vlad!"

He swivels again and resumes his stride. "See you tomorrow, then!" he shouts, waving.

* * *

Fiesta is followed by another chat and another chat, replacing the wine glass with a cup of coffee, with an ice cream profiterole, or just with a stroll. In a different park than fifteen years back.

And they talk. Or they walk in silence, undisturbed.

Vlad is slowly melting, *Remember when we...?, This is where...*

No wife and kids are waiting for him. Never did. The playground slide of memory is free of obstacles. They put back together the now with the younger version of things, from chatters to laughs to shy compliments.

Vlad is there, by her side, listening, sometimes chuckling, latching his turns on to hers in what becomes a tight-knit conversation, a bubble enveloping them as they move on across the city, across the map of their convergence.

"How are your parents?" she asks at some point.

He smiles. "They're good. As you know them, more or less. Keeping busy when they're not on duty, tinkering at the cottage in Busteni."

The cottage in Busteni. That convenient home away from home.

"They kept bugging me about settling down, starting a family and so on. But at some point they gave up. I told them, look, I've got my post at the hospital, the specialisation is on track, that should be fine. The rest is my business. Thank goodness we don't live together any longer," he adds with a chuckle.

"Oh! The sunlit flat on the stylish boulevard across the big park? You moved out?"

"Yes, I did. I had to move on. On my own. And I'm happy about it." He looks her in the eyes. Vlad is a happy man – or at least, a man who's happy with his achievements. There's a fleeting shadow sometimes in his eyes, but it must be a ghost.

* * *

...and one afternoon, the sun sinking behind the city's grey buildings like the yolk of a countryside egg, they're facing each other, suddenly flustered by some insignificant detail, whether it be a casual remark, some replay of an old refrain, the beauty of colour splashing over the greyness of the surroundings – and with their eyes locked in an intense gaze, they reach out for each other until fingers latch on, lips touch with a brief twitch of electricity, they chuckle like teenagers, and then, finally, comes the kiss.

There's a plunge down the slide, deep and deeper and

faster as it goes, as their arms hold on to each other as if it was the end of the world.

"I want you," she whispers, almost anguished when their lips come apart. His eyes are dark, but not with sadness. He wants her, too, beyond words.

He nods and runs his hands over her hair, smiles, and whispers, parodying an old dictum, "your wish is my command."

They laugh, letting go of the embrace. They hurry home. Her place, after all these years.

(*Wait, would she no longer live with Mother?*

No, she'd be that adult, self-providing woman, living in a small studio near the Observatory, one of the tiny streets with ivy-shaded houses of old Bucharest.)

They rush along, earnest, with occasional bursts of laughter seeing themselves like two crazy young lovers. They burst into the flat, slam the door behind them with their feet, crash against walls in a dizzying embrace, hands not knowing what to do first, hold, caress, grasp, snatch clothes off. They stumble and fall on the bed, the race carrying on, chasing the ultimate togetherness, hands, knees, arms, shoulders, skin on skin, gasps, until suddenly she's lying naked and he pulls back, contemplating her.

(*She doesn't know how to go on from here. She's never experienced it. Vlad penetrating her in a way that's like a first time, a first knowing of what it can be. A plunge down the slide into something no one can define.*

But it would be Vlad, tellingly, the one coming from her past, bringing the true fulfilment of a girl's nebulous dream. The second go at it.

Just like her, countless, second attempts after first failing mindlessly.

And then?)

* * *

"Vlad, we need to talk."

He pulls back and gazes at her. His arms are still holding her shoulders.

"Something wrong?"

Her lips twitch into a queasy smile.

"Depends how you look at it."

"I'm looking at you now, and holding you. What is it?"

She unlocks his arms and walks over to the window, a hand on her head, as if wondering how the hell she can get out of this kettle of fish.

"Lili," Vlad calls to her in a tone of caution, "don't give me that, will you? Don't give me your walk-away. Tell me what's wrong and we'll fix it, the best we can."

Oh yeah? Fix it? Will it be better than last time?

"I'm pregnant, Vlad." She lets her eyes wander outside the windows. At least the bushes are harmless.

Next, he's upon her and turning her around to face him.

"Say that again!"

She can't see him properly. It must be something in her eyes that makes everything fuzzy.

"I'm sorry, Vlad. I'm pregnant. We can do whatever you think's right and fix it," she whispers between gasps.

His eyes gaze at her as if searching for something unsaid.

"Do you want to have it fixed, Lili?"

"Would it be impossible?" She sounds as if she's begging.

"No. Not at all. We can arrange it, carefully. But is this what you want?"

She's startled and returns his gaze, her turn to search.

"Is there a choice?"

He smiles and holds her cheeks.

"There's always a choice. Well," he adds, correcting himself, "at least on this. At least with me," he adds, winking at her.

She's not sure she gets him; or not sure she can trust what she thinks she gets.

"I mean, Lili, it's entirely up to you. For my part, we could be happy with the little guy in the world – or the little girl."

He plants a kiss on her lips, brief, but reassuring.

"We can get married anytime, if you'll have me, after all these years, Lili. No more fooling around with silly blabber, like when we were silly kids. It might have been nicer if you could have made this decision without any pressure, but – I'm okay with this pressure, you know?" he says with a playful smile. "Take a bit of time to consider, and let me know what you think's best. I'm here, not going anywhere."

She feels her knees surrender and clasps his arms. She'll have him, oh, yes, she'll have everything, the whole thing, love, mama-papa, shared household, shared holidays, but above all – this loving and holding, this being-here-not-going-anywhere.

But wait—

"What will your parents say?"

He raises his eyebrows in surprise and then laughs.

"You kidding me? What do my parents have to do with this? They'll be happy for me, happy for us, and if not, well, it'll be them missing something. But they know what a blessing it is to have a home where there's love. Don't you ever worry about my parents, Lili! If you'll have me, they're not part of the bargain. We'll have our own lives."

There are tears and kisses and tears and kisses again, tenderness and passion spiralling up and melting together in quick breaths and deep pleasure moans.

... and the months roll by in an idyll of togetherness, Vlad holding her hand, her waist, her cheeks, checking on her, standing by her, fusing with her, then some time later calling at her to push, "You're doing great, love, just keep doing that, I'm here to catch her," amid her screams he's composed and solid, there, focused, competent, there.

It's a girl. What shall we call her?

(*What was it back then, that Sunday, she suddenly feels the pinch of the question. The parcel Vlad packed in a newspaper and then in a plastic grocery bag and then he drove away with it, he never told her where or if he took a peek inside, and she never asked...*

This second go will redeem everything.)

Days are drifting by, peacefully. She can breathe. No more race. No more holding tight. The spinning plates are lying on the shelf and the rods stored backstage. Performance over, back to the trees, back to real life.

One of these days the phone rings and Mother is the first to pick it up. It's about nine in the morning, and she's considering the options for today: taking a book and going out in the park to read on the grass, or calling Dana to go to an outdoor swimming pool—

"Thank you so much Mrs Stojan," she hears Mother's voice, loud with excitement. Mrs Stojan is not a usual caller. She lives next door and works in an administrative office in the Physics Institute. The Stojans are more or less bohemian freethinkers. They smoke a lot, wear black and baggy clothes, and although both of them are in their late fifties, they often get visited by young people who seem to be artists or other sorts of freethinkers. Do they do anything subversive in their gatherings, is the question lurking around in the neighbourhood.

Why is Mrs Stojan calling, and what is Mother thanking her for?

Mother hangs up. Lili can hear her dashing along the corridor, heading towards Lili's room. The door is opened abruptly.

Mother barges in with tearful eyes.

"Lili my love!" she cries out.

Lili gazes into Mother's wide open blue eyes, as if watching something unusual going on there.

"You're in!" Mother's voice is going shrill. And loud. Very loud.

"The first on the list!" Mother adds and holds out her arms to her girl.

Lili keeps on gazing, her limbs petrified. Her mind standing still.

"Mrs Stojan has seen the lists, they've only just been put up and she's run over to have a look for your name."

Danes, Lilian.

"And you got the first ten in physics in the past two decades of admission exams, Lili!"

A flood is welling up inside and all around her, is carrying her, gently defying gravity, and she's giving in to it, closing her eyes, feeling soft in every cell of her body, soft and alive, throbbing, flowing, floating, gliding. Something in her recognises unerringly what it is that has just come into being: it's that bit of perfection she has never for a second contemplated, but ached towards nevertheless.

The perfect symmetry between where she is now, and where she was last year.

The uncompromising statement the symmetry is making. Doubts about her performance, however subliminal and latent, thoroughly crushed and blown away.

And her name. The Danes have done it again. Defied, and moved beyond ambivalence. Yimmi Papa's name echoing along those corridors. She knows that many people will be looking down when crossing her path in the Institute, even if that is but the least significant retribution.

What matters most is: her self and herself are one, full and complete. That place to be brave is here, in every fibre of her body.

There are tears and confessions of pain long withheld, promises of a sunny openness between mother and daughter, and professions of unconditional love.

Until a white Lada is stopping in front of their windows.

Lili wipes away her tears and knows what there is to do. The dangling is over. Mother rushes off and hides in her bedroom, so she doesn't give the news away.

Vlad knocks at the door, and Lili manages to articulate a casual "Come in!"

He enters in a somewhat agitated mood.

"Anything new about the results?"

Lili shakes her head and looks down. She hasn't got a plan, but she can't just tell him. He needs to see it for himself.

"My goodness, why is it taking so long? Come, let's drive over and have a look, or ask someone. We can wait there if they're to put them up later today."

She nods and changes her clothes. Vlad looks out of the window, not sure if he's supposed to look away from Lili getting undressed.

She puts on a smart skirt and a matching T-shirt, then picks a small handbag to go with the outfit. It's been long while since she minded her outfit.

On their way out, Lili cries out for Mother to hear, "Mom, we're driving to the Institute, to see about the results in case they're being put out today!"

They get into the car and off they go. Vlad is nervous; the rictus across his lips is tighter than usual. She glances at him every now and then and wonders when he grew so old. He has chattering binges and heavy silence spells. There are so many traffic lights, corners to take, buses to wait behind, and he's drumming with his fingers on the wheel. Lili's mind is clear.

She recognises the streets, the bus she took on the

exam days, the grey people scurrying along in the street, carrying bags filled with various things, from milk bottles to bread loaves, onions or watermelons, or tools to repair some broken household item or other. She looks up towards the flats in the high buildings, noticing the repetitive square pattern of the windows looking like tiny cells of a huge dormant organism; she wonders briefly how people can live in these matchbox flats, and takes in the full view of the streets with their meagre uniformity.

She's so lucky, she tells herself with certainty, not having to live in a matchbox. And she's been lucky this year to have had Vlad around, or else she would have hopelessly sunk in the grimness. But the year is over.

Above the gloom of the grey blocks, the sky is already bleached by sunshine, although it's only just past ten in the morning. The trees hemming the street look dusty, but still alive, doing their job of casting their shade for the people waiting at bus stops.

And why isn't she telling Vlad what she knows? She glances at him. Is he worried what his mom and dad are going to say when there's no excuse left and his sweetheart has failed again? She smiles inwardly. He's only a kid, seeking approval and a pat on his shoulder. One more reason she can't tell him: he needs to see and understand who she really is.

She wants to see it, too. To stand there, in front of the lists, and look at the names, at her name, at the ranking, at her unprecedented top mark. She must take it all in.

"Oh, just so you know," Vlad says as if only just remembering. "My precious mom has done a thorough cleaning and moved furniture around, and guess what? She found the necklace. It was behind the chest of drawers."

"Oh!" Lili nods slightly, wondering what else to say.

"Yes, I know, I told her. I scolded her, next time think twice before you – well, something along that line," Vlad ends abruptly and sinks back into his gloom.

So that has neatly come to light, too, as will the rest

now, in just a little time. The last one or two miles.

She can feel something like a flutter of wings at times, lapsing into the quiet of a pond inside her. What if Mrs Stojan was wrong? What if it's all been a dream?

She'll see. But she already knows.

Vlad pulls over with a bump, both wheels on the kerb. She looks at him questioningly.

"Yeah, well, it should do for now, let's see, no time to drive around looking for a proper place to park," Vlad explains, irritated, already one foot outside the car. She gets out calmly, as if measuring her steps.

"You know something, don't you," Vlad teases her. "You're so composed, I can't get you, how can you be like that?"

She smiles condescendingly.

"I'm composed because there's nothing I can do about it, is there?"

They can see the crowd ahead of them, all scrumming against a window.

"They're out!" Vlad exclaims and points at the crowd. "The results must be out, look at that!" Vlad almost shoots away but checks his impulse and gets back into Lili's measured pace.

They manage to squeeze past the people at the edge, making their way through the heart of the scrum, getting nearer and nearer. She can see the lists just a few feet away, white, some grey machine-typed lines neatly arranged one under another. Vlad is ahead of her; she's stepping behind him, cautiously.

"You go on, you're taller, can you read it?" She's standing half a step behind him, holding his left arm so they don't lose each other in the billowing crowd. Vlad nods and stands still, squinting.

And he stands. Squinting. Squinting on. What's taking so long, where is he looking, Lili wonders remotely, is he reading the list of those below the line? In that case, it's going to take a while.

And then his arm starts and he swivels around.

"You're in!" he shouts. "You're in, my goodness, and you're right at the top, you hear me, right at the top, the first one!" His voice is going shrill. Yes, she can hear him, and so can all the others.

"Oh, stop fooling around," she replies, smiling like a knowing mother.

"You're the first, my goodness, you really are," Vlad repeats, reading the list again. "And you got a ten in physics, didn't you say they never give tens?"

She smiles on, nodding. The crowd is listening, it seems.

"Yes, Vlad, I did, do you mean I really got a ten, are you sure you see it clearly?" She looks up innocently.

"Of course I do, it's a ten all right, with a plus next to it, you can't take it for anything else – my goodness I don't believe it, I don't believe it!"

She pulls him gently.

"I need to see it too," she says in a soothing tone. The crowd has had its show, now it's her own moment.

The few guys in front of them pull aside to let her through, watching her dazed. She has a smile dwelling on her face, and she looks down shyly, watching her steps.

Here she is.

And here they are, the lists. Face to face. Lili and her name. Up there, high up, reading unequivocally: Lilian Danes. Physics: ten. Mathematics: nine fifty-five.

Lower down the sheet, the line. And beneath the line, sheets of paper with endless rows of names. She knows. She's been there.

She stands there for a few moments longer. Then she turns around. Vlad is out of the crowd, smoking a cigarette. He smiles and waves at her. He looks so relieved. A few years younger again.

She finds the shortest way out of the scrum and meets him. He takes her in his arms and holds her. "Have I told you how much I love you, you're such a brilliant girl!" he declares.

She laughs and thanks him, nodding.

He finishes his cigarette and there's no more reason to hang out there. The searching, the reading, the name spotting, the standing in contemplation have been accomplished. Now life can move on.

On the way back to the city, Vlad chatters continually.

"My goodness, my old ones are going to go crazy when they hear, they'll be looking sheepish, I can tell you, and Mom had better be sorry for everything she said to you, and not just to you," he pauses here allusively, but then, too happy to dwell on past conflicts, he carries on. "And Daddy will surely regret, he wasn't himself, I can tell you, I guess Mom put him under quite some pressure, and you know, people are human, Daddy's also human, he started having doubts and wanted to do the right thing, but now – hey!" Vlad exclaims, struck by a sudden idea. "Let's go to the seaside tomorrow, I can find a holiday flat, and money, well, I'll borrow some, Dad can keep his money, that'll teach him something, too – what do you say?" Vlad turns to her with enthusiasm spread all over his swarthy face.

Lili keeps smiling, the smile that has been lingering the past half hour or so.

"No, thanks, Vlad," she answers quietly. Why is he suddenly able to get the money on his own and take his girlfriend – his fiancée? – on vacation?

"Oh, come on, Lili, you made it!" he insists, as if asking her not to spoil his joy.

"Vlad, please. You know just as well as I do that we're over. We have been for some time now."

Vlad is speechless at the composure in Lili's voice. He stares ahead, eyebrows pressed against each other at the root of his nose, like two magnets stuck together.

"Besides, I already have plans," Lili adds after a

moment. “I’m going to the seaside with Cora Balş. Mother has borrowed some money for me. Now that I’m a student, I’ll qualify for social assistance as a half-orphan, you know, which will be about a third of Father’s salary, so returning the money will be much easier.”

“How about our engagement, how about our getting married and stuff?” he insists.

“Yes, that might have been a legitimate question all these last months,” Lili replies pondering. “But neither of us posed it. Maybe because all that getting married stuff – it was never real. Other things were real instead, which kept crying out for our attention. Attention which I partly failed to give, guilty as charged.

“But then again,” she adds once more, turning her head to give Vlad her full smile, the final blow of her detachment, “I’m just a nineteen-year-old girl, and I made mistakes.”

“Oh, I see,” Vlad nods with some resentment, “so all’s well that ends well, so to speak.”

Lili glances at him.

“So to speak, yes,” she assents. “Just – before ending well, it’s been a hell of a ride. All the more reason to thank you, Vlad, for this ride today, and the whole of it, this past year.”

She gets out of the car with the composure she has acquired today.

“I’ll call you later,” Vlad says before revving his father’s white Lada and driving away.

She nods, watching him go.

EPILOGUE

Lili spent that August light as a feather.

Mother took the car out of the garage and had it checked, preparing it for the long drive over the mountains.

Lili used to dread it when they went to her grandma's countryside house, as the car always held some nasty surprise in store: windshield wipers getting stuck in torrential rain, engine going dead when the brake was held, fourth gear choking and coughing when overtaking some huge truck, and anything else that Lili hadn't yet discovered could go wrong.

But this summer, she didn't worry. She and Mother alone in the car, Lili in the passenger's seat, they chattered and laughed and munched through the bag of sandwiches and boiled eggs prepared as supplies ahead of the trip.

Grandma's house was again overgrown with ivy. They couldn't push the gate open because of the rank weeds that were standing tall like soldiers. Lili laughed, Mother laughed, and they called the neighbour with his scythe.

After sunset, they got a fire going with kindling the neighbour gave them. The next day they would fetch their own wood from the forest. For now, they were fine with a bowl of cornflour porridge with cheese, milk and eggs from the other neighbours down the street.

And then, the night sky. Just as Lili remembered it.

The darkest hue of blue, spread with the densest web of twinkles she had ever seen.

"The sky here is like nowhere else," Mother would say, looking up.

The sky of her childhood. She used to hold her head back, looking up until her jaw would gradually go down in what looked like gaping. The wonder of it.

She was now on track to dive in and explore it.

The error had been remedied, in Mother's words a year before.

Maybe sometimes one needed to lose before one won, so one could learn what it was they were after.

The weeks spent in the village were active and serene. Fetching wood, making fire, tinkering with the fence where a plank was loose, picking up the tools that only Father had handled, getting used to their heaviness and to the application needed in hitting a nail on its head – it was all an adventure.

And then, in the last days of August, returning home to get ready for the seaside with Cora Balș.

Lili sorted her clothes with a remote smile on her face. Light shirts and dresses, for the last time this year, bidding summer goodbye from the beach. What could be better?

Cora would be sharing her exciting people stories, filling up the days with a lighthearted humour that was in harmony with Lili's mood.

Would Greg Talu visit them again? She shook her head briefly while folding the laundry. What if he did? He could learn about her victory, and congratulate her like everyone else, no more minister's privilege. But she would be happy to give him the news. At least he'd tried to be on her side.

All the unfulfilled promises were a thing of the past now, neatly shelved, some for remembrance, like Gabriel's passion, others for detached storage.

Vlad had come by once or twice, faking a light-hearted chatter, but had soon driven away again. Mrs Baci had called, in the first days after the results, to congratulate Lili. Mother had picked up the phone, but Lili had shaken her head, meaning "I'm not here." Mother had thanked Mrs Baci with an icy smile on her face and in her voice, and was quick to hang up.

The next day is the first of September. The train leaves at seven in the morning. Lili has packed her rucksack and a travel handbag, with the beach mat laid between its handles. They're to get up at five thirty, and Mother will drive her to the station. On the way, they'll pick Cora up from her house.

Lili and Mother have a long dinner and light-hearted chatter until late at night, then Lili goes to bed knowing that Mother will take care of things in the morning.

She sinks into the blanket of sleep.

But soon there is a buzzing sound nagging her dreams. Going on and off. Like a muffled pain in the bones. Again. And again.

It's the telephone.

Who could it be that late at night, she wonders. Why isn't Mother picking up?

She gets up from bed slowly, grumbling about the unfortunate caller.

She heads along the corridor to the cubicle where they keep the telephone.

Lili picks it up and says, "Hello?"

"What the hell are you two doing? Cora's got a taxi!"

It's Cora's husband. What's he talking about? Cora got a taxi in the middle of the night?

"Well, we were asleep. Why did she get a taxi?"

"You're missing the train, you fool! It's six thirty!"

Lili hangs up in shock.

"Mom! Wake up, wake up! It's six thirty!"

She rushes to her bedroom, yanks the light on and dashes to the clothes on the chair. She hears Mother trampling to the bathroom, then to the kitchen.

"Are you getting dressed? No time for coffee now!"

"Yes, I'm ready, honey, no coffee."

Lili picks up her rucksack and hurls it over her shoulders, then grabs the bag and dashes through the door.

It's the longest drive to the station. She's now aware of every junction, every bus halting at every stop, every tram crossing. The watch on her wrist could give her precious information about the time, but she won't check. Maybe just this once, time will dilate and accommodate her trip against all probability.

Things do happen against the odds, against equations. Against the classical ones, at least.

Mother pulls up at the station entrance closest to the platforms. They exchange a rushed goodbye-take-care-love-I'll wait here-if-you-get-back, and she flings her rucksack on, grabs her bag and starts running.

Across the hall, searching frantically for the display, line 5, there it is, the train is a few yards away, already slowly moving away.

She starts down the platform. Her thighs are tense with the effort, her breath is sending splinters into her guts, but she won't stop now.

Just hang on and it'll be good. I gotta get on this train.

She's running for the train of her new life. The weight of her rucksack and the banging of the bag against her right knee are slowing her down. If only she could drop them so she could run free.

But she must carry it all nonetheless and hop on that train.

The last car, the last door, still open, someone standing there, the conductor maybe, watching her, reaching out his hand and bending to help her hop on, dragging her bag inside, the beach mat miraculously still lying there, she's now on the train, still gasping, the race is over, she's safe now, she's done good running, carrying her stuff too, now she can find her seat and let herself drop.

Her mother, her father, the neighbours' wisdom, the dull streets with the people scurrying about in a half-trance.

And her own choices, ordeals, mountains, or grains of sand.

To embrace and carry them all, but then be lonely, as a foreign body amid everyone else's absenteeism.

Or to join in the absenteeism and be displaced.

How far away can you manage to keep, to be safe? And what does the achieved safety amount to? Leaving her mountain behind and going astray?

How that exactly works out, she'll see some other time. Life, like summer, holds the promise of a long way ahead.

Lili Danes relishes her newly gained wholeness. For a while.

AFTERWORD

Thanks for reading through to this last page; I hope you enjoyed the book. If you did, perhaps you'd consider leaving a review on Amazon, and tell a friend about Lili's story?

I'd love us to stay in touch. Check out my website https://zoe-carada.com/ and sign up for the newsletter there. Occasionally I might send you extra material related to this book or other writing projects. I promise I won't flood your inbox.

You are most welcome to get in touch yourself. Fill in the contact form on my website, and I'll get back to you.

www.ingramcontent.com/pod-product-compliance
Lightning Source LLC
LaVergne TN
LVHW050533160826
845677LV00011B/2022

* 9 7 8 3 0 0 0 8 1 2 9 6 5 *